Davin's Quest

Praise for Bianca D'Arc's *Davin's Quest*

Rating: 5 Angels & Recommended Read "Bianca D'Arc has done it again. She has followed up a book with an equally fabulous book!"

~ *Serena Polheber, Fallen Angel Reviews*

Rating: 5 Blue Ribbons "...finely written and ultimately satisfying...I laughed with the characters successes and shed tears at their sadness...Bianca D'Arc is my new 'to watch for' author!"

~ *Natasha Smith, Romance Junkies*

Rating: 5 Klovers "Once again, Bianca D'Arc has delivered a story full of steamy sex, emotional romance, and gripping suspense all wrapped up in a beautiful story of boundless love and human resilience."

~ *Jennifer Ray, CK2S Kwips and Kritiques*

Rating: 5 Red Tattoos "...wonderfully created...Highly sympathetic characters will have you perched on the edge of your seat as you await their ultimate fate... a work of art that you will find yourself unable to put down."

~ *Megan, Erotic Escapades*

"...a fabulous story of human nature and the role emotions play in our makeup...a great storyline with sensual love scenes that I enjoyed reading."

~ *Literary Nymphs*

Look for these titles by
Bianca D'Arc

Now Available:

Wings of Change
(I Dream of Dragons Volume 1 Anthology)
Forever Valentine
(Caught By Cupid Anthology)
Sweeter Than Wine
One and Only

Dragon Knights Series:
Maiden Flight
Border Lair
Ladies of the Lair—Dragon Knights 1 & 2 (print)
The Ice Dragon
Prince of Spies
FireDrake

Tales of Were Series:
Lords of the Were

Resonance Mates Series:
Hara's Legacy
Davin's Quest
Jaci's Experiment

Davin's Quest

Bianca D'Arc

A SAMHAIN PUBLISHING, LTD. publication.

Samhain Publishing, Ltd.
577 Mulberry Street, Suite 1520
Macon, GA 31201
www.samhainpublishing.com

Editing by Angela James
Cover by Anne Cain

First Samhain Publishing, Ltd. electronic publication: February 2008
First Samhain Publishing, Ltd. print publication: December 2008

Dedication

To my own Special Forces hero—now lost to this world—
Colonel, you were the best uncle a girl could have and an
example to live up to. I miss you.

Prologue

Human

Richard St. John was a hard case. Raised in the Waste since his early teens, he had only scattered memories of the way the world had been before the aliens came—before the attack from orbit tore apart the fabric of the world.

He'd wanted to be a doctor in the old days, but the crystal bombardment destroyed everything long before he was old enough to go to medical school. His mother died in the first wave, leaving his father heartbroken. But Rick's father, Zach, was a survivor. He'd packed Rick up and they'd headed for the mountains in his pickup truck. They'd just barely made it before the next orbit when the attacks began anew.

Zachariah St. John had been both a doctor and an Army Ranger in the old United States and he taught his son everything he knew about living off the land and surviving in the wild. Rick's old man had a sixth sense about nature and was able to keep them both safe through the waves of attacks that followed, each time the Earth rotated fully on its axis. They'd moved farther into the mountains, working their way north, into the deepest recesses of the Rocky Mountains. They kept up with radio reports about the decimated coastlines as tsunamis spawned by the massive crystal shards hitting the Earth's oceans killed by the millions.

One day, their small transistor radio stopped working entirely. Only static met repeated attempts to tune in a station—any station at all. Civilization, as they'd known it, was over.

"Guess that's it," Zach said, stowing the antenna and

switching off the radio. "We're on our own now."

The last broadcast had listed details of nearly unimaginable devastation. Coastlines all over the world under water from giant tsunamis. California separated down the line of the San Andreas fault. Massive earthquakes brought on by the crystal bombardment from space had finally clipped the golden state nearly in half. The ring of fire was more active than ever with two or three volcanoes erupting violently in the Pacific and Pacific Northwest.

The sky was dark with soot covering the sun, and autumn came early that year, but by the following summer, temperatures started drifting back to normal. The sun shone brightly in the sky—but so did alien craft.

Zach St. John took in the news spreading through the wastelands of the Rockies—now called simply the Waste—with his typical calm. They'd run into a trader one morning who told of tall, fair-haired aliens building a silver city on the plains. Rick asked his dad about it that night at dinner.

"I figured it was something like this, son," Zach said as he dressed the rabbit they'd snared for dinner. "The attack came from orbit. First thing to go down was my sat phone and GPS. Not many world powers who could do that, and none that could launch an attack on the entire planet. Had to be something from outer space."

"Aliens?" Rick wasn't entirely surprised. They'd talked about various possibilities often during the early days. "So they're not little and green like in the old movies."

"According to the trader, they look a lot like us, but with elf ears." Zach finished with the rabbit and looked at his son. "This changes things. Now that they're on the surface, they might just start hunting. Up 'til now, all we had to worry about was other men. The stakes are higher now, because any race that can do what they did to our planet has got to have superior weaponry. You're going to have to learn to defend yourself, and we'll make plans for when they come."

Rick thought it significant that his father said "when" and not "if".

He spent the next ten years learning from his dad and growing to adulthood. They'd met a few fellow survivors along the way, but not many, and not often. They grew close in those years.

Zach shared an amazing secret that helped keep them both alive. He had a strong gift of empathy with animals, and could sometimes pick up their thought images and see through their eyes, sensing when the animals of the forest were scared or felt threatened. He could also read people, but only when he touched them.

Rick had his own secrets. He finally let his father in on the biggest of them. He could heal most wounds by simply laying his hand over them and thinking real hard. That was why he'd wanted to study medicine—to find out how he did what he did, but also to help people with his gift.

Through their infrequent interactions with other survivors, they realized they weren't the only ones with psychic abilities. It seemed like every single soul they met had something different about them. Many had small amounts of precognitive ability that had led them out of harm's way before the attack began. Some were telepaths, some could move things with their minds. Others had combinations of skills that were often benign, but some were downright deadly.

All in all, Rick preferred to be on his own—just him and his dad. They didn't need the society of others, except for one thing, but hetero sex was hard to come by since there were so few women among the survivors of humanity. Still, Rick grew into a good-looking young man and the few women he was able to charm were as eager for him as he was for them.

But dalliances were few and far between as the lack of females turned many of the male survivors into beasts. Women went into hiding for their own protection, though few towns existed with even fewer inhabitants.

"I pity women today," Zach would often comment after contact with others. "They're traded like commodities, forced into whoring or multi-partner families. That's not the way it was, son. You should always remember that. You were old enough to know the way it should be. The way our family was. God knows, I miss your mother more every day, but I wouldn't have wanted her to see the level of depravity to which we have sunk."

Rick took all his father's teachings to heart, but especially that one. He'd just been starting to date when the cataclysm happened and felt strongly that girls should be protected, not exploited. Every time he saw some poor, frightened creature creeping about a settlement under guard by one of her protectors, the lesson was driven home again. He'd never sink that low.

The likelihood he'd ever have a woman of his own was close to nil, but Rick didn't curse fate—at least not too often. He had his dad. That was more family than most people could claim nowadays. So the St. John men lived off the land in their own small cabin out in the middle of nowhere.

Until the Alvians came.

They heard the ships fly by in the night and then the miniscule sounds of one landing not far away. Silently Zach signaled his grown son to head for the woods behind the cabin. They'd planned for this kind of thing. Each man would fend for himself, since two together were more likely to be captured or killed. They had a rendezvous and backup plan already in place.

Zach grabbed his son for one last hug before they headed out the doors—Zach out the front, and Rick out the back.

That was the last time Rick St. John saw his father.

Alien

"Chief Engineer, it is an honor to assist you." Young Selva's gaze lowered, almost submissively, but Davin knew she was ambitious.

Perhaps too ambitious.

So much so, she was even willing to work closely with him. There'd been few volunteers to act as his private assistant, regardless of his important position. Most of the Alvian race shunned Davin for having primitive, excessive emotion.

"Come here, Selva 56." Davin slid his console chair back from the huge work station. She stood in front of him with a questioning smile. Like the rest of their race, she didn't really experience emotion, but she was a smart woman. She could see the hard-on in his trousers.

"Can I help you with that, sir?" Her dark gaze traveled the length of his erection.

"Yes, you may." Davin got comfortable in his chair. This was going just as he expected. The Alvian race was nothing, if not predictable. He spread his knees to make room for her.

"Kneel in front of me, Selva, and see what you can do about this." He slid one palm over the bulge in his pants and her smile deepened. She probably thought she was getting her way, but in reality, it would be his way or no way at all. He was in charge here, as she would soon learn.

She sank to her knees and freed him with practiced movements. She had dark skin and wide brown eyes, a rarity among their race. He liked the look of her darker hands against his cock. Her nails were neatly trimmed and softly tinted. Her looks were exotic and he soon learned her hot little mouth was very talented indeed, as she took him deep.

Davin gasped. He hadn't quite expected that. She was certainly no novice at sucking dick. Perhaps he'd keep her around for a bit longer than he'd originally planned.

Her gaze swept upward, the fringe of lashes flirty. He couldn't help but wish she could feel even a flicker of the emotions he experienced on a daily basis.

But that would never be. Davin was isolated in his ability to feel and these moments of purely sexual relief were all he would have. Among his kind, he would never find a true mate—a resonance mate—to share his life. Just schemers like Selva who thought they could get ahead by throwing the big man a bone once in a while.

"Suck harder. Take me deeper," he instructed, clasping the back of her head and pushing her more firmly onto his cock. "Use your tongue and swallow it down."

She complied readily, apparently willing to do just about anything to please him. Davin appreciated that. It would come in handy with his strong sexual needs.

Still, something about her didn't add up. She was beautiful, even sexy in her own way, and Davin was not immune to her planned seductiveness. The way she brushed up against him, touched him when she had no real need to do so and used her big, dark eyes, was not lost on him. She was rather obvious in her attempts to tease. For a woman without emotions, she didn't know quite how far to go in trying to fool a man who saw more than she would ever realize.

Still, she was pretty, and eminently fuckable. And he needed relief.

"Massage my balls, pretty Selva," he ordered, almost too gratified when she used just the right pressure on him. "I'm close." He gave fair warning, but she didn't let up. He took that as a good sign and let go completely.

He came hard in her mouth, holding the back of her head so she had no choice but to swallow everything he gave. Not that she was complaining. She obviously wanted to please him. She'd made it more than clear over the past few days.

For a brief moment he felt a sense of blessed relief, an almost blissful feeling of completion. He soared. But all too soon, it was over and he plummeted back to earth. Davin relaxed back in his chair, straightening his clothes.

"Where'd you learn that?"

"I spoke to some of the women who service the soldiers." Her expression didn't change and her clinical tone set his teeth on edge.

Soldiers were considered lower life forms because their race's aggressive tendencies had not been completely bred out of them. Certain women were given the job of serving their needs, but someone like Selva 56 would never have been chosen for the task. Her crystal gift alone kept her from such menial jobs, but even if she had not had crystal ability, the line of Selva was usually gifted in business and politics. She was highly ranked for her age, at 56th on this planet. She would move up swiftly—especially if she used him to speed the process. He knew her game.

The pleasure he'd taken in release was dimmed by the thought. He meant nothing to her beyond a possible stepping-stone to greater authority and more power.

"Thank you, Selva 56. That will be all."

She stood and smiled, but it was a smile devoid of feeling that left him cold. "I'd be happy to assist you further, Chief Engineer. Anytime at all. Just call me."

Davin nodded. "I just may take you up on that. I'll let you

know."

"Thank you, sir." She smiled once more and turned gracefully, leaving him without a second thought.

Davin was not too proud to take the sexual release she offered, but he also wasn't above admitting his needs were fiercer than the other males of his race. Unless they had hints of aggressive tendencies like the warrior lines, the males of his species didn't have strong sexual needs anymore. Neither did the women. Procreation was taken care of in a lab more often than not, with genetic designers manipulating almost every aspect of the process. They'd taken an ancient and proud race from overly aggressive killing machines to unfeeling automatons in less than ten generations.

Davin was a throwback. He was like his ancestors, with all the emotions and fierce needs that had since been bred out of almost every other Alvian. His new assistant had done her research and found one way in which she could serve the Chief Engineer—and her career ambitions as well—by submitting to his sexual needs. He'd watched and listened carefully, and realized that while she was somewhat talented in crystal work, she was still young and unskilled. Careful questioning of his colleagues had revealed that she'd jumped at the chance to assist him, when everyone else tended to avoid him. Throwbacks were known to be unstable, after all.

So he questioned her motivations—both the obvious ones and the not so obvious. She probably wanted his job. Being the Chief Engineer for the new planet was a very big deal. Davin had power few of his kind ever attained, and unlike young Selva, he'd gained his position based solely on ability. There was simply no other way the Council would have let a throwback advance.

But they were conquering a new planet. They needed his skill. They watched him carefully and did not trust him, except where the crystal was concerned. He had proven time and time again he was the most gifted crystallographer in generations and only with his leadership and diligent work could the Alvian people tune the remainder of Earth's wild crystal deposits to their own uses.

Without Davin, the process would have taken many generations, but with Davin on the job, they were far ahead of schedule and increasing their ability to maintain the new settlements with each passing day. Expansion plans could move ahead and the High Council was happy. They had much to do to reestablish their race on this new homeworld.

He thought again of seductive Selva 56. He really should take her up on her blatant offer, but he'd keep his eyes open. He didn't trust her, but he wouldn't mind a little more sexual relief. In return he would make sure she experienced a level of sexual satisfaction she had probably never experienced. Perhaps he could make her want to be with him for more than just career advancement purposes. He knew he could make her crave the satisfaction she would find in his bed.

But first he needed some space. Davin's people didn't want him. They didn't understand him. They thought him inferior in all ways.

He was a freak, but he would rather be a freak with feelings and emotions than an automaton like the rest of his people. The geneticists had bred out aggression to end the constant warfare, but with it, they'd removed all other emotion. Once in a while a "throwback" was born, like him, with deeper emotions than the rest of the population. They were studied and patted on the head, but otherwise misunderstood and even reviled in many quarters.

Eventually, there would be an accounting. The day was coming when his people would learn the error of their ways. They would learn as they interacted more with humans—or Breeds, as they called them, a word borrowed from the human lexicon and used to disguise the higher echelon's knowledge that the native survivors were descended from the first explorers his people had sent to this remote system. The Breeds had survived because of the extraordinary mixture of human DNA with his people's genetic code. Gifted with extrasensory perception and psychic abilities of all kinds, the Breeds survived the crystal seeding of the Earth that had raised the resonance of the entire planet, making it habitable for Alvians. In their arrogance, Davin's people had stolen this beautiful blue planet and murdered most of its native inhabitants. It was a heinous crime he feared they would never understand.

Chapter One

"She's coming." Harry spoke into the silence of the ranch house kitchen. Callie felt the waves of fear his words inspired with her strong empathic gift, and wanted to go to him, but he caught her eye and sent a short burst of telepathic thought. He had to do this alone. She understood, but still wanted to stand by her brother as their family turned to look at him with varying degrees of alarm.

"Your mother? Mara's coming here?" Mama Jane's cheeks went pale as Harry nodded. "Dear Lord, why?" Her voice was a terrified whisper.

It had been a long time since the alien scientist called Mara 12 had come out to the O'Hara ranch for any reason. Harry's biological mother literally had the power of life and death over all the human inhabitants in the small, protected valley. Harry's gaze shifted to the eldest of the three O'Hara brothers.

"Papa Caleb knows why."

"What's going to happen, Caleb?" Jane whispered. The whole family knew Caleb had a strong gift of precognition. He knew things about the future.

He sighed and leaned forward, resting his hands on the table. "She's coming for me."

"No!" Her mother got up and went to him. Callie felt the sorrow, fear and flat out denial that surrounded them, but knew from past experience Papa Caleb's visions were never wrong. "Is there anything we can do?"

"It's okay, sweetheart. It'll be all right." He stroked his wife's hair with deep affection, turning to nod at Harry. "Tell her, son."

Mama Jane's gaze focused on Harry, Justin's son by the alien Mara 12. Compared to his human half brothers and sisters, Harry had almost supernatural powers, but today he looked fragile where he rarely had before. Like Callie, he was only fifteen years old, and just getting comfortable with his incredible gifts of both intellect and psychic ability.

"I worked out a deal," Harry said softly. "It was the best I could do."

"You did good, son." Papa Caleb reached out and patted Harry's arm, comforting the nephew who was more like a son to him. "You did the best you could for this family and I thank you."

"What sort of deal?" Papa Justin demanded Harry's attention. "What are they going to do with Caleb?"

"They want to study him, sample his DNA, mix it in with their own." Harry collapsed into a chair by the kitchen table as if he'd run a very long race, ending in defeat. Callie went to him then and stood at his side, touching his arm and giving him encouragement using her empathic gift. He was full of pain, and she soothed it as best she could. She loved her brother and didn't want to see him hurt.

"But why?" their mother sobbed. "Why Caleb?"

Harry's sad gaze shifted to her. "My mother thinks the Hara DNA is strongest in Papa Caleb, though it runs true in all three O'Hara brothers. She wanted to take them all at first, but I argued against it. Surprisingly, she listened. She does have some respect for the line of Hara, after all, and I convinced her to compromise."

"What's the compromise?" Papa Mick was the youngest of the three O'Hara brothers, and the family doctor.

"You know Alvians don't age like humans. It's a gift of their DNA. They're not quite immortal, but they do live for hundreds of years. My mother's tests confirm you all carry that part of their genetic code within you, but it's not active, so you age like humans. She's agreed to develop a process to turn off your human aging genes in return for Papa Caleb's cooperation. She wants to keep him for a decade, and she'd already planned to try to stop his aging when she got him. I convinced her to do it to all of you. Even Mama Jane, though she has no Hara DNA. And when the time is right and they're grown enough, she'll do the same for every one of my brothers and sisters."

"Jeez! She agreed to this?" Papa Mick looked stunned as Harry nodded.

Jane crumpled. "Ten years? That's an awful long time to be apart."

"Alvians live a lot longer than humans. They think of time differently because of it." Caleb's tone was contemplative.

"She's convinced extending your lifespans will give her more time to study you all and keeping Mama Jane around is supposed to keep you and your brothers cooperative," Harry said.

"Then she'll probably come for each of us at one time or another." Papa Justin slammed one hand down on the tabletop. "Damn!"

"She won't let the current test subject go for any reason while she's performing her study, but I'll be able to go back and forth, to keep the lines of communication open. And of course, there's no way she can monitor our telepathy." Harry was the bridge that would keep this unconventional family together, even in the direst of circumstances.

"I don't want you to go." Their mother wept as she hugged Papa Caleb. Callie knew he'd been Jane's husband in the old world, before the cataclysm. Only later, she'd been told, when it became clear there would be no mates for the other O'Hara brothers, had Jane and Caleb expanded their relationship to include Justin and Mick. Callie understood it wasn't the way things used to be, but she'd grown up with the three men all acting as fathers to her and her siblings. Each of the kids knew pretty well which of the brothers was their biological father and Jane was the mother of all the O'Hara children, except Harry. He was half-Alvian, but Jane had opened her heart to Harry when he was just a baby and he and Callie had been raised as brother and sister, here on the ranch.

Caleb quieted Jane, stroking her back with his big, capable hands. "It's only for a few years, and in return for my time in purgatory, you'll stop aging. Think of all the time we'll have to be together when it's over. And think what we can do with the extra years we'll have for the rest of our kind." He took both of her hands in his and looked into her sad eyes. "Janie, I saw this coming. Not all of it, but enough to know this is the way it's got to be. A few years in return for the possibility of saving countless human lives. It's worth it, Jane. It's got to be."

Harry spoke up again. "My mother also agreed to stop killing captives. She knows from studying us that she could be responsible for losing more traces of their Founders' DNA if they continue to let their human prisoners die."

"So we've accomplished that much already," Caleb said with a satisfied smile. "But we have more work to do, right Harry?"

"Much more work," he agreed. "And I promise, I'll be there with you in the city. I won't leave you."

Caleb smiled at his nephew. "You're a good boy, Harry."

Weeks later, thousands of miles away, Davin sat eating his breakfast. The yellow sun of this new solar system warmed his skin as it rose above the treeline. His workday was about to begin, but he had a little time yet to reflect on his observations of this new planet.

Few realized just how easily he could access all aspects of data kept in the crystals he cared for. Even fewer realized just how much he knew about the High Council's plans for Earth, or their observations of the rather surprising Breeds they'd discovered once the crystal seeding was done. They didn't understand the natives and seemed to think nothing of the fact that while they'd spent hundreds of years traveling to Earth, the primitive people initially found on the planet had advanced.

Davin kept tabs on the various scientific studies of the natives from his office in the main engineering facility, nestled in the mountains of what the humans had once called South America. He rather liked the name. Most of the human languages had a very lyrical ring to his ears, though his translator implant allowed him to comprehend and speak almost fluently in all the native tongues of this planet, as well as his own. Only a small percentage of words were missing from the databases—some, he knew for a fact, had been left out on purpose—like the term "half-breed" and the shortened form they'd adopted to call the native human population.

Davin had hacked into the crystals that transmitted from

the Breed observation labs in the northern city for the first time the week before, and was appalled by what he saw. He'd tapped into fertility reports and discovered the scientists were not pleased that their test subjects had such short lifespans. As a result, they were deliberately trying to breed more and their methods didn't take emotion into account at all, though emotion was the very thing they wanted to study. That, and the way human and Alvian DNA mixed to create amazing mental powers. But standard Alvian testing methods could take decades and these short-lived Breeds were a problem. Having been raised in the wild, they were uncooperative in captivity. Some in the scientific community had settled on the idea of raising a new generation in captivity that would be more docile and amenable to their plans.

Davin watched, helpless, as a lab tech separated a naked female from three males who'd been fighting with a fourth male in the same enclosure. His heart ached for the pain on the woman's face and his primitive anger erupted when he got a good look at the damage done to the injured male. Instinctively, he knew that man had tried to defend her.

The lab tech took the injured male and the woman to a separate cell. Davin followed their progress, hacking into various observation stations. He had to do this work delicately, lest the scientists discover him.

It was a couple of days before he could track down the woman and her protector. Work had interfered when he'd wanted to see how they fared, the crystals demanding his attention before he could find the time to hack back into the science center. Then he had to find what cell or cells the subjects had been placed in and hack into those specific observation posts.

It was tedious work, but it kept him occupied and his curiosity would not be denied. He wanted to know the man and woman were all right, though what he could do to help them, he had no idea. He didn't have regular access to the science center. By rights he shouldn't even be aware there were Breeds being studied in the cities. But he did know, and it preyed on his mind. He had to make sure the woman and her protector were all right.

Davin found them hours later, in a darkened cell. He could

see them both clearly through the enhanced viewing device. They probably didn't realize they were being observed, but he knew the test subjects were kept under constant watch.

He was somewhat surprised when he realized that the male was on top of the female, quite obviously in the midst of fucking her. Also odd, she didn't look like she objected. On the contrary, she appeared to be eagerly cheering him on with her passionate whimpers and soft moans of enjoyment.

Davin was shocked to feel his own body respond.

He'd never thought of himself as a voyeur, but found it nearly impossible to look away from the Breeds enjoying sex in a way his people never did. His people had sex, of course, but it was never so carnal, so primal, so downright enjoyable as it looked when these two Breeds did it.

Davin watched as the man rolled, placing the woman on top of him, still impaled and encouraging her to ride him. Her breasts bounced enticingly and Davin's mouth went dry and his dick hard. He watched the emotions playing out across their faces, building a hunger within him for that kind of feeling, that kind of love—both physical and emotional.

He didn't have any doubt as he watched the woman sweat and bounce on her partner that she looked on the man with the eyes of love. It was clear for him to read. Davin didn't understand how he knew, but even over the monitors, he could hear the hum of rightness between the couple. The crystals in his chamber reflected the brightness in their eyes, even if it was only a transmitted image.

Resonance.

The very idea stole his breath. He'd never witnessed resonance between two beings, though his culture's history was full of such pairings. In fact, it was something ancient Alvians—those who'd had emotions—strove their entire lives to find.

The woman came with an intense moan and the man spasmed a moment later, caught in the depths of her body. She collapsed on him, his arms coming around her, stroking her hair and sheltering her against his heart as he whispered words of tenderness and thanks. He kissed her in a way Davin's people would never recognize, with deep caring and love—

something that was bred out of their very DNA by the geneticists who had seized control of their culture generations ago and still ruled with a cold, calculating, scientific precision.

Davin wouldn't live by their rules much longer. He had a plan, and seeing this couple and the love they shared only made him more resolved to seek his destiny outside the city, away from Alvians. Perhaps among the Breeds he could find acceptance, some kind of understanding, someone to love him, even if he was a throwback.

Decision made, he finished his breakfast and started to plan. He had a few things to do before he could leave on his quest, but he wouldn't wait any longer. He would leave the Alvian city behind as soon as possible.

Davin saw her first from afar. She was petite, as most Breed women were when compared to the females of his species, but she was like a breath of spring to his starving senses. She was laughing, playing with a small four-legged creature inside a fenced area. Davin recalled that these creatures were called horses and this one had to be just a baby, judging from its wobbly legs and the larger version of itself that hovered some yards distant, watching attentively.

But it was the Breed girl who caught his attention. She was so full of life and emotion, her happiness shining in her eyes as she played with the baby creature, coaxing it and crooning to it. Her voice was a thing of beauty. Of course it wasn't the musical tones of his own race, but instead the slightly deeper, sexy human tones that made his blood hot with desire as her soft murmurs reached his sensitive ears.

He was so absorbed watching the small woman in the paddock below, he didn't hear the two men who came up behind him. He didn't even know they were there until a cold metal barrel made startling contact with his temple and a low voice breathed a warning.

"Don't move," the taller of the two said, deadly menace clear in his voice.

"I won't. Just don't shoot. I'm not what you think."

25

"And what's that?" the other man asked, watching him with observant eyes.

"I'm not part of the research team. I'm not like them at all."

"So what are you doing out here, watching our valley?" the first man asked. "They promised we'd be undisturbed as long as we cooperated, which we are doing—fully. What's your story?"

"I'm a throwback. I have emotions."

They smiled. He didn't know what to make of their reaction, and he was further surprised when the rifle barrel lowered to rest toward the ground, still ready, but not trained on him any longer. The darker man motioned for him to rise.

"No shame in that among us, stranger. What are you called?"

"I am Davin." He faced the tall man squarely.

"What? No numbers?"

Davin shook his head. "Throwbacks are not given numerical designations since we're not desired in the gene pool. Davin is the name I chose for myself at ten years of age."

The big Breed nodded. "I'm Justin O'Hara and this is my brother Mick."

"What are you doing way out here, Davin?" Mick asked.

Davin sighed, running one hand through his hair. He wasn't accustomed to explaining himself, but he needed their understanding. It was important these Breeds not report his presence here to their keepers. If the Maras knew he was sniffing around their experiments, there would be increased scrutiny from the High Council, which he definitely didn't want.

"I need to leave the others every once in a while. It's hard to be around them. I go into the Waste and try to learn about your planet firsthand rather than from their observations. It helps me in my work and helps me stay as sane as I can among them."

Justin's eyes narrowed. "I guess it would be hard to be the only one with feelings for miles around. I'd probably take off into the hinterlands myself. But that doesn't explain what you're doing up here, watching us."

Davin shrugged, unable to give them the full truth. "Curiosity. I've never observed Breeds in their natural environment, interacting with each other and their surroundings on an emotional level. It's fascinating."

"We're not *Breeds*." Mick emphasized the word as if it were a curse. "We're human. That's the name of our race."

"I stand corrected," Davin allowed graciously. He hadn't realized they were so touchy about the term, but he'd remember in the future.

"Well," Justin shouldered his weapon, "there's only one way to be certain you're telling the truth."

"What's that?" Davin wasn't sure he liked the man's tone.

"Not what, but who," Mick said with a thoughtful look. "We have several strong empaths among our family. Jane, especially, will be able to feel your emotions—if you really have them."

"One of your females is empathic?" Davin wondered privately if it would be the gorgeous young woman he'd glimpsed in the field. "I'd heard about your mental powers but I've never experienced it firsthand." In truth, he was fascinated by the idea of the Breeds' extra-sensory abilities. Fascinated and a little concerned they might be able to harm him, even with his advanced technology, but it was worth the risk. He would risk his very existence to connect with another being on an emotional level—something he'd longed for his entire life.

"You are a miracle, Jane O'Hara." Davin was humbled by the warm reception he received from the mother of the O'Hara clan. Justin and Mick moved to flank her, their arms coming over her shoulders protectively, one on either side as Davin sank to one knee in respect.

"Just so you understand," Justin said with soft menace, "Jane is *our* miracle. Women are rare in our world now and we protect them fiercely. Your own people have guaranteed our safety in return for our cooperation."

"Justin." Jane turned to him, stroking his chest with one small hand. Seeing her unthinking gesture of love and comfort toward the man who so fiercely defended her, Davin was struck again with the emptiness of his own existence. He held up his palms in a gesture of peace as he remained vulnerable, on one knee before them.

"Jane O'Hara, your males are right to protect you. I mean none of you any harm. I only seek to learn and, unlike those of my kind you've dealt with before, I do understand the emotional aspects of what my people have done to your kind and your planet. I am deeply ashamed and filled with sorrow at our actions that have caused such death and destruction."

Jane reached forward and took both of his hands in hers, tugging to indicate he should stand. He did, looking down at her as he struggled for calm. It was a shock to be in the presence of beings who felt so deeply and understood him on an emotional level.

"I feel the truth of your words." She put one arm around each of her male protectors' waists in a reassuring gesture. "My love belongs to the O'Hara brothers, as theirs belongs to me," she said formally in words he could easily understand so there would be no confusion. "But I can offer you friendship. I think you need a friend, Davin, and I think perhaps you might find a few of them here at our ranch."

Davin met each of their gazes. "I know you have young living here. I want you to know I would never harm a child in any way."

Jane merely nodded as if she knew that already, and he realized she could probably read every emotion that festered in his damned soul. It was an uncomfortable thought.

"We have a rather non-traditional family, considering human history, but it works for us." Her smile was accepting and gracious. "Our children are curious and if you stay here for any length of time, they will no doubt plague you with questions."

"Do any of them share your amazing gifts?" he couldn't help but ask.

She nodded. "All of them have some amount of empathy, some stronger than others. But they share their fathers' gifts as well, so beware of telekinetically sprung practical jokes."

"The nosy little eavesdroppers are already listening in," Mick said with mock disgust as he opened a door from the kitchen, revealing a small group of chagrined children of various ages.

But Davin only had eyes for the tall female he'd seen frolicking with the infant horse in that green pasture. His mouth went dry and his insides flamed as he saw her features clearly for the first time. As delicate as her mother, but taller, probably owing to her father's height. Davin wondered idly which one of the O'Hara men was her sire, but it really didn't matter. What mattered was that she was here, and her innocent beauty inspired him to hope.

Jane came up beside him, her gaze moving from his dazed expression to where her oldest child stood, equally dazed in the doorway behind her younger siblings. The others were all making loud excuses to the two O'Hara men who teased them.

"I feel your fascination with my daughter, Callie," she said in a low, almost worried voice. "She's very young, Davin, and strongly empathic. Please make an effort to conceal your desire from her if you can. Mick might be able to show you how."

Davin turned. "I would never harm her. You have my word of honor."

"You don't understand the empathic gift. You can literally make her feel your own desires and she's too inexperienced to know whether her feelings are her own or merely reflections of yours. I wouldn't want that for her, Davin. She's too precious to my heart."

The mother's entreaty touched his emotions. "I will endeavor to comply, but I fear I'll need further instruction in the control of my emotions."

Dawning realization showed on her features. "This must be so new to you. I'm sorry, I didn't consider it. I think subjecting you to the whole family at once might be rough." She summoned Mick over, motioning Justin to keep the kids in the other part of the house for now.

Mick, Jane and Davin moved from the kitchen to the outbuilding that had been made into a combination laboratory, examining room and office for Mick's medical work. Davin was surprised to learn that the youngest O'Hara brother had been training to be a veterinarian before the cataclysm, and now was the closest thing the family had to a doctor.

"Did you plan to stay in the area?" Jane asked once they were seated in Mick's lab.

"I've been sleeping in a nearby cave for the past two nights. I stored my flyer within. Before departing, I told my subordinates I'd be gone for a week. They didn't understand what I might want to do on my own in the Waste for a week, but they're used to me being odd."

Mick sat back in his chair. "Well, there's an old human saying, 'Keep your friends close and your enemies closer'. You might as well stay here at the ranch than in a cave. It's got to be more comfortable."

"And you will know where I am," Davin agreed, trying not to take insult from the man's blatant distrust.

"There's still the complication of Callie," Jane said while Mick bristled.

"What about Callie?" Mick's expression grew stern, the male's protective instincts coming out as Davin watched with interest.

"Um," Jane seemed hesitant, "Davin here is quite attracted to her. I was hoping you could show him how to hide it." Jane addressed Davin. "You see, of all the brothers, only Mick ever mastered the ability to hide his emotions completely from me. Maybe he can show you how it's done."

"If he can't hide it from her, we'll have to keep them separate," Mick said. Davin didn't know if he was capable of the task, but it immediately became imperative to try. He didn't want to be kept away from the girl. She was quickly becoming an obsession.

Jane made a rude noise. "Easier said than done, Mick. And I don't want Justin to know. He'd go insane. It's only for five days." Jane turned to Davin. "Justin is Callie's biological father and he's extremely protective of her. Well," she admitted with a small grin, "he's protective of all the children, but he has a special need to protect the really empathic kids. He knows how I suffered with my gift and he wants to keep them from doing the same."

"Justin was an officer in our military special forces before the cataclysm," Mick warned. "He has skills the rest of us don't even want to know about and is deadly when riled. We don't want that kind of trouble here, Davin."

Davin nodded, understanding the gravity of the situation. "I didn't come here to cause trouble. I'll do what you ask to hide my emotions from her, if I can. But I tell you this now..." his eyes narrowed, "...if she has her own true feelings for me, they will not be denied. I came to the Waste knowing I could never find a true mate among my own kind. I came here with the idea of either finding my true mate among the Breeds or ending my existence before I follow the rest of my throwback brethren into madness."

"Throwbacks go mad?" Jane asked quietly, and even Mick seemed curious. Davin realized the man was a scientist, after all. Davin had been studied his entire life for his oddities. It seemed nothing had changed, even among these strangers. Davin was the odd man out, the freak of nature to be studied and dissected. Still, these folk had more of a chance than his own people at understanding. He would give them an explanation, since of all the beings he had ever met, these Breeds might just hold the key to his salvation.

"I have studied my people's histories closely over my lifetime, seeking answers," Davin said shortly. "I've found evidence in early writings that when our people had strong emotions—before they were bred out by the geneticists—our males often spent years of their lives on mate quests. For each male, it was said, there was one female who resonated on his emotional wavelength. Males outnumbered females about two to one when our people bred naturally. If the male found his mate, they would join for the rest of their lives and breed the next generation. If he did not find her, he would most often put his energies into his work. Many would become warriors to focus their aggression and anger at not finding their mate. Ours was a very violent race and we would war amongst ourselves endlessly. The supply of young warriors was large and most would die in battle. It was deemed preferable to do so than go into old age and madness alone. Without a mate, most often, our males would go insane as they aged." Davin ran a hand through his hair in frustration. "I'm like them. I have the emotions the geneticists sought to remove from our race. Throwbacks like me almost always end in madness. Still, I have hope I might find my mate among your people and avoid that terrible end."

31

"You think Callie...?" Jane breathed.

Davin shook his head. "I have no idea if Callie could be my resonance mate, but I would like to see if such could be the case. There are ancient tests our males performed to find their resonance mates."

"What sort of tests?" Mick asked with suspicion.

Davin held up the hand of peace. "Nothing that could harm her in any way. The first stage is merely the Hum. If we are compatible, there are further tests."

"The Hum?" Jane asked, "What's that?"

Davin looked surprised. "You haven't noticed it between you? The air fairly throbs with the Hum when you touch."

Mick looked intrigued. "Is it a physical sound you hear?" At Davin's nod, Mick turned to his big computer station and flicked the switches, warming up the machine. "Human hearing is probably not as good as yours. Can you tell me the frequency range you hear this Hum in?" Mick had auditory testing equipment on a low bench. He motioned Davin over and asked him to help him find the right frequencies. Adapting some of the computer equipment, Davin invited Jane to stand beside Mick in front of the auditory pickups.

"Touch her and you may have your answers," Davin said softly, backing off to the other side of the room so as not to interfere in the experiment.

Mick held his hand up to Jane and she placed hers within it, starting when he squeezed as the monitor registered a jump in the frequencies the alien had shown him. He let go and the lines on the monitor stilled. He grasped her hand again and they jumped and he laughed outright as he tried it again and again in different ways.

"I'll be damned," Mick finally said, turning to the alien. "You can hear this?"

Davin nodded. "You may test the range of my hearing, if you wish."

Mick smiled at the offer. "I would definitely like to do that. I've tested Harry, of course," he said to the woman who still stood by his side, "but I had no idea!"

"Who is Harry?" Davin asked as they turned back to him.

Mick laughed. "If you think Justin is protective of our daughter Callie, he's got nothing on her brother Harry."

Jane motioned for Davin to sit as she resumed her seat at Mick's side. "Harry is the son of Justin and one of your scientists, Mara 12."

Chapter Two

Jane felt Davin's shock. "I'd heard rumors," he said softly, "but I didn't dare believe."

Jane grew concerned. "Why is the existence of Hara DNA on Earth such a big deal to your people?"

"You are definitely of the line of Hara?" His breathing quickened in excitement.

"Not me," she said, watching him carefully. "Caleb, Justin and Mick have the Hara DNA, as do our children."

Davin slid into a chair as his emotions swelled in a way Jane felt he was unprepared to handle. Mick came over, ready to assist with his medical training, but Davin held up a hand to fend him off.

"I'm all right. Blessed Hara! I can't believe it!"

"I think he's just overwhelmed," Jane said, battling to keep the alien man's emotions from battering her. "This is really important to him, Mick. He felt a huge burst of hope when we started talking about Hara." She moved beside him. "Why is this so important to you, Davin?"

He held her gaze as if it were a lifeline. "Hara was like me. He had emotions. He lived before the geneticists were able to completely rid our people of them. He and his explorers found ways to avoid the madness that is coming for me. He was the greatest of us and he was lost to us, but now..." He looked over at Mick. "Now he's reborn in you and your family. It's a miracle and a hope for the future that you cannot comprehend. I doubt even my people can understand what the reintroduction of Hara DNA will do to us."

He seemed happy, so Jane figured he was no threat to any

of the Hara descendants on the place. If she were any judge, in fact, she'd bet he would only redouble his efforts to protect them all now that he knew.

"And you say Harry is the son of your brother Justin and Mara 12?" He shook his head as if in disbelief. "Does he have emotions? Does he have your mental powers?"

Jane beamed, feeling the awe and respect in the other man. "Yes to both. Harry is...well, he's just the greatest."

"And he is brother to Callie. By the First Crystal! She is a descendant of Hara!" He seemed stunned by the realization. "If we Hum..." He trailed off, contemplating the enormity of his thoughts, Jane realized with some satisfaction. Here was a man who would value her daughter...as long as they "Hummed".

"So after the Hum, what are the other tests?" Mick asked in a skeptical tone.

Davin started at the question. "Next there's the Kiss."

"I don't know if I like the sound of that," Mick said darkly.

"It's not as intimate as it sounds. If your equipment is still on, I can show you." Davin stood up and moved toward the computer, reaching into his pocket for a small crystal that he placed on the desk in front of the small microphone pickup. "Stand here." He motioned to both of them and they complied with raised eyebrows. "Now raise your hands and let your palms kiss." Immediately the Hum registered on the monitors. "Good, now bend your lips to hers," he instructed Mick, who complied with a grin.

When Mick's lips touched hers the familiar fire blossomed in her gut, even after the years they'd been free to explore their passion for each other. She responded to his kiss, losing herself in the moment until she heard a sigh of satisfaction from off to her side. She raised her eyelids to find Davin nodding at them with more than a bit of envy.

"The crystal glows, the Hum escalates. You are true mates, I am certain. But the next test will tell for sure."

Jane looked down at the crystal, which indeed was glowing with an orangey red light from within, and the lines on the monitors had increased dramatically.

"What's the next test?" Mick wanted to know, his breath a little bit ragged.

"The Embrace," Davin said. Jane could feel he wasn't unaffected by watching them, his envy vying with his yearning and his own lust as he educated them in the ancient ways of his people. "Take her in your arms, kiss her and fit your body to hers. This test is best done with as few clothes as possible between you, but you'll get the idea, I think, when you see what the monitors and the crystal do."

Mick didn't need to be told twice, though Jane was a little shy around the Alvian. Still, she went willingly into Mick's tight embrace, feeling his cock stir against the juncture of her thighs as he lifted her off her feet and kissed her deeply. The room was suddenly glowing with bright yellow light and Jane realized it was coming from the crystal. Mick broke the kiss long enough to check the monitors and she was able to see the lines waving crazily as the Hum increased exponentially.

She also felt the waves of lust coming from the alien man and it made her a little uncomfortable. He was undoubtedly older than both she and Mick, and had seen plenty in his lifetime as an interstellar traveler, but he'd never seen two beings with emotions behave so intimately in front of him, she would bet. And then she remembered he was showing them these things so he could try them out on her little girl.

"You're not going to grab Callie like that, are you? She's very innocent, Davin. You could scare her half to death. You're so much older and worldlier than she is."

Jane was touched by the immediate compassion she felt from him. "If we do not Hum, there's no need for further tests, Jane. Don't worry."

"Is there more after the Embrace?" Mick asked.

Davin sighed. "Only the Joining. But that is a formality. If the crystal glows as the sun, then you are truly mates. The Joining will only make it shine with the light of a thousand stars."

Mick released Jane, allowing her to catch her breath. "What sort of crystal is it?"

Davin picked up the clear pointed object and handed it to Mick for inspection. "It's quartz, but tuned. The fact that your planet had so much raw quartz made it ideal for us. It only needed the introduction of our home crystal to tune it to our needs. Now your Earth sings with our tones and your quartz is

Davin's Quest

tuning all over your world to the new frequencies. It is something we need to survive and we use the tuned crystal in many diverse ways. It powers our cities and our machinery. It also heals us and renews us. I am a crystal engineer, by training and temperament. It is very satisfying work, but the thought of how we brought your planet's crystal deposits to life pains me at every turn. Had I known our reports of primitive life on this planet were so very wrong, I never would have helped put the crystal seeding plan into action."

Jane watched him, feeling his deep remorse. "We all have some guilt to bear in our lives," she said softly, surprising him, she could tell. He'd probably expected nothing but condemnation for his admission about taking part in the destruction of their way of life and the deaths of millions of innocent people. "What's important is that we learn from our mistakes and do not repeat or compound them."

Davin nodded at her with respect. "You are wise indeed, Jane O'Hara."

She smiled. "I hope you'll still think so when I ask you to give my daughter Callie some space. She's very young and innocent. And very empathic."

"I'll do my best not to let my emotions influence her. But you must realize that if we Hum, I will want to test her further to see if we are true mates or not. At that point, my emotions and her empathy will have little to do with what must be between us. For each male there is only one true mate, or so the legends say. If it is meant to be, then she will be mine."

"Only one?" Jane asked, her face crumpling in a way that made Davin feel guilty.

"So it is written. Although there have been a few notable exceptions in our history."

"But..." Jane moved her stricken gaze to Mick as he stroked her cheek.

"It doesn't apply to us, Jane."

Not understanding, Davin moved closer. "But it does. You Hum and you make the crystal glow. You are true mates." Jane was on the verge of tears now, and still he didn't understand how his words were hurting her.

"Davin, after your people destroyed our world, there were

37

few women left," Mick said softly. "Jane was already married to my older brother, Caleb."

"I don't understand."

"You haven't met Caleb yet because he's in your city being studied by Mara 12 right now, but Caleb is our leader, our guide. He has the gift of foresight and everything we've built here, we did because of his visions. He gave us time to prepare before your people's attacks on the Earth began." Davin was staggered by the thought of the older brother's power and how it had saved his family. "Caleb also foresaw the coming of Mara and how we had to stand united in order to survive. Justin and I..." Mick trailed off, seemingly embarrassed.

"What he's trying to say is that Caleb and I expanded our marriage to include Justin and Mick when he foresaw there were no mates in their future. He knew unless they were able to express the love we all share, none of us would survive. You see, I grew up with the O'Hara brothers. They've protected me and nurtured me all my life and I love each one of them with all my heart." She smiled softly, touching his own fragile heart. "It's not conventional—or it wouldn't have been in the old world—but all three of them are my mates. I'm willing to bet if we performed your tests, all three of them would make that crystal glow."

Davin simply shook his head at this small woman's generosity of spirit. "It's true that when you touched Justin I heard the Hum, but I thought I must have been wrong. I don't pretend to understand it, but then yours is a very unique situation I will admit. What my people did to the Earth and to your people is criminal. Perhaps this is a manifestation of the Divine's work to aid you in rebuilding your world and your people."

Further discussion halted when the door opened and Justin walked in. Mick turned away to study his computers, his expression closed while Jane just looked nervous. But she was definitely willing to dare, extending her hand to the other man and beckoning him forward.

"Justin, we've just been discussing Davin's people and their traditions."

"Anything interesting?" he asked idly, taking his woman's hand and Davin immediately heard the Hum. Mick noted it too on the computer and turned to show the others. He explained shortly about the Hum Davin heard, not going into full detail as Jane took the experiment to the next step. Mick replaced the crystal on the desk as she placed her palms over Justin's, beckoning him down for a kiss. He complied with a bemused expression, but didn't ask too many questions.

Davin was surprised to see the crystal glow red orange and the Hum increase. Jane didn't waste time deepening the Kiss into a full Embrace, not giving Justin a moment to think. Davin watched as the tall man aligned her supple body with his, plundering her mouth and delving deep within. It made him hot to watch this raw emotion and he only prayed he found a woman as compatible with him as this one was with her chosen mates. The crystal was glowing like the sun now and the Hum had increased in pitch.

Jane looked relieved when Justin set her down and she smiled at them all.

"Now what was that all about?" Justin demanded, a small quirk of his mouth showing that he knew something was going on, but was willing to indulge his woman.

"Just testing a theory," Jane said with a saucy smile. "Apparently only a true mate can make the crystal glow, according to Davin's cultural traditions. I'm happy to report that both you and Mick are my true mates."

Justin tugged her close for a quick hug and peck on the cheek. "Hell, I could've told you that even without his fancy parlor tricks. You were born for us, Janie. You are our salvation."

"You have to go back soon, don't you?" Jane asked as she shared lunch with Davin a few days later.

Davin nodded. "Tomorrow night, actually. But, if you permit..." he felt greatly daring as he approached the woman who could undoubtedly feel how important his next words were to him, "...I would like to come back."

Jane nodded and smiled. "I think I'd like that. But I may have to convince Justin and Mick a bit. Mick says you've been working hard on the exercises he's given you."

It was Davin's turn to nod. "Yes, and I will continue to do

so. This way, when I return, perhaps I'll be able to shield my emotions more completely from your daughter. I still want very much to know her."

Jane sighed. "She's only fifteen, Davin."

"I understand your objections. But I really need to know."

"Why is this so important to you? Even if you do Hum and make the crystals glow, she's too young. She's still a child, Davin. Still a little girl in so many ways."

Davin cursed silently. "Knowing that I have a mate, even if she is too young to claim right now could be the difference between sanity and death for me, Jane. They monitor me all the time, and though I'm too important to dispose of right now, at the first sign of madness I will be put down, discarded and forgotten like so much rubbish."

"That's awful!"

"That's the truth."

Jane stood to go, pausing by the door as if coming to some decision while Davin held his breath. So much rested with this one compassionate woman.

"I'll send Callie to you with dinner. You won't be alone, but perhaps you can manage to test your theories about whether or not you Hum if you touch her." She turned wide, scared eyes on him, driving home how hard this was for her. "But please don't let her know what you're about. She won't be able to hear the Hum. Please don't tell her. Give her time to grow into the woman who could possibly be your mate. If she's meant for you, she'll come to you on her own terms, not because of some resonance tests your people have. She's human, Davin. Not Alvian."

Davin bowed his head. "She is at least part Alvian, my lady. As are you." He didn't want to correct her, but he knew this point was important.

Jane nodded. "Okay. I accept that. But she's more human. She doesn't understand your traditions. She's been raised to expect to love the man she ultimately commits her life to, and always thought it would be a human man, or perhaps more than one human man, not one of your kind. There are so few of our women left. She knows this. She's seen the reality of what I had to do to keep my family together. All I ask is that you let her get used to the idea of you in our lives as a friend." She looked out the doorway into the distance. "The only Alvians we've had contact with are Mara 12 and the soldiers she brings with her. All we've known of your people up until now has been fear. Give Callie time to get used to the idea that you're different."

"What you say has merit, my lady. You are truly wise." Davin sighed. "I'll do as you wish and you have my word I won't rush her. Besides," he smiled at his reluctant hostess, "all this may be for naught. We may not even Hum." But in his heart of hearts he knew this brave woman's first-born daughter would be his. They would Hum. He just knew it.

Callie followed Mick into the office later that evening, bearing a tray. Mick was similarly laden, but he motioned to Callie when Davin came forward to help him with his burden. Holding the door wide for the young woman, Davin took the tray from her hands, making sure to brush her skin with his own.

And his heart nearly stopped.

The brief touch of her hand to his brought about a rush of sensation the likes of which he had never known. The air vibrated with the Hum of their energies meeting and meshing, then parting as she moved back from him. It was all he could do to stop himself from reaching out to pull her fully into his embrace, touching her skin and reveling in the Hum that he hadn't dared hope he would ever hear—the woman he hadn't dared hope he would ever find.

Callie looked up at him, her wide, dark eyes bemused as he stood frozen in the doorway. Davin was struck momentarily speechless as he got his first up-close look at the woman who he believed now more than ever had been born for him. Luckily Mick was there to fill in the silence, or Davin's promise to Jane might have been broken. He wanted so much to tell Callie about his discovery. He wanted to take her with him right this minute, regardless of her youth. She was his!

Or she would be. In a couple of years.

That was the bargain he'd struck. He saw the sense of it in his mind, but his heart was screaming out for him to stake his claim on this woman here and now.

"Come all the way in, girl," Mick said briskly to his niece.

Callie blushed prettily and ducked under Davin's outstretched arm, moving fully into the room. She went about setting the platters and plates out, working efficiently and stealing looks at Davin from beneath her lashes when she thought no one was looking.

But Davin had eyes only for her. She was so beautiful, she took his breath away.

"Davin, you haven't met Callie yet. She's our oldest daughter." Mick hauled her close and tickled her 'til she giggled.

Davin let the door close and put the second tray on the table near her. He braced himself, but their skin didn't touch a second time and he found himself regretting that even so slight a touch was denied him. He pulled a special purple crystal out of his pocket. It was a perfect amethyst, already tuned to his energies. He'd tuned it specially as a gift for this girl, the one he hoped would be his resonance mate.

He lifted it in his hand now, holding it to the light to allow the natural facets to pick up and refract the light in a show of splendor. He was happy to see Callie's eyes follow the glow of the crystal. He saw the expression of awe and wonder on her face. It was touching to see her reaction. Her easy display of emotion was a miracle to him after all the years he'd spent among his own people.

Davin stepped forward. "I think this a fitting gift for so beautiful a young lady." He took her hand in his, prepared but still surprised by the loudness of the Hum between them. He placed the amethyst in the center of her palm and closed her fingers over it, holding her hand a bit longer than strictly necessary, but he was reveling in the Hum that reverberated through his senses as her eyes locked with his. "Please accept this as a token of my friendship."

Davin was gladdened by her reaction. She stared back at him as if entranced. Even if she couldn't hear the Hum on a physical level, it was good to know she felt something inside when they touched. He could see the fascination in her beautiful hazel eyes.

"Thank you," she breathed, her voice a mere whisper. But still it enchanted him. "It's beautiful."

"No more lovely than you." Davin smiled at her as Mick cleared his throat from across the room. Looking up, Davin noticed Mick was at his computer, recording the evidence of the Hum, and he was glad. Now the family would have proof of his claim since they couldn't hear it with their human ears. But he'd made a promise to Jane and he made himself release Callie's hand. She was still too young to subject to the rest of the tests.

Callie blushed at his compliment, clutching the amethyst to her chest when he released her hand.

"That's a very special crystal, Callie." Davin watched her with hungry eyes. "It's pure. There are no flaws in the structure, even on a molecular level. That's a rare thing in itself, but I've also tuned the crystal to my energy. I think it will be soothing to your senses."

"You mean like a worry stone?" Callie seemed intrigued and he was pleased by the quick intellect he could sense in her.

"In a way, but this crystal has been prepared to both store and release energy. Should you need it, this crystal will supply you with soothing energy. In times of plenty, it will recharge itself from the world around it. And should you have desperate need, it may help amplify your natural abilities." Davin looked over at Mick, who'd rejoined them near the table. "I've never had the opportunity to test our tuned crystals with Breed abilities, but I wouldn't be surprised if you could use this crystal to strengthen your telepathy or whatever other gifts you may have."

Mick looked intrigued, as Davin had hoped. "Can we experiment with this?"

Davin smiled and pulled a similar small quartz crystal from his pocket and tossed it to the other man. "I was hoping you'd be interested. I tuned four crystals as parting gifts for you and your family. I've made one for Justin and one for Jane, as well as these for you and Callie. Clear quartz for you and your brother, amethyst for Callie and citrine for Jane. Keep them with you at all times so that they attune to your individual energies. And yes, you should experiment with them, but don't let Mara or any of the other Alvians see them. It would be my death if they knew I'd given them to you."

Callie reached out and touched his hand, startling him. "I

43

don't want to put you in danger."

"What my people did to you and your world was wrong, Callie. You have amazing gifts that have meant the difference between life and death for you and your family. If these crystals can help you strengthen those gifts, I'm willing to take the chance."

He covered her hand with his, pressing lightly to emphasize his point. "I want you to keep that amethyst with you. If ever you need me, touch it and focus your thoughts on me. It should open a secure channel of communication between us."

"You're not like the other aliens I've seen."

"No. I'm not like them at all. I have feelings. I'm a genetic throwback. I'm more like my ancestors than my contemporaries."

Callie nodded, seeming years older than she really was. "Harry told me about that. He thinks he's kind of like that too, being half-Alvian, yet having such strong emotions." Her wide eyes softened as her gentle voice lowered. "I feel sorry for you."

"Don't. I'm the luckiest man among my people. Most of them will never know the true beauty of a sunset or the magical wonder of dawn. They'll never feel love or hate or any other emotion. Pity them, not me."

"You have a wonderful way of looking at things." She pulled back and he released her. "I'll keep your amethyst with me always."

Davin nodded, happy she would take his gift to heart. He'd struggled with what to give these fine people as a parting gift and had settled on the crystals for two reasons. First, he really did want to know if the crystals could enhance Breed abilities. His people weren't researching this yet and he knew it would be far down the list of things to study about Breeds. But the information could be vital in helping the Breeds hold their own against the Alvian scientists who continued to capture and subject them to all sorts of brutal tests, in their ignorance. The scientific community was trying to understand Breed emotional response with no frame of reference. It was an exercise in futility, as well as cruelty that made Davin angry to even think about.

Second, he wanted to give Callie a way to contact him. He

hoped she would initiate contact. He needed to talk with her and know she was safe and happy. The crystal he'd given her was special. It would allow him to monitor her well-being without really spying on her. He considered it insurance. If she got into trouble, he'd know and might be able to help. It was the best he could do for now, until he could claim her and keep her with him always.

Mick examined the clear crystal, his sharp eyes thoughtful. "Thank you, Davin. I'll do some experimenting and see what we can do with these."

Davin nodded and Mick sent Callie back to the house. She left with a last long look in Davin's direction and he couldn't help the pang of regret at her departure. When they were alone he turned to Mick.

"You saw the proof, didn't you? She and I Hum."

"I saw it. I can't say I like it, but I saw it. And when the time comes to take this further, I won't stand in your way."

"Thank you for that, Mick. I won't hurt her, but when she's older, I'll want to perform the next test. For now, it's enough to know there's hope."

Mick clapped him on the shoulder companionably as they sat down to dinner. "There's always hope, my friend. Always."

"Do you have some kind of data storage device that can interface with my computer system?" Mick surprised Davin with the question as he was packing his few meager belongings in preparation for leaving the ranch.

"I think I could rig one of my smaller crystals to do the job. What did you have in mind?"

Mick seemed to be considering his response, looking him over in a way he didn't quite understand before making his decision.

"A parting gift. I have some digital images of Callie as she grew up. I think you should have a few of them."

Davin was dumbfounded. He thought all the adult O'Haras were against him pursuing a relationship with their daughter.

But perhaps he'd been wrong.

"Why would you do that for me?"

Mick met his eyes with determination. "I was in love with Callie's mother from almost the moment I met her. She was only about five years old and I was only a little older. I wouldn't have traded the time we had together growing up for anything. And then I had to put aside my feelings for her forever, I thought, when she married my brother. It wasn't easy. Neither was resurrecting those feelings when your peoples' actions left us no alternative. But I've come to peace with it for the most part. Still, I think I have a little bit of an understanding of how you may be feeling right now. Callie is too young, but you have hope. In a few years, who knows? In the meantime..." He calmly pushed a few buttons on his keyboard and images of Callie at various ages appeared, entrancing him. "These may help you get through the wait."

Davin felt a wave of longing as he saw the images of the woman he thought might be his resonance mate. She was beautiful to him, and so full of life and emotion as she laughed into the camera, so unlike his people. He realized Mick was right. These images would be something to hold against the bleakness of his existence, a ray of hope to cling to as he waited and fought against the madness.

Davin grasped Mick's hand the way he'd learned humans did, and pulled the other man in for a quick, thankful embrace.

"This is the nicest thing anyone has ever done for me, Mick."

Mick tried to shrug off the moment, turning to the computer and preparing the files he wanted Davin to have. "If she is your resonance mate and you two do get together at some point in the future, I just want your promise that you'll always treat her with love and respect, and protect her with your life."

Davin nodded solemnly. "You have my vow, Mick O'Hara."

Chapter Three

Rick St. John had learned survival skills at his father's knee. There was no better man to learn from than Zachariah St. John, former Army Ranger and medical doctor. He knew how to survive in the worst conditions, how to hide and how to fight. But the day the Alvians finally caught up with him, Rick was not at his best. Sick with a high fever, he wasn't able to use his gift of healing or his extensive knowledge of either medicine or self-defense. His reaction time was way off and when the soldiers captured him, they took him not to prison, but to a hospital ward where he stayed for the first three weeks of his captivity.

He didn't make a lot of friends during that time, but he'd used the opportunity to learn more about his new situation. He didn't let on about the true extent of his psychic talents. As far as they knew, he was a minor telepath. He wasn't about to become the subject of study when they realized just what he could do. Healing talent as strong as his was rare. He'd be damned if he'd give the Alvians another lab rat.

In the end, it didn't make any difference. Rick was transported to the pens below the city and stuck in a cell with a few other men. From time to time their jailors would come and take one or a few of them elsewhere for a while to be used in their experiments. Sometimes those experiments were as innocuous as being weighed, measured and given a medical exam. Sometimes they were downright depraved, owing to the fact, Rick believed, that the aliens had absolutely no clue what impact emotions had on their captives' responses.

He'd become a sort of leader of his small group of cellmates and when the Alvians tested their mettle by throwing a naked girl in with them, nobody moved. The girl couldn't be more than eleven or twelve and while Rick was as hungry for pussy as the next man, he wouldn't become subhuman, as their jailors no doubt expected.

Rick tore a sheet off one of the cots as the girl cowered in fear by the door. Approaching slowly, he used his small gift of telepathy to try to calm her, but her thoughts were too chaotic. Calling on memories of his father and the way Zach St. John had been able to tame wild animals with calm movements, words and thoughts, Rick tried to imitate the soothing sounds and motions as he crept forward, holding the sheet out in front of him.

He kept an eye on his cellmates too. They were edgy, but they respected his abilities and let him lead. Of course, he was ready to fight should one of them forget who was in charge here, but he didn't think it would come to that. Most of them had learned not to mess with him, and every one of them was what Rick would consider a good guy. He didn't think they'd stoop to attacking a child. They were hungry, but not yet driven to perversion.

Rick gave the sheet to the girl and wasn't surprised when she grabbed at it like a wild thing, covering herself as she regarded him with terror. He squatted down a few feet away from her and tried to project calm, but the poor creature was too far gone. The Alvians had essentially thrown this little lamb to the wolves. Rick felt compassion and rage in equal measures—compassion for the poor girl and rage at their captors for the unfeeling use and abuse of such a frightened creature.

He stood and faced the camera he knew was monitoring their every move.

"It won't work, you bastards." His anger burned through his veins. "We're not animals to be thrown a piece of meat. We won't cooperate and we won't hurt her any more than you have already, you unfeeling savages."

The men in the cell shuffled a bit, but one by one they stepped forward to stand with Rick, facing the camera, turning their back on the shivering girl by the door.

"Does this one answer for all of you, then?" a new voice asked from near the doorway.

Rick spun to find one of the scientists watching them. He was one of the older ones, though guessing the age of Alvians wasn't easy. The pale man was flanked by two big soldiers, so he was probably one of the more highly ranked aliens. Rick stepped forward as the girl cowered between them.

"We won't participate in rape. You should be ashamed for what you've done to this girl. She already needs psychiatric help. For that matter, your people could use a shrink—or a beating—to straighten a few things out. Probably both."

"Is that a threat?"

"It's a fact." Rick walked right up to the man, staring him down. These Alvians were so damned unemotional, it was hard to deal with them on any level. But for the girl's sake, he had to try to make this one understand.

"And what do you know of medicine, Breed?" The Alvian couldn't quite carry off a sneer, but Rick felt it all the same.

He didn't want to give the aliens any ammunition against him, but the girl needed someone to speak for her. It went against his conscience to even talk to the damned cold bastards, but someone had to. The more time he spent in the pens, the less human he felt and he knew the others felt the same.

"Quite a bit, as it happens. My father was a medical doctor, with an interest in psychiatry. He taught me most of what he knew. You've traumatized every human in your grasp without the slightest understanding of what you've done. Your ignorance is unforgivable. This girl may never be the same after what you've done to her. I know you have no feelings, but surely you take an interest in your test subjects? Torture for torture's sake is not the way of science. At least not any kind of sane science. And from what I've seen you people aren't insane, just intensely misguided."

The alien picked him apart with his gaze. "Curious." He turned on his heel and left the room, signaling to the guards to take both the girl and Rick with them.

Rick followed along silently, wondering what he'd gotten himself into. The girl whimpered, but fled the cell eagerly, and followed the Alvian soldier without much prompting. The scientist entered a white room that looked like the medical exam rooms he'd been in when he was first captured and so gravely ill.

The scientist stepped through a portal that lit up as he entered and stood there for a moment before proceeding fully into the room. The guards waited outside, motioning for the girl and Rick to enter the same way the Alvian man had. The implication was clear. The soldiers weren't entering the room but would be watching all in case Rick got any funny ideas. Rick was a big man, but these guys were even bigger and the odds weren't in his favor. Rick was smart enough to know this wasn't the time to make a break for it. He'd pick his time—and better odds—when it came. For now, he had to help the girl.

He felt a slight buzz against his skin as he stepped through the lights. They looked vaguely ultraviolet and Rick spoke before he thought better of it.

"Some kind of sterilization beam?"

The scientist looked at him with a raised eyebrow. "Very good, Breed. The sanitizing rays keep our examination rooms, patients and personnel clean during medical procedures."

Rick shrugged, trying for nonchalance. "Makes sense. And my name is Rick, not Breed."

"I am Mara 36," the man answered, surprising Rick with his almost friendly tone. He then signaled for the girl to take a seat on the exam table.

"Now," the Alvian turned to Rick again, "will you procreate with this female?"

Rick stepped back, appalled, and unable to hide his horror at the idea. "Not on your life."

"Is that a negative response?"

"You bet your ass it is."

"Excuse me?" The scientist displayed only confusion on his pale features.

Rick sighed. "I will not have sex with this girl for your entertainment."

"It is for scientific purposes, I assure you."

"The answer is still no." Rick clenched his fist at his side, wanting badly to plant it in the face of one of the Alvians, but he had to play it cool for the girl's sake. He noticed she was watching him with wide, frightened eyes as she huddled on the table.

"Why?"

Rick discarded several replies before settling on the most innocuous one. "I prefer willing partners. This girl is clearly frightened and much too young."

"Age is a factor? She is fertile, according to our observations."

"Fertility is not the only factor in whether or not humans become sexually active."

"I don't understand."

"Look—" Rick sighed, amazed at how little the aliens knew after all their testing, "—human children go through a period of years called puberty, during which their sexual organs mature and hormone levels rise. Judging by her size, this girl is at the very beginning of this portion of her life. Among rational humans, she would not be considered eligible for mating for several more years until her psyche has time to mature along with her body."

"Interesting. We had concluded fertility was the main factor in Breed mating."

"Your conclusion is wrong. We're not animals, contrary to the way you treat us. We had an advanced civilization before your people attacked. Society functioned according to rules generally agreed to among civilized people. If you managed to save any of our books or databases, you should look for a title called *The Social Contract* by a fellow named Rousseau. He was just one of our philosophers who articulated the ideals of human society. There were others—Descartes and Locke to name a few."

"How do you know of such things? I thought you were too young to have been educated in the time before our people claimed the Earth."

"I was fifteen when you attacked. I'd been through roughly ten years of schooling and would have studied more advanced subjects and specialties for another five to ten years after that before I was considered fully educated for the profession I wanted as a doctor. But my father was an educated man and he taught me from those books and others. I had a small solar-powered computer unit before I was captured that had the text of hundreds of books on it. I don't know what happened to it. Maybe it's still in my last camp." Rick shrugged, trying not to indicate how deeply the loss of his books had hurt. But then, the aliens probably wouldn't understand regret any more than they understood fear or emotional pain of any kind.

"If I had the soldiers search for it, would you show us the books?"

Rick wondered at the question. He knew damn well the aliens didn't need him to show them anything. If they wanted to see the books, with their advanced technology they'd discover a way to download them. It wasn't as if they were encrypted or anything. This Mara 36 had to have some motive in asking, but Rick would play along for now. He was curious about these aliens. Perhaps if he learned more about them, he'd discover some weakness and be able to give them a little payback for what they'd done to humanity—or more specifically, for what they'd done to his family.

"Yeah, I'll show you the books, if that's what you want. I'd like to read some of them again myself. There's not much to do when you're stuck in a prison cell twenty-four/seven."

"Twenty-four/seven? What does this mean?"

"It's an old expression meaning literally all the time. Twenty-four hours a day, seven days a week. It's how we count time. Seconds, minutes, hours, days, weeks, months, years, etc. All based on the Earth's rotation around the Sun."

The alien looked startled for a scant second before the usual bland expression reclaimed his face. "Interesting. Will you discuss this with one of our chronomaticians? I believe they would be interested in the primitive measurements. We use a similar system for each planet we inhabit."

"I'm not an expert, but I'll tell you what I know. There are probably some folks in the pens with more knowledge on the topic than me. I know for a fact, there's a woman named Sadie in the cell across from mine who was an astronomer. She'd be able to explain it all in much more detail."

Sadie was also sickly and the damp cells—though not dungeon-like, but still subterranean—were not good for her lungs. Rick would be happy if she got a chance to come up here once in a while to breathe less humid air.

Mara 36 nodded. "A good suggestion. I will pass it along." He turned abruptly back to the girl. "Now, as for this one. What is your opinion as a medical professional?"

"I never claimed to be a professional, but right off the bat, I can tell you she's scared."

"This is something we don't yet fully understand. Fear is foreign to us."

Rick felt his anger rise again, but did his best to control it. "That much is obvious from the way you torture some of us. Human women were habitually treated gently in our society. They were to be protected and nurtured so they could in turn nurture their chosen mates and children. Not always, of course. There are exceptions to every rule. But women, generally, were treated as the gentler sex, to be respected and protected."

"And you still adhere to these ways? My observations have led me to believe that most males will mount any female presented to him."

Rick wanted to curse, but kept his cool. "Starve a creature and most will turn feral. Men have strong sexual drives and since the destruction of our society, more than a few have become no better than animals. I'm not one of them."

"Commendable, but impractical for the continuation of your species."

"Perhaps extinction is the best course for a species that has lost everything. Existing as guinea pigs in your prison is not any kind of existence."

"What is a guinea pig?" Mara 36 asked.

"A small, furry rodent," the girl spoke for the first time. Rick looked at her, surprised by the change in her demeanor. She sat up straighter on the table, cloaked in the sheet, holding it around herself with white-knuckled hands. "I had one as a pet once, but my father said they used to be used in experiments."

"Your dad was right," Rick said softly, not wanting to scare the girl.

"He was a biologist in the old world. He taught me a lot about plants and animals," she said with a hint of shyness.

Rick stayed where he was, not wanting to frighten her. "He sounds like a good man. Do you know where he is now?"

53

"Probably still in the cell with my mother and little sister. They took me away last week." She nudged her chin toward the soldiers by the door.

Rick stepped closer, projecting calm as best he could. "Did they hurt you?"

She shook her head. "They hurt Daddy when he tried to stop them. I hope he's all right." Tears threatened and Rick knew he had to help her in whatever small way he could. Perhaps he could find some angle that would appeal to the scientist. He looked at the alien with shrewd eyes.

"Do you know the condition of her father?"

"He is well, though the soldiers did have to restrain him with some force. I believe they broke one of his arms, but it is healing well."

"And your plans for this girl? I have to tell you right now, putting her in with a group of hungry males is a very bad idea. Gang rape will do nothing but traumatize a youngster like this. She is not mature enough physically or emotionally to endure that kind of treatment."

"How do you know this?" Mara 36 asked.

Rick wanted to pound his fist against the wall in frustration, but restrained himself. "If you'll find my handheld device, I have a number of medical texts on human development. If you had familiarized yourself with the subject before beginning your experimentation, you could have avoided reinventing the wheel."

The scientist pursed his lips, almost smiling in amusement, but Rick couldn't see a damned thing that was funny about this situation. "A quaint expression, but one I understand. I will give this matter some thought."

"In the meantime, will you allow this girl to go back to her parents? I can assure you, she's way too young for what you had in mind. Subjecting her to the kind of experiment you intended could bring on despondency, thoughts of suicide and major psychosis."

Mara 36 sighed. "Perhaps you're right. I can delay this study for now and dispatch a team to find your device. If you agree to help me study your people's old texts, I will wait. Otherwise, the study will proceed as planned. Do I have your agreement?"

Rick saw no way out that would not harm the girl. He had no choice but to help his enemy. He'd have to make a deal with the devil.

"I agree."

Callie turned sweet sixteen a few weeks after Davin left and the family had a party for her. They'd had a celebration of Harry's sixteenth birthday just days before and he'd stayed with them at the ranch for the occasion. Harry spent a lot of his time in the alien city, getting an education and surreptitiously looking after his Papa Caleb, but he didn't want to miss Callie's special day.

The party lasted for hours with music and jokes, all her favorite dishes and a big cake. Jane had also managed to make some new clothes to surprise her daughter with and the girls of the house had oohed and aahed at an impromptu fashion show.

Harry found Callie alone by the paddock the next day, just before he was going to return to the city. She had the beautiful amethyst crystal Davin had given her in her hand, watching the play of light through the facets, almost mesmerized by its beauty.

"That's a special gift he gave you." Harry propped up his boot on the split-rail fence next to her as he watched a yearling colt gallop over the grass.

"Harry, you know about their technology. What can you tell me about this amethyst?"

Harry looked at the stone with a critical eye. "I can tell it's one of the more powerful crystals I've ever seen. It hums with energy."

"Davin said it was flawless, and that he'd tuned it."

"Well, he's the best crystallographer they have. If he did the tuning, no wonder it's good. I asked a bit about him, you know. As much as I could without raising suspicion. Our parents were a little concerned about him, but as far as I could tell, everything he told them was true. He is a throwback, but he's also one of the most powerful of the Alvians. He's the Chief Engineer for the whole planet, and he got that position solely on merit."

"Sounds important." Callie fingered the crystal, watching the play of the sun off its natural facets.

"It is." Harry nodded. "He's interested in you, I think."

"What?" Callie blushed and didn't quite meet her brother's eyes.

"I overheard Mama Jane talking about resonance mates and I did a little digging in the Alvian histories. It used to be, when they still had emotions, the males would search for their destined mate. They called them resonance mates. Without a mate, most of the males eventually went insane. I guess Davin came to the Waste looking for a human mate who could return his feelings and maybe his eye turned to you."

"No way." Her blush deepened as she protested.

"Then why did he give you such a valuable gift? He only gave crystals to Mama Jane, Papa Mick and my dad. And I've seen those crystals. They're not half as powerful as the one he gave you."

"Really?"

Harry touched her hand. "Really. We're sixteen now, Cal. In the old world we would have been dating other kids already and in a few years we might've thought about getting married. I, for one, don't want to miss out on that if I can help it and I don't think you do either." He smiled at her kindly. "Am I right?"

Callie shrugged one shoulder. "I'd like to get married someday, I guess."

"But where are we going to find potential life partners?" Harry slapped one hand down on the fence railing. "I don't want an Alvian woman. First off, none of them would understand me and my emotions, and they'd probably only want me because of my Hara DNA anyway."

"Harry, that's awful!"

"Awful, but true. You haven't been around them much, but Callie, regular Alvians are just coldhearted. They don't understand or want emotion and it's hard for me to live among them." He turned back to her. "Which is why I think I understand a little about Chief Engineer Davin. If I were him,

I'd be looking among the human women for a mate. Hell, I will be, when the time is right."

"But there are so few human women, Harry. It may take you a long time to find the one for you."

"Well, I don't have anything against having sex with Alvian women. That's what Dad did to make me after all, right?"

"Harry!" She punched his arm, blushing again at his bold words.

"Well, I'm not a virgin, Cal."

"You're not?"

Harry laughed. "One of the benefits of having a mother who's a scientist. She arranged for me to learn about sex in a rather hands-on way. She even monitors me in my sleep. And she's collecting my DNA for study and comparison."

"What's it like? Sex, I mean." Callie was bright red with embarrassment, but intrigued.

"It's hard to describe." He hesitated. They'd been raised on a ranch. They'd seen animals doing it, but it was hard to reconcile the harsh reality of the act with the rush of pleasure he'd learned could be coaxed and prolonged, or hard and fast. "And I can only guess what it's like for a woman, but for me, it's...amazing."

Callie watched the yearling gallop closer. "I want to try it, but..."

Harry tucked her under his arm and hugged her to his side. "It's okay to wait. In fact, I think you should. I know that's old-fashioned of me, but you're my sister. I love you and I want you to share it with someone who loves you and who you love back. Without love, it's just sex, Cal. It feels great, but a little empty."

"Well it's not like there's a bunch of men courting me, so I'll probably never do it. The only men I really know are members of my family."

"And Davin." Harry nodded toward the purple crystal still in her hand.

Her breath caught. "I only met him once."

"But he gave you a tuned communication crystal, Cal. You can talk to him through it, if you want, and get to know him."

She turned the crystal in her hand. "This is a communication device?"

"Among other things." Harry reached out one finger to touch the surface, pulling away quickly. "It's a powerful emitter, and tuned perfectly. It's probably a direct link to Davin, and totally untraceable because of the way he's tuned it. The other crystals he left aren't like this one, Cal. I think he gave it to you, hoping you'd talk to him."

"You mean it's like an old-world telephone? I can just call him and talk back and forth?" She seemed fascinated by the idea.

Harry nodded. "I think so, Cal. I've seen crystals similar to this in the city, but nothing this small or fine. Davin's reputed to be the best of the best when it comes to crystals, so I'm not surprised he gave you some of his best work. It tells me he really is serious about you—or at least wants to learn more about you."

"Really?"

Harry squeezed her shoulder once more. "Really. And Cal, think about it. He's the only Alvian with emotions I've heard about. His work keeps him separate and apart from everyone— even most other Alvians. I think he's probably a pretty lonely guy."

"Are you trying to convince me to talk to him?" She eyed him suspiciously. "I don't think our parents would want me to."

Harry sighed. "You're probably right, but I can't help but think maybe this was meant to be. I get this feeling..." His eyes took on a faraway look that she'd come to recognize a bit from Papa Caleb. Harry's amazing gifts were still manifesting as he matured and it wouldn't surprise her at all to learn he'd somehow gotten the clairvoyant gift as well as all the other things he could do with his powerful mind.

"Did you see something?"

But Harry shook his head. "It's more a feeling. I don't know, Cal, but this feels right. Davin is important to the Alvians and I think he's important to this family too. I think he's going to be important to you, but I can't say just how. But I can say this—he needs you, Cal. He needs a friend." His eyes turned serious as he focused solely on her. "Even if it never amounts to more, he needs to know there is someone out there who can feel—who can commiserate and talk with him about his day. He has no one. Absolutely no one he can talk to. You could be his friend, Callie."

She seemed to consider his words. Her empathic gift was no doubt making her feel sympathy for the lonely Chief Engineer. Harry couldn't say why this was so important, but he'd been waiting for something to give over the past few weeks and he thought this had to be it. There had been a feeling of waiting about the ranch and about Callie in particular since she'd started carrying that amethyst crystal. It was as if the universe were waiting for her to call on the massive power stored within the small shard, waiting for her to bridge the gap between her empathic soul and the lonely man who had given her the means to make contact.

"I don't think our parents could object to that," she hedged, palming the crystal more strongly. "I don't think they'd mind if I made friends with him."

Harry felt the energies sliding toward completion with some satisfaction. He'd given her the nudge and now she would see it through. He knew he'd done the right thing, but he still didn't know exactly how it would all play out. His powers were growing stronger as he grew, but there was still so much he didn't quite understand.

"No, they wouldn't object to your making friends, Cal. You should call him."

"But how?"

He spent just a few moments telling her how to work the crystal as he'd seen similar crystals work in the city, then left her to it. He'd planted the seed and as he walked away, the flower blossomed.

"Davin?"

Callie's voice was hesitant, but it was music to his ears, half a world away.

"Is that you, Callie?"

"Yes. It's me. Harry showed me how to work the crystal. I hope you don't mind."

Mind? She had to be joking! He was ecstatic that she'd

59

initiated contact. He quickly secured his chamber and lay back on his couch, ready to hear whatever she would choose to share with him. He hoped he could keep her talking, but he wasn't much of a conversationalist.

"I don't mind, Callie. I'm actually very happy to speak with you."

She could feel that, even over the distance that separated them. Her empathic gift was an odd creature. Sometimes she felt resonances of feeling from people just by hearing their voice. It was that way with Davin, and it was that which had made her sneak around Papa Mick's office when Davin had been staying there, hoping to hear the deep rumble of his voice and experience the shivers it sent down her spine and through her empathic senses. She didn't quite understand it all, but she knew his voice, his raw emotion, made her feel good in a way that was entirely different than what she'd experienced with her family members.

"I was hoping..." She took a breath for courage. "I was hoping we could be friends. I know my parents didn't want you talking with us kids while you were here, but Harry says you might be lonely, and you might want a friend to talk to once in a while."

Davin was silent and she was afraid she'd said too much. But when he sighed, she felt it down in her bones.

"Harry sounds like a very wise man."

Callie laughed, liking the respect she could feel in his voice. "Harry's the best. But he's going back to the city today. Maybe you'll see him there."

"I doubt it. I imagine he's going to the northern settlement. I live in the Southern Engineering Facility, which, if I'm reading the old human maps correctly, is roughly in an area that used to be called Brazil, though the coastline is much changed now."

"Wow, you mean in South America? Mom taught us the old geography, but warned us it was probably all different since the cataclysm. I didn't realize your people had more than one city, but I guess that would make sense."

"We have several cities, settlements and facilities all over this globe. I'm in the largest engineering facility."

"Because you're the Chief Engineer, right? Harry told me about that."

"Yes. I'm working on the crystal deposits here and will be for many years to come, so I don't know if my path will ever cross your brother's, but I'd like to meet him someday."

"I think he'd like that too. He has a hard time sometimes, being half-Alvian. I know the city life is hard on him, but Papa Caleb is there, so he's not completely alone."

They talked for a bit longer and she promised to call him back in a few days. After that, they set a time each week when she would call him. Eventually their calls became more frequent. Davin admitted to being lonely and she did too. With Harry spending most of his time in the alien city, she was missing her brother sorely. Davin helped her as much as she thought she helped him during the lonely times and they talked frequently, long into the night when they both should have been sleeping.

Through all this, she managed to keep the crystal's communication properties secret from everyone in the family except Harry, of course, but he wasn't telling. She normally wasn't a secretive girl, but she hugged her growing friendship with the Chief Engineer close to her heart. It was private and she wasn't ready to share her burgeoning feelings for the man who talked her to sleep each night.

"I really enjoy talking to you, Davin. You're as sensible as Harry, and you don't treat me like a child."

She was wrapped up in bed, snuggling into her blankets against the chill mountain air. As she did almost every night, she called Davin, knowing that he was alone in his quarters, relaxing, his workday having drawn to a close as well. She cherished these moments when they could talk.

They talked about all sorts of things. He told her about spaceflight and the wonders of his people's homeworld, now gone, and he told her stories from their ancient past. She told him the things her mother had taught her about the old world and the way things used to be. Sometimes they talked about their daily routines or funny things that had happened to them that day, but always, they talked.

She felt she knew him perhaps better than she knew anyone, including Harry, who now spent so much time away from home, she felt a little estranged from him. Davin had filled a place in her heart that had been emptied by Harry's embrace of his mother's culture, and though she loved Harry dearly and always would, she found there was room in her heart for Davin as well.

"Are you trying to tell me your esteemed brother treats you like a child? I refuse to believe it." Davin's voice was pleasant, warm and entirely yummy, she thought, especially when he was engaging in teasing banter with her.

"Well, you should," she protested. "He's been here for two days and he refuses to answer any of my questions seriously."

"What sorts of questions have you been asking him?"

She hesitated. "Well, I heard something perhaps I shouldn't have heard and I wanted to know more. From his expression, Harry knows what it means, but he won't tell me. He keeps teasing me so much, I'm ready to punch him."

Davin's chuckle warmed her as she snuggled further into her bed. "What is this thing you perhaps shouldn't have heard? Maybe I can clear it up for you."

"It's a term. I heard Papa Mick say something about something called a resonance mate, and then he saw me and got all quiet. I think they were talking about me and I want to know what it means."

Davin's sigh filled her ears. "They probably were talking about you, Callie, and I'm sorry you had to hear it, but I will tell you, if you wish. It has to do with an ancient tradition of my culture and the way my people used to join with their mates. While I was at your ranch I passed on the information to your parents and we discovered that they were true mates, much to my surprise. I didn't realize our traditions could apply to humans as well, but then I realized that you all have at least some Alvian DNA, so perhaps it is that side of your nature that allows the tests to work."

"Tests?" She was more confused by his words than enlightened, but she was willing to let him explain.

"In ancient times, when my people still had strong emotions, males would seek their life mates by the use of three tests. If a pair succeeded with all three tests, they were proven as true mates and they joined forevermore."

"Like marriage," Callie thought out loud.

"Yes, but there is no way true mates can divorce. There is no recorded history of any true pairing ever *wanting* to divorce. This joining is permanent. Resonance mates are each others' perfect matches. Theirs is a bond that is completely unbreakable and soul deep. Or at least, that's what the ancient texts all say."

"So when you were here my parents took these tests and passed?"

"Yes. To my amazement, your mother and her mates are all truly bonded in the ancient way of my people. I've done a lot of research on the matter since returning here and I've found only rare instances in my culture's past where more than two people were mated together."

"But there were some," Callie prompted him. She knew her parents' arrangement was different than the way it would have been in the old world. Her mother had been honest with her about that once she'd been old enough to understand, but she also knew that every one of the O'Hara men loved her mother truly and deeply. They belonged together.

"Under extraordinary circumstances there were a few notations in the ancient records of unions of three or more resonance mates and they all were happy, true unions, but they were a rarity."

"What sort of extraordinary circumstances?"

He sighed before continuing. He sounded tired, she thought. "In one case, there was a crashed interplanetary shuttle that landed several families on a small moon with no way to communicate their location. They weren't found for many, many years. In that time, the children had formed true bonds and there were several multi-partner joinings. There was an overabundance of males in relation to females, so somehow more than one male managed to resonate with each female. The phenomenon was studied once this group was rescued, but each of the joinings was true and legitimate, and lasted the rest of their lives."

"Well, isn't that like what happened here on Earth? There

are so few women left, maybe God or nature or whatever made allowances for the lack of women."

"That's something I've been tossing around in my mind as well but I don't know how to prove the theory. It's not my area of expertise, after all." He smiled and she relaxed a bit. This was, by far, one of the more interesting conversations they'd ever had.

"So what are the tests? Are they hard?"

"Not especially hard, no," he told her softly. "Actually, you've already passed the first one, without even knowing it."

"What?" She felt a bubble of excitement shoot through her at his sexy, low voice in her ears. His tone had turned rumbley and she felt her skin heat, though she didn't quite understand her reaction.

"The first test is called the Hum. When two compatible people touch, a Hum sounds as their energies join and multiply. Every time your mother touched one of her mates, I heard the Hum."

"But I've never heard anything when Mama touches one of my dads." She was truly confused.

"The sound is outside the range of human hearing but I proved my point to your Uncle Mick. He had equipment that could pick up on the sound energy and he was satisfied it was real."

"And I passed this test? How? When? And with who?" Her voice was a whisper.

"With me, sweetheart. I touched you last year, right before I left your family's ranch. Remember when you delivered that meal? That was your parents' way of letting me test my theory. Our hands brushed and I immediately heard the Hum. Mick was at the computer and he saw the readings too, so your parents know the truth of the matter." His voice dropped even lower. "We Hum, Callie."

She couldn't speak for a long moment, breathing rapidly as something skittered through her insides.

"So that means we're compatible or something?"

Davin grinned at her. "Compatible? Yes. But there are other tests before anything more important can be proven or disproven."

She gathered her courage. "Would you want me to be your resonance mate?"

"More than anything." His quick, decisive answer made her blood sing in her veins. "But we have a long way to go before that, Callie. You are young. Too young, according to your parents, and I have to sadly agree."

"So you're not saying you're too old for me—it's that I'm too young for you? I don't get it."

Davin laughed. "In human terms, I'm probably much too old for you, but Alvian lifespans are much longer."

"Just how old are you, Davin?"

"Over one hundred Earth years, Callie." He paused while that sank in. "I spent a long time in stasis on the ship coming here, so I'm actually older than that, but I've lived just over 102 years the way you'd count them on Earth. I'm considered quite young for an Alvian."

"Wow."

"With long lifespans, Alvian children are considered eligible as soon as they finish puberty. After that, chronological age means little among my people, but I know it's different with humans. You're not finished growing yet, Callie, and I'm the only male you know outside your family. You should have a chance to mature fully before we go much further."

"But what if I want to?"

"Want to what? Join with me?" Davin seemed a little shocked by her forwardness, but she was feeling unusually reckless.

"If that means have sex with you, then yes. Harry's already had sex and as you pointed out, you're the only man I know that I'm not related to. So what if I want to try it with you? Would you say no?"

"By the Crystal, Callie! I wouldn't say no, but it also wouldn't be right. Not yet. Not before you're old enough."

"I think I'm old enough to know my own mind, Davin," she said in a small, daring voice, but he shot her down.

"I don't." He sighed heavily. "I'm sorry, sweetheart. I don't mean to hurt you, but this has to be done carefully. My position is not the safest and I need to find a way to give you security if indeed you prove to be my resonance mate."

She wanted to argue but she relented after a moment. She didn't want them to go to sleep mad at each other, so she mentally tabled the discussion for another time.

"So then, what's the second test?"

He was silent so long she wasn't sure he was going to answer, but then he relented.

"You'll find out when it's time."

"That is just not fair." She laughed, knowing he'd already told her far more than Harry would have. "And don't tell me I'm too young."

"But you are, sweetheart."

He laughed but she grew dejected. "Do you know, I've never even been kissed. There's an old-world saying, 'sweet sixteen and never been kissed'. Well, that's me. It's so depressing."

He chuckled, which was not the response she'd expected, but his next words made her feel better.

"What if I promise you, right now, that you won't turn seventeen without being kissed?"

Her breath caught in her throat. "You mean it?"

"I do. I want very much to kiss you, Callie. You're a beautiful, witty, attractive young woman and I'd truly enjoy the honor of giving you your first kiss."

She felt a little overwhelmed but she had to keep it light. "Then you'd better get up here and deliver it. I don't think it can be done over a communication crystal."

Chapter Four

Rick St. John formed an uneasy truce with Mara 36, working quietly behind the scenes to help the humans penned up beneath the alien city. He couldn't do much, but he did have Mara's ear and was able to convince the scientist of the fallacy of some of their more brutal experiments. He spent hours each week above ground with Mara 36, discussing the medical texts they'd recovered from his handheld device along with others he'd never seen before. Mostly he acted as a translator for words and proper names—especially those in Latin—that were not in the Alvian databases or sometimes, even their lexicon. There were many diseases the Alvians had no understanding of, since their own race didn't have anything similar. Rick realized the Alvians were either disgustingly healthy, or they'd genetically engineered most kinds of disease out of their population so long ago, they no longer had any recollection of them.

He also managed to get a few of the others above ground for short periods of time, including poor old Sadie, who was still coughing, but doing better with periods away from the damp of the cells. Mostly the folks who had the ability to translate foreign languages and some technical expertise were picked for the above-ground forays into the alien complex, to help Mara 36 and those like him figure out the growing collection of human books.

Rick didn't like cooperating with the aliens, but he felt like he had no choice. Misguided as they were, the Alvians would continue their harmful behavior unless someone tried to coax them in another direction. That role had fallen to Rick, though he'd never asked for it. Just as he'd never intended to become the unofficial leader of the human prisoners kept locked up beneath the city. But he accepted the responsibility and did his best to improve conditions for as many as he could.

It was a hard life. Rick, like most of his fellows, had been born free. He detested being caged like an animal, but he was making the best of it. For now.

But he would never give up the idea of escape. As soon as he saw his chance—and as soon as he could be sure the people he left behind would come to no harm because of his escape— he'd be gone. He was only biding his time.

A little over one year after his first visit, Davin returned to the O'Hara ranch. He hid his ship in the cave that shielded it so well and walked to the ranch, gratified to see that things hadn't changed much since he'd been there last. Jane saw him first from the kitchen window, and she came out onto the porch to greet him. It was like a breath of fresh air to see her open happiness as she greeted him. It was like coming home.

She sent one of the younger children out to the office to tell Mick they had a guest and in the time it took for Jane to pour him a glass of fresh milk, the other O'Hara brothers were there, shaking his hand in greeting and asking how he'd been. Davin had never experienced anything like it. He thought this might be what it would feel like to have a family—a loving, caring, feeling family. He had never experienced such a thing and it was more precious to him than pure crystal.

He was disappointed at first to not see Callie among the young faces peering at him from around the ranch, but Jane interpreted his searching looks, covering his hand with hers and smiling softly. "Callie's out riding. She'll be back shortly. You might want to wait for her near the barn, if you're eager to see her."

He was glad to have her mother's implicit permission to seek out the daughter. Still, he searched her face, turning to seek out Mick and Justin as well.

"We talked this over at some length," Mick said seriously, "and we don't think it's fair to either her or you to keep you so far apart."

"Even in the old world she would have been dating by now, but that doesn't mean we have to like it." Justin's grin was a bit self-mocking. "Still, she's almost seventeen and she's got a good head on her shoulders."

"So long as you continue to block most of your feelings from her, we won't keep you two apart."

Davin couldn't believe how generous these people were. "May I perform the second test?" His voice was modulated low, barely daring to hope they'd agree. So much was riding on their cooperation. He didn't want to overstep their boundaries, so he had to move carefully.

"The Kiss, right?" Justin growled as Davin nodded. "Hell."

"Yes, Davin." As usual, Jane was his light of hope. "If she wants it, you can Kiss her. But keep in mind, she's never had a suitor before. I had a long talk with her, and I can feel she's curious and hopeful. She has all those yearnings young girls have and no outlet for them. It's kind of sad, really."

"But don't take it too far," Mick cautioned. "She's inexperienced. It's up to you to protect her."

Davin bowed his head. "I am honored by your faith in me, and I give my vow she will come to no harm in my care."

As Callie rode up, a huge grin broke over her face when she saw Davin, and it lightened his heart to a degree he never would have expected. He was glad her parents remained within the house. As it was, he'd have a hard time explaining how quickly he'd convinced her to Kiss him. They didn't know of his almost nightly talks with Callie over the communication crystal. As far as they knew, she'd only spoken to him the one time, but he couldn't hold himself in check. She was near and he wanted— no, he *needed*—to Kiss her.

She jumped from her horse, caring for it before turning to him, and he sensed her shyness. With a determined step he strode toward her, covertly placing a small, tuned crystal on a fencepost where it would be clearly visible to the watchers in the farmhouse.

"I can't believe you're here," Callie whispered as he moved to stand in front of her. His back was to the house, blocking their view, so they couldn't see her face as they talked, but they could see she was safe nonetheless.

"I can hardly believe it either, sweetheart." He raised one hand to trail the backs of his fingers over her soft cheek. Her skin was even softer than it looked, a sensual delight to his starved senses. "I've wanted to touch you and see you smile. I've wanted to hold your hand and spend time with you for so long."

"Me too," she breathed as he stepped closer, closing the distance between them.

"I promised you I'd make sure you didn't turn seventeen without being kissed." His whispered words made something in her tummy clench with pleasure. She blushed, hoping no one could see, though she knew they weren't completely hidden by the barn. She pulled back, tugging him toward the barn, but he let her go on without him. "If I go in there with you now, I'll want to do a lot more than just kiss you, Callie. And you're not quite ready for what I have in mind yet."

"But what if I want it too?"

"Oh, sweetheart—" he tucked her hair behind her ear, "—you're killing me, but I'm trying to do the right thing here. I promised your family I would take this slow."

"You talked to them about this? About kissing me?" Her face flamed red as his fingers touched her again, so softly.

He nodded. "I had to. I have to do this according to their wishes, Callie. You are too precious to them, and to me, to rush things."

"I've been waiting forever, Davin!"

He chuckled at her youthful impatience. At times he really felt the difference in their ages, but he couldn't stop his desire for her, no matter what lay between them. They would work through the age difference and in a few years, it wouldn't really matter. They would both live long, hopefully healthy, Alvian-length lifespans and any age difference would cease to matter beyond their first few decades together.

"Then it would be cruel of me to make you wait any longer." With an indulgent, yet excited smile he opened his arms and she flew into them. The Hum sounded as his skin touched hers in places.

He moved slowly, savoring the moment of discovery, sliding his cheek over her hair, down her temple, nuzzling her sweet face with his lips and nose. He inhaled her fresh fragrance, stunned by how much her simple, sweet scent turned him on. He kept a small space between their lower bodies, as he'd promised her family he would, but it was just about killing him. He wanted her so badly!

Still, the little taste he would have of her fired his senses as he moved downward, toward his goal. He gave her every opportunity to change her mind, telegraphing his movements as he reached her lips. He moved back momentarily, searching her eyes. He read yearning and hope there, along with a naïve excitement that stirred him so deeply. If it were up to him he would keep her as innocent of fear and fresh as she was now. He would never do anything to destroy that joy in her eyes.

"I'm going to Kiss you now, Callie."

"Oh, Davin. Hurry up!"

He chuckled, bringing his amusement into their first Kiss as his lips covered hers in a light touch that soon became much more. He'd promised not to take this to the full Embrace, but there was much within the discretion of the Kiss they could enjoy nonetheless. He drew her upper body more closely into his arms as he traced her innocent lips with his tongue.

Her eyes shot open, questioning the sensation but he soon had her relaxing into the feel of his tongue playing over her lips. When she sighed, he slipped within, shocking her yet again. This time, though, she was eager to explore what he could show her, opening her mouth naturally to his exploration. Her tongue tangled with his curiously, sucking lightly as he taught her by example how he liked to be kissed.

His senses were on fire with the taste and feel of her. She was everything he'd imagined and dreamed—and more. She tasted like sunshine and warm honey, unique and special in his otherwise bleak world. He opened his eyes briefly, turning so he could see what he knew would be happening to the crystal over his shoulder. He had no doubt in his mind now that such pleasure could only be found with one's true mate.

The crystal shone bright red and swirling orange, enough for him to see with only a quick glance, and he knew her family could see it from the window of the farmhouse where they were no doubt staked out. Thinking of them watching their first real intimacy put a damper on his libido, but he still couldn't quite let her go. He eased back, kissing her lightly, drawing away when he wanted nothing more than to kiss her for the rest of their lives.

She clung to him as well. He was as gentle as he possibly could be with her. It was there in her eyes how overwhelmed her senses were at that moment and she swayed in his arms as if drunk on the pleasure they'd found together.

"Wow," she breathed, leaning heavily against his supportive arms.

"I agree." Davin's voice was tender, intimate, in her ear. "You are so beautiful to me, Callie. So perfect and lovely."

Her long eyelashes swept up so she could smile at him. "I feel that. I feel your emotions and they're...you're...so amazing, Davin. Why is it I've never felt your emotions like this before?"

He pulled another few millimeters back, working on releasing her entirely, but he just couldn't bring himself to do it yet.

"Mick taught me how to withhold some of my stronger feelings so I wouldn't unduly influence you. Do you feel unduly influenced?" His teasing smile made her grin.

"No. I just feel...I don't know...cherished. I like the feeling, Davin. I like it a lot."

Her honesty made it even harder to set her away, but he must. He'd promised her family he'd take this slow. She was still too young. She had to grow into her womanhood and he wouldn't take that magical time of childhood away from her, no matter how desperate he became. It was enough to know she existed in the world and was thinking of him. They would talk as they had before and learn more about each other, and when the time came, he would claim her for his own. After that, there would be no going back, for either of them.

"I do cherish you, Callie. I cherish the friendship we've built and the future yet to come." He kissed her forehead, his eyes tightly shut as he finally found the strength to release her. She clung for a moment more but finally stood on her own.

Letting her go was the hardest thing he had ever done.

But he had hope once more. A greater hope than he'd had

before and a promise of a future with her as his mate. If only he could Embrace her now! But it was not meant to be. Not yet.

He turned toward the house, picking up the crystal and pocketing it where she couldn't see.

"Did you like your first kiss, Callie?"

An impish smile crossed her beloved face. "Like it? I loved it! Thank you, Davin. You're truly a man of your word."

He bowed his head slightly. "I aim to please, but, Callie, it's I who should thank you for entrusting me with such an important—and pleasurable—task. You're sweet to kiss, and if your parents weren't watching, I'd kiss you all day."

"I wish you could." Her voice was soft, her words brutally honest with the innocence of youth.

"I do too, Callie, but not today. Someday, when you're older, I promise, if you still want it, I'll kiss you for hours."

She nodded mischievously as she headed for the barn and the small chores awaiting her before she could head into the house. "I'll hold you to that, Davin."

Davin returned to his base in what used to be called Brazil and stayed there, working hard on his crystallography for the next year or so. He and Callie talked often via the crystal he'd given her. It was the high point of his existence, talking to her and getting to know her hopes and dreams, hearing about her day.

She had a natural aptitude with the crystal and Davin finally sought out the Council so he could test his theories about humans and the possibility that some of them could have the crystal gift. With their hard-won approval, Davin set out for the northern settlement and a quest he'd put off until Callie turned eighteen. She was of age now, and he couldn't wait much longer to claim her as his own, but first he needed to meet the rest of her family. Getting them on his side—or at least acquainted with him—before he made his bid for her was all part of his plan. They were a close-knit family and he needed them to accept him.

Especially Harry.

Callie talked of her brother all the time and Davin knew he'd have to have Harry's approval or Callie would never be happy. So Davin devised a way to meet Harry and set it into motion. He had a legitimate reason to travel to the city and meet Callie's brother, but it would also suit his personal plans very well indeed.

Davin moved swiftly toward the apartments where he'd been told Harry lived, but was somewhat surprised when he ran into the young man in the hall. Harry was taller than he'd expected and much larger than an Alvian youth his age would have been. The human DNA's influence was clearly seen in his physical development.

Harry eyed him carefully as they stood facing each other in the hall. The knowledge in his young-old eyes startled Davin for just a moment as they appraised each other.

"You're Davin."

"And you're Harry." He nodded, holding Harry's challenging gaze steadily. This young male was evidently feeling protective of his sister and Davin was glad she had such a strong—if young—protector. Time would bring great power to this man, if everything he'd heard and ferreted out about him was true.

"Your people call me Hara." The words were clearly a challenge.

"I'm not like them."

"Yes, I've heard you're a throwback. That must be difficult for you."

"No harder, I imagine, than being half-human is for you, Harry."

The younger man nodded in acknowledgement. In all probability they were being monitored. Davin spent his life under surveillance, as undoubtedly, did young Harry.

"My mother monitors all my contact with others—Alvian or human. Be careful what you say."

The voice sounded in his mind and if he hadn't had contact with Mick O'Hara, he would have been alarmed. But he'd been told Harry was a strong telepath. He wasn't surprised he would use his gift to speak privately with him, even though Davin couldn't do the same in return.

"I've heard of your work in the Southern Engineering Facility. They say you are a genius at crystal tuning." Harry began to walk down the corridor and Davin fell into step beside him.

"It's why I've come. Mara 12 has granted me leave to test a theory and you are to be the subject."

"I was made aware that I should cooperate with you, but I have no idea what you want to test. If there's something about me that hasn't been tested and analyzed by now, I'd be amazed."

Davin laughed just once. It wouldn't do to show too much emotion where his people could see. Davin had learned over the years to curb his responses in front of other Alvians, but he already felt comfortable around this young human—like he did with the other O'Haras. Davin followed Harry into a small sitting room that was part of his private quarters.

"Nice place," Davin commented, looking around.

"Thanks. I like it. My mother allowed me to move to private quarters when they brought Papa Caleb to the city for study. I'm not too far from his place, which is great since he has little company. I try to see him as often as I can."

Davin knew the scientists' personal quarters, where Harry's mother still resided, were up two levels. This section of housing was also closer to the other test subjects, Harry's human brethren in the cells below the city. Davin knew from his time spent with the O'Haras that they all missed Caleb, but he couldn't disclose his knowledge, so he pretended surprise.

"I didn't know you had family here. Mara 12 suggested your father and siblings were closely monitored, but allowed to live somewhere in the Waste." Davin made small talk as they were both seated in the front room. There was a couch and two chairs around a low table. The furnishings were comfortable and functional, like most Alvian abodes, but Harry had colorful pillows and knickknacks here and there that were undoubtedly gifts from his human family. The childish drawings of stick figures and horses were especially enchanting. Gifts from Harry's younger siblings, Davin guessed.

"The rest of my human family lives on a ranch in the mountains, but my mother decided to take each of the O'Hara brothers here for study, one at a time, for a period of ten years each. She started with the eldest, Caleb O'Hara. The plan is to study him, then swap him for the next brother, my biological father, Justin, and so on."

"But I didn't think Breeds lived that long. How can she study each of them for ten years?"

Harry winked at him. They both understood that Harry was laying the groundwork of Davin's knowledge about the O'Haras to help avoid any slipups. If the Alvians knew Harry had told Davin a lot about his family, they would be less likely to notice any mistakes either man might make in talking too freely about them.

"All the O'Haras have some Alvian DNA, Chief Engineer. It was a simple matter for my mother to switch off their human aging gene and activate the Alvian DNA that lay dormant. The O'Haras will age like Alvians from here on out. In fact, I wouldn't be surprised if my mother hasn't done the same for her other test subjects. There are great advantages to having them around longer for study purposes."

"Undoubtedly," Davin agreed, but privately wondered if allowing humans to live hundreds of years was more cruel than kind. Who really wanted to live so long as a prisoner?

But some humans were doing a little better. Caleb O'Hara, for example, was given a suite of rooms adjacent to Harry's so they could visit easily. Mara had wanted to make her prize specimen as comfortable as possible, openly acknowledging that he was at least part Alvian and of the line of one of their most respected leaders.

The conversation hit a lull and Davin took that as his cue to launch into the reason for his visit. So far, it was going very well. They'd managed to get a lot of information out in the open to protect both Davin and the humans from possible slipups while they were being monitored so closely.

"This is a quick test, and nothing invasive." Harry was seated on the couch as Davin faced him from one of the chairs. "As you know, my specialty is crystal tuning. It is a gift among our people and all Alvian children are tested at the age of thirteen for even a hint of the crystal gift. No matter their genetic line, if they have even a little bit of the gift, they are segregated into a special training program. We need every crystallographer we can get as we try to tame this new world.

There are not enough of us, and our scientists have not come up with a way to predetermine which children will have the gift and which will not, even with all their skills and knowledge of our genome."

"So you want to test me? I'm eighteen, Davin. Aren't I a little old?"

"As you may already realize, crystals are the basis of all our technology. They power our cities and machinery, store our data, facilitate our communications and so much more. They are our most precious resource."

"So you wouldn't want just anyone handling them, huh? I can see why you're cautious about it. So then, why are you testing me now?"

Davin sat forward. "I have a theory that some Breeds may have the crystal gift, but the Council didn't have a suitable subject for me to test until now."

"Until me."

"Yes. Because you are half-Alvian, you are better suited to the test."

"And they expect me to be more tolerant of Alvian society than the people whose planet they stole." Harry's voice echoed through Davin's mind.

Slowly, Davin nodded just slightly.

"What do I have to do?"

Davin sat forward and pulled an untuned crystal from a special container he'd had in his pocket. "It's simple really. I want you to take this in your hands and concentrate on it." Davin emptied the crystal from the container, directly into Harry's outstretched hand. "Do you feel its energy?"

Harry tilted his head, watching the lump of crystal in his hand. "It feels warm. And it hums."

Davin smiled, excited by the idea that Harry had displayed at least this much ability. Now for the crucial test.

"Good. Now tell me what you feel when you think deeper, look deeper, into the facets."

Harry's face screwed up in concentration. "It's murky. Sort of cloudy. There's a flaw, but the energy is routing around it. It's an integral part of the whole, but like a sheer face inside the crystal structure."

"Excellent. Now think about aligning the energies with your own." Harry had already easily demonstrated ability far above that of the average crystallographer. Davin hoped the Maras were watching every moment of this and he knew the Council would be watching the recording within the hour. He'd send it to them himself.

"It's being stubborn," Harry said after a moment. "It doesn't want to shift."

Davin was impressed. "I purposely gave you a difficult specimen." He smiled as Harry chuckled. "How are you feeling? No lightheadedness?"

Harry shook his head. "I'm fine."

"Okay, then try this trick." Davin pulled an already-tuned crystal out of his pocket and placed it on the low table in front of Harry. "Pick up that crystal in your dominant hand, get a feel for it, then align the raw one with it."

Harry did it with little effort, earning a broad smile from Davin.

"Thank you for proving my theory. You could be a very gifted crystallographer with a bit of training."

"Think they'll let me take the training?"

Davin shrugged. "That's up to the Council, but I will argue in your favor, if it's something you want to do."

Harry seemed to think a moment, then nodded. "I'd like to try. I've finished most of the classes for my age group already. My mother is a Mara, but I have little interest in specializing in genetics."

"Well, Hara was an explorer and leader of some renown. He had a broad-based knowledge and as I recall, no small crystal gift. It was what made him well suited to finding new worlds with strong crystal deposits." He paused and continued in a more pensive tone. "There are few Maras among the crystal gifted in each generation, so it's doubtful the ability came from your mother's side, if it is an inherited gift."

"You think Callie has the gift too, don't you?" The question sounded only in his mind, but Davin nodded as if thinking. "I'd like to learn more, if the Council is willing for me to have the knowledge. I have yet to find my true path in life, though I'm

well past the age where the decision should have already been made."

"But they've made allowances for your heritage, haven't they?"

Harry nodded. "My human side and the fact that they need to continue to study me. It's both kept me back and propelled me forward. Because I don't have a job, I spend a lot of time studying. As a result, I've surpassed my age group in most areas of study, but I haven't found the one thing I want to make my life's work."

"If you were a regular Alvian, I would say your life's path would be in crystal work, but it's not for me to decide. I will tell you that you have enough of the gift to make you one of the strongest candidates I've seen in many years. You could hold a high position in the engineering sector, but as it stands, I don't know if that path will be open to you."

Harry stood, putting both crystals on the low table. "I know someone who might have an idea about my future, if you'd like to meet him."

Davin knew full well that Harry was probably referring to Caleb O'Hara, but he had to be circumspect. He stood and tried to look only mildly interested.

"I'd be pleased to meet anyone you wish," he said formally.

"Then come on next door. It's lunchtime and I promised Papa Caleb I'd share the meal with him today. He'll be happy to have one more guest, I'm sure."

The two men moved to the apartments next door and Harry was unsurprised when the door opened before they'd even reached it. A large, older man stood in the entry, his expression clouded with a mixture of concern, question and not a little bit of worry.

"Chief Engineer Davin, this is Caleb O'Hara." Harry made the introductions before Caleb stepped back to allow them entry.

"Better come in. Lunch is already here." Caleb closed the door as the other men entered, but stood facing them as they moved into the room. "I've already engaged the privacy. Since I knew Harry was coming, they won't take it amiss, but they may try to take it down, so we have to talk fast." He turned his green-eyed gaze on Davin, pinning him in place. "I've seen you before, in my visions. What are your intentions toward my girl Callie?"

Davin stood firm. He should have expected something like this from the man who was clearly the leader of the O'Hara household.

"I sincerely hope and believe she is my resonance mate. If I am so lucky, I will cherish and love her for the rest of our lives. And I will protect her with my own life, should it come to that."

Caleb seemed to lose some of his rigidity at Davin's heartfelt words. "All right then," he conceded, moving forward into the room. "I've seen you with her in my visions, and it might come down to your life for hers, so be warned. There's trouble coming, but I haven't seen much more than the feeling of a threat."

Davin's thoughts turned grim at the idea that someone or something would threaten his Callie, but he vowed to be there for her. He would keep her safe from harm. He had to. There simply was no alternative.

Davin left the northern city later that day after an enjoyable lunch shared with the O'Hara men. On the flight back, he received a call from Callie and spent over an hour talking with her as he flew back to his home base. He told her about his meeting with Harry and Caleb and gave her a firsthand report of how they looked and sounded. He even related some of the jokes they had shared over lunch and they laughed as he sped through the skies, back toward his work.

It was late by the time he returned to the engineering facility. Most of the workers were gone for the evening, but he found Selva at his desk. A picture of Callie was up on the screen when he entered and it was clear his overzealous assistant was rooting through his personal files.

"What do you think you're doing?"

The screen went blank as Selva turned and stood from his desk. She faced him squarely, clearly unable to feel fear or embarrassment at being caught spying.

"Surely you know that as a throwback you are under constant surveillance. You had hidden contraband files on your personal crystals that had to be reported to the Council."

"You sent those images to the Council?"

Selva nodded and suddenly it all clicked into place. The danger to Callie was from the Council—or the soldiers they would send to apprehend her now that it was known she was somehow involved with their unstable Chief Engineer.

Rage filled him, hotter than any anger he'd ever felt before. But Davin knew if he stalked over and choked the life out of Selva—as he longed to do—he would never be able to see Callie ever again and more importantly, he wouldn't be able to help her. So he tamped down his rage and quickly formulated a plan.

"Selva, you're a bitch." The unfeeling woman didn't even flinch at his curse. "You are no longer my assistant. Pack your things and leave this facility."

Chapter Five

"You don't have the authority to demote me," Selva challenged him.

"I'm still Chief Engineer here. You have little crystal gift. I've tolerated you because you are easily mounted, but you are a mediocre crystallographer at best and not gifted enough to be of any real use as my assistant. Get out or I'll have the guards throw you out."

She walked past him to the door. "I will take this up with the Council."

"You do that. But you should also realize that I'm more valuable to them than you are. It's my request they will honor, not yours."

He watched her go, all the while planning his next move. He'd have to leave right away if he wanted to beat the Council's soldiers. He'd alert Callie and tell her to tell her parents, but as skilled as they were, they wouldn't stand a chance against Alvian assault troops.

He grabbed a few necessities and ran back out to his vehicle. He fired up the engines and took off before anyone even knew what he was about. Fiddling with the crystals, he made his trail untraceable—a trick that few other crystallographers would have thought of or even been able to accomplish. But he'd planned for all contingencies for some time now. As a throwback, he never knew when they'd come for him and he hadn't wanted to die that way. Better to become a mad hermit in the Waste than die in a government cell.

He pushed the little craft, headed as fast as he could possibly manage to the Waste. While he flew, he activated the communication crystal and hoped Callie would answer.

After about five minutes of intense sweating, she answered.

"Callie!"

"What is it? We just talked less than an hour ago."

"You're in danger."

"Yeah, Papa Caleb just communicated his warning through Harry. Everyone's on alert over here. It was hard to get out of the house to talk with you."

Davin knew it was time to reveal their secret communication. "I want you to bring the crystal with you into the house and get your parents. I have something I have to say to them."

"But they don't know about the crystal!"

"I know. But this is too important, Callie. You have to tell them. I have to tell them what's happening. It's a matter of life and death."

She hesitated. "All right."

He knew she might get in trouble for keeping their secret, but he couldn't think about that now. Her very life was in danger. That had to take priority now. He heard the commotion as she reentered the house, then the quiet as she gained everyone's attention.

"Everyone's here now, Davin. Go ahead."

He took a deep breath. "First, let me say I'm sorry. Caleb was right. Callie's in danger. My assistant found those photos you gave me, Mick, and sent them to the Council. I can only assume they're sending soldiers to take Callie into custody. I'm on my way, but I won't be able to get there for another hour at least."

"I can set up some surprises at the perimeter but I don't have anything that will stop an assault force for long." Justin's calm words had a chilling effect on the gathered family.

"If I can get there before the troops, I'll take her someplace safe. I promise. It's the safest place I know and no Alvian would dare come after us there."

"But for how long? You can hide her for a while, but what about the future?" Mick wanted to know.

"I have a plan. It's not fully formed yet, but I think I can persuade the Council that Callie is better off with me than as a prisoner. If she's willing to take the chance. Callie, I'm sorry your choice has been all but taken away. I want you with me, but I wanted it to be your choice. I'm sorry things are happening this way."

"Are you kidding?" Callie's voice was taut with emotion. "I want to go with you, Davin."

The next hour passed in tense vigilance. Justin and Mick scouted the perimeter. Justin had taught his brothers most of what he knew about warfare over the years of exile in the Waste. They'd set up some surprises—man-traps, some explosives Mick had cooked up, and early warning signaling devices they'd contrived.

Callie waited in the nursery, the most secure room in the house, with her mother and siblings. Davin kept the communication crystal active and updated them on his progress though most of his concentration was geared toward moving his little ship as fast as it possibly could go.

He arrived in a little less than an hour, setting down right in the home pasture without regard for the frightened horses that scampered away from the craft. Callie ran out to meet him as soon as he landed and he scooped her into his arms with obvious relief, kissing her right there, in front of her mother and siblings. She was a little overwhelmed, but thrilled beyond measure to have him declare his feelings so openly.

When he put her to his side, her mother was there, tears in her eyes.

"I feel your love for my girl." Her mother's empathic senses were the strongest of all the family, though she'd passed on some of her talent to each one of her children. Most of her brothers and sisters were grinning like fools, happy for her, and she smiled back, shy but elated.

"I'll take care of her to the best of my ability."

"I know you will." Jane stepped forward and reached up to kiss Davin's cheek. "Be safe. And be happy." She hugged Callie again, tightly. "Call us when you can."

"I will, Mama. I love you! Tell Dad and Papa Mick that I love them."

With a few more words they were airborne. Callie sat in the passenger seat, just behind Davin. The tension was thick as he maneuvered the small craft out of the area as quickly as possible. He'd left the untraceable communication crystal with Jane so they'd have a way to contact the family and let them know when all was well. If they could just get that far.

Callie put her hand on his shoulder, feeling his turmoil with her empathic senses. "It'll be all right. Have faith."

"The only thing I have faith in, in this whole crazy universe, is you." His words were low, serious, and she wished in that moment she could see his face.

They were about halfway to the southern facility when the communication crystal pinged. It was Justin.

"Grady Prime just left here. He's heading south, Davin."

"Shards! I was afraid of that."

"You can't go home."

"I know. I have a place in mind. I didn't expect they'd send Grady Prime, but even he won't be able to follow where we're going. We'll be out of contact for a little while, but we'll be safe. Don't worry." He altered course as he spoke, shifting slightly to the southeast.

"Davin, I know you'll take care of my girl. Just take care of yourself as well. She needs you, now more than ever."

Davin took Justin's words to heart. Now that his people knew Callie was important to him, she would be the subject of study. It was unavoidable. The only way to protect her was to keep her with him. He had to find a way for them both to live safe and free. He had a plan, but a lot of it was contingent on variables he didn't have solid answers for yet.

Either way, their fate would be decided soon.

"We'll take care of each other." Davin looked at Callie as he reassured her father. "We'll both get through this. Together. That I promise. We'll be in touch when it's safe. Until then, try not to worry, and thanks for the warning about Grady Prime."

Callie leaned forward to speak into the communication crystal. "I love you, Dad!"

"I love you too, Callie mine. Trust Davin and do what he

says. There's no man on this Earth I'd trust more to see to your safety at this particular moment."

Davin was floored by the trust and confidence Justin O'Hara had just voiced. He'd try hard to live up to the man's faith in him.

They signed off moments later and Davin concentrated on flying. He'd made some modifications to the power systems of this little craft that should make it untraceable, even by Grady Prime, but he still flew carefully, avoiding detection from the ground bases scattered throughout the jungle.

Before long they arrived at their destination, a patch of jungle that looked no different from the rest of the dense jungle, but this particular place held a miraculous secret. It was a secret only someone with Davin's gifts could hope to uncover and use, and use it he would.

They disembarked from the small craft and he hid it with vines and fronds from the dense foliage all around. Callie helped, working steadily at his side. When it was well hidden, he guided her through the dense growth to the hidden entrance that only he knew. It led to an underground passage.

They went down the long, natural tunnel to the first turning, until they were in the deep gloom of a subterranean tunnel with Davin's superior night vision as their guide. He'd brought a pack of items he'd had in the ship, but wanted to conserve power until he discovered if this place would welcome Callie as he hoped it would. He stopped her with a gentle hand on her shoulder, turning her to face him in the gloom, his expression deadly serious.

"Before we go any further, you must promise me you'll tell me if you feel any discomfort at all. This place isn't entirely safe."

She tilted her head and smiled. He knew she felt his concern, his love and his protectiveness. Her empathy was so different than the response he was used to from his own people. Each time he saw evidence of her innate ability to understand his emotions, he was touched anew. It was a miracle. *She* was his miracle.

"I trust you, Davin. With my life." She reached up and kissed him lightly on the lips. The walls around them seemed to come alive with a peculiar kind of glow. She eased back and looked around, clearly startled. "Where are we?" Her breathy voice conveyed her wonder.

The walls of the tunnel were spotted here and there with glowing crystals. Most were clear or a cloudy white, but some were golden and some a deep, rich purple, like amethyst. She realized a moment later, they *were* amethyst, and citrine and beautiful pure quartz crystals, and they were lit somehow from within.

"You feel no pain?" Davin was anxious, she could tell, but also felt a deep satisfaction with her rapt expression. Clearly, she realized, this place was important to him.

"I'm fine. But this place! Davin, it's beautiful!" Her voice was pitched in low, almost reverent tones.

He smiled. "I'm glad you think so. It gets even better, but let me know if anything makes you uncomfortable. The next chamber would be dangerous for most of my kind to enter."

"But why?" She moved to the end of the corridor where a dark opening loomed.

Davin held her elbow, guiding her. Their brief Kiss had lit up the raw crystal in the corridor sufficiently for them to see easily in the darkness of the tunnel.

"The chamber contains massive quantities of untuned crystal, which can be dangerous to my kind."

She stopped short. "Is it dangerous to you? I don't want you getting hurt because of me, Davin."

He pulled her in for a quick, reassuring hug that brought the Hum of crystal around him to a pleasant tone as he listened to its song.

"No, my heart. I am one of the few who can handle wild crystal. Every Alvian child is tested no matter their lineage, and those with even the slightest ability are trained as crystallographers. It's an increasingly rare ability and I can say without conceit that I'm probably the best crystallographer my people have seen in generations. Only one or two of my colleagues would dare come into this chamber without protection and even then, they could only stay a short while." He moved with her into the darkness of the chamber. He watched her carefully for any signs of distress while he attuned his own senses to the raw energy in the air.

"This is the safest place I know. And the most beautiful. I've longed to bring you here, to share this with you."

He removed a small light from his pack and shined it around the chamber. The beam glinted off a myriad of sparkling surfaces sending out dark rainbows of shimmering light.

"Will these crystals glow like the ones in the corridor?"

Davin looked uncertain for a moment. "I believe so, but it could be risky."

"How so?"

"That much unregulated energy... I'm not really sure what it could do. But we do need to conserve the light and I refuse to go another moment without kissing you."

He pulled her into his arms, still near enough to the exit to make a dash outside if they needed to. This place was one of those rare, sacred spots—a natural resonance chamber. The crystal deposits in this chamber played in harmony with each other, in massive quantities that could easily kill an Alvian with less crystal talent than Davin possessed, by way of sensory overload. Davin was one of the rare few who could tame the wild crystal and live in harmony with it. He was perhaps the only Alvian on the planet so gifted. He knew he'd be safe here. But what of Callie? As his resonance mate, Davin was betting she vibrated on the same plane—that she'd be able to withstand the wild crystal harmony as easily as he. It was a risk, but she was so perfect for him in every other way, he'd stake his life—her life too—on her being compatible in this most basic of ways.

Callie laughed, distracting him, as did the Hum that sounded when he touched her, skin to skin. His senses were caught up in the wonder of her as he lowered his lips to touch hers in the sweetest kiss they'd yet shared. The chamber began to glow in waves of purple, gold and spots of dazzling white here and there, but he barely noticed. Only when she pulled back, looking around them in wonder, did he realize the energy they'd created. The cave was studded on every surface with large shards of amethyst, citrine and clear quartz that sparkled at them with throbbing energy.

"We did that?" She sounded amazed by the idea.

Davin nodded, reaching down to lick her lips before rejoining their kiss. When he finally came up for air, the chamber was brighter, the various forms of quartz lit from within and beginning to resonate with the Hum they created. He stepped back and took note of the amazing reaction. Never before had he seen such an immediate reaction from raw crystal. It was as if it wanted to attune itself to them—to their Hum. Could this be the secret long lost to their people? Could mated pairs work crystal more efficiently together, as was hinted in the ancient texts?

"What causes the glow?" Callie clutched his arm as she stood beside him, taking in the wide expanse of glowing crystal.

"Our energies together cause the glow when we Kiss. The mingling of our energy causes our souls to resonate. The crystal reacts by shining from within, refracting our energy into visible and audible waves."

"I can't hear anything."

He brought her hand to his lips and kissed her palm gently. "I can. Every time I touch you, we Hum. Mick said it's outside the range of human hearing, but it is quite beautiful to my ear. It's a sound I've waited all my life to hear. The most beautiful sound in my universe—the sound of my resonance mate, touching me."

"Resonance mate? Truly?"

Davin pulled her further into the chamber since it appeared she was as safe as he was in the crystal cavern.

"You're my mate, Callie. I knew it from the first moment I saw you. You were just fifteen then, and your family forbade me to even talk to you alone, but I knew. My soul recognized you. Especially on that last day, when I touched your hand and we Hummed. That gave me hope."

"So that's why they let you test me, even then."

Davin nodded. "They took pity on me. Mick knew what it was like to have the woman you need be out of your reach. He recorded that first Hum so he could show the evidence to your mother and his brothers."

"They knew." She thought about that for a moment. "What other tests are there?"

"The Kiss is the second test." He leaned in and kissed her

sweetly on the lips once more, as if unable to resist. "I Kissed you that day by the barn, the second time I visited the ranch, remember? I knew you were the one, but I put a crystal on the fencepost and Mick and your mother saw it glow when we Kissed. I needed them to see the proof with their own eyes."

"They saw that?" She blushed becomingly and he kissed her reddened cheeks tenderly.

"Yes, and it's been torture waiting for you to get older so I could perform the final test and finally claim you as my own."

"What's the final test?" Her words were a nearly breathless sigh as she watched him.

"The Embrace. Callie, I've wanted to Embrace you—to take you in my arms, fit my body to yours and kiss you so deeply we wouldn't know where you began and I ended. I've wanted it for so long."

"So why didn't you do it before? Why did you wait until now?"

"Your parents wanted me to wait, but with the threat to you, time has run out. They probably think you're still too young, but I can't wait any longer, Callie. The madness is creeping closer each day and I need you to be mine completely, to drive it away with your sweet Embrace." He pulled her in closer.

"I'm here now, Davin, and I won't leave you."

He kissed her again, forcefully, sealing her promise with his kiss. He shrugged out of his shirt, pushing her jacket off her shoulders and down onto the ground a moment later. All the while, he kissed her, baring as much skin as he could so they might Embrace properly. When he was bare from the waist up and she wore only a tank top, he pulled her into his arms and fit her body to his.

She was made for him. He'd known it all along, but the feel of her lithe form against his hardness was enough to make him cry. Or drive him mad. Or save him from madness.

Yes, that's what Callie was—his sanity in the chaos of this world. He blended their lips in the deepest Kiss they'd ever shared, allowing her to feel his rigid arousal against her softness. She squirmed and moaned in his embrace, music to his ears. As was the Hum that grew to surround them, reflecting off the untuned crystals all around and sheltering them in a cocoon of sound that soothed and protected.

Davin knew the crystals accepted them, though with any two other beings the results could have been alarmingly more dangerous. But it seemed the raw crystals merged with the resonances created by true mates, amplified it and sent it back to them, almost becoming part of them. It was a wondrous experience. Almost as wondrous as having Callie answer his Embrace with all the enthusiasm he could have wished for, and an eagerness that was extremely flattering.

He broke off, only peripherally aware of the brightness in the chamber. He opened his eyes to look and noted the bright sunny glow of the crystal. Here was proof beyond doubt, though he'd held little doubt in his heart after that Embrace. Callie was truly his—as he was hers. They were without question, resonance mates.

"I can never part from you again, Callie. We've passed all the tests. We are mates. All that's left now is the Joining."

"It's so bright in here." Her voice held awe as she looked at the shimmering show of crystal all around.

"As bright as our hearts, Callie. We were meant to be together. To be friends and lovers for the rest of our lives. If I can find a way for us to be together." Doubt crept into his mind as he realized they were in quite a bit of danger, resonance mates or not.

"Aside from Harry, you're my best friend in the whole world, Davin." She stroked his hair back from his face. "I trust you."

Davin laughed at that. "I'll try not to be jealous of your illustrious brother, but sweet, I can give you something your brother can never give you."

She knew what he was talking about and it made her blush, but she couldn't hide the eager smile in her eyes as she thought of what he was promising. She'd waited so long to discover the truth about making love. Harry had discussed the mechanics with her, but she wanted what her mother had. She wanted a man to love her and make love to her with his body, his mind and his heart.

And she felt all of that from Davin. She felt the emotions he wasn't all that great at expressing verbally. She even felt the emotions he tried to hide. She knew he loved her and she loved him too. The years of long talks in the darkness and gentle words of sharing had bonded them together and now she was ready for the next step.

"I want everything you can give me, Davin. I love you with all my heart."

He pulled her close and hugged her. "As I love you, my heart. I'll try to be gentle, but I must have you now, or go completely insane."

She could feel that too, from him. He was close to the edge of madness. The threat to her had shaken him badly, as had her very nearness. He needed her on a cellular level that went beyond emotion and physical need to something almost spiritual. He needed her in a way no other being had ever needed her and it touched her heart deeply.

"I don't care what this first time is like. I know it's going to hurt," she said bravely, "but I don't care. I want this. I want you, Davin. I *need* you. As much as you need me." She shucked her clothes quickly as he watched, distracted, only half-sane. "I love you, Davin. Take me. Take me now."

He pulled her into his arms and made for the far side of the chamber where he'd secreted a bed and some camping necessities. He'd thought to use this cave as a refuge for himself—a place to get away from it all. He'd never counted on bringing his mate here.

But the time for recriminations was past. There was only one thing on his mind now. Only one thing that mattered.

Callie.

He had to have her. The need was primal and stronger than anything he'd ever experienced. Still, she was a virgin. He had to give her time to accept him. He was a big man, even among Alvians, and he didn't want to hurt her. He'd rather die than hurt her!

His emotions weren't too stable, his senses devolving into moments of madness, but still he knew he had to treat her carefully. He removed the rest of her clothing and then tore his own in his rush. He left the shreds on the floor next to the bed and came down on one knee next to her.

"I'll do my best to make this good for you, Callie, but I'm afraid I waited too long." His voice shook as he took her shoulders in his big, hot hands. "I don't want to hurt you."

"You won't hurt me." She spoke softly, but with the firm conviction of love. "Nothing you could do when we make love could ever hurt me, but I'm prepared for some discomfort, Davin. From what I've heard, it's unavoidable the first time." Her crooked smile touched him deeply and gave him the strength to hold back.

He leaned down and kissed her, noting the glow of the crystal all around them. This was going to be an explosive joining in more ways than one, he realized absently. Maybe making love to her for the first time in the middle of a huge deposit of raw crystal wasn't his best plan ever, but he had no choice now. He had to have her. He could delay no longer.

Their kiss built into an inferno as he moved over her, his skin sliding along hers. He felt hot, burning from within, the only ease he could find was her touch. Davin moved, twined his fingers with hers and coaxed her hands onto his shoulders, encouraging her with little tugs of her hands to stroke him. She caught on and he released her fingers to let her touch him at will. It felt so good to have her hands on his bare skin, her touch igniting the thrilling, pulsing Hum.

The sound bathed him in warmth, a low rumble of delight underpinning all the energy as it began to swirl between them and around the vast crystal chamber. The very Earth sang the song of their love as Davin pressed Callie's soft body into the mattress. She went willingly, her touch encouraging him as she spread her legs for him to settle between. He broke the kiss, hanging on to sanity by a bare thread.

"It's got to be fast this first time, my love. I'm sorry."

"Don't be sorry, Davin. I don't think I can wait either."

Shards! This woman was perfect for him in every way. She'd been his friend for the past few years—a voice in the darkness when no one else could understand him at all—and now she would be his lover. His. Forevermore.

"I love you, Callie." His voice broke as he began the slow

entry into her tight body. She was wet and slippery, eager for him, but still, there was resistance. Davin eased out and then pushed back in, just a little farther than he'd been before. Callie squirmed, making little sounds of distress at the back of her throat, but Davin was lost. He only had enough presence of mind to ease his way inside. Other than that small concession to her virginity, her protests were lost on him.

The beast was in control now.

Davin rocked inward, easing his way, but pushing relentlessly forward. He had to claim her, to take her, to make her his own. It was the driving force behind his near-blind need, the thing creeping in to cloud his thoughts, the beast that might well drive him mad. The beast wanted only one thing—its mate.

Callie pushed at his shoulders as he slid past the barrier, tearing her maidenhead. She cried out and her eyes closed tight in a wince of pain, but he was beyond the ability to stop or slow down. Davin shoved home with one last mighty push until he was fully embedded within her tight sheath.

"You're mine now, my love. Mine."

Her hands gripped his shoulders as she opened her eyes and stared up at him. Pain glazed her expression, but beyond the pain was...love. Davin recognized it and it calmed him enough so he could give her the time to get used to his presence within her untried body. He lay over her, soaking in her love, reveling in the feel of her hot core around him as he waited for her discomfort to subside.

Davin wanted her to enjoy her first time. So far, he'd only been able to give her pain, but her love steadied him. It gave him the strength—the sanity—to wait for her to catch her breath.

"Better now, kitten?" He licked her throat as her shivers eased. The beast calmed momentarily, now that he was in full possession of his mate. "Can you feel how much I desire you?"

The pain in her eyes receded, to be replaced with wonder. "I feel it." Her breath came in short pants. "Davin, I love you so much!"

He growled as the beast reared up, thrilling at the words of love from his mate. This would bind them. All he had to do was come inside her and bathe her in his possession.

"Hang on, Callie, my love."

Davin truly lost control after that, pistoning into her with little finesse. She whimpered, but luckily they were sounds of enjoyment, not distress. He couldn't have stopped for anything, but he didn't have to. Callie was with him. For all he knew, she was feeding off his unrestrained emotions, his own mindless desire reflecting back at him from her soul.

She watched him as he rutted, his body claiming hers, their eyes locked and holding. That connection meant more to him than anything. That connection calmed him when he would have gone mad. That connection blinded him to all else while at the same time making him aware of every last-minute detail.

The drip of water on wild crystal, the harmonies reaching out to mesh with theirs, the way their two beings bonded and became one. No longer separate. Never again to part. This was resonance on the most profound scale. There was no Davin. No Callie. Only the two of them, together, as they joined fully for the first time.

Davin stiffened above her, crying out in a tone that could have deafened him, resonating against the crystal chamber, taunting the dormant energy of each shard and bending it to his will. Callie cried out as well, her human voice echoing in the cavern, blending with his and complimenting his tones as they, together, retuned an entire chamber of wild crystal. All without even trying.

Davin collapsed over her, his eyes shut against the glare of the glowing crystal. For all he cared, the cave could collapse over them right this minute. His life was complete. He had his mate and he was still part of her.

He had no idea how long they lay there, breathing hard as their bodies came down from the highest high Davin had ever experienced. He wasn't sure about Callie, but he knew she'd experienced pleasure. He counted that as a miracle, considering just how out of control he'd been. Wearily, Davin opened his eyes and levered himself off of her as much as he could. He refused to leave her completely, but he wanted to see her reaction, watch the dawn of expression over her lovely face.

"Callie?" His question was barely a whisper, but it resonated through the chamber, reflecting off every facet of every crystal, a whisper of love from the Earth itself.

Callie's expression held wonder as she smiled up at him, then looked past him, over his shoulder to the brilliance of the chamber itself. She caught her breath and squinted against the bright rainbows of light.

"Davin!" The awed tone of his name held many meanings and the crystal reflected and heightened every one, straight into Davin's heart. Born to wrangle wild crystal, he knew its ways better than anyone else on this planet. He twisted his head to the side and noted the wonder all around them.

The crystal deposits were lit with nearly blinding intensity, but their power couldn't hurt the two beings at the center of the storm. The energy of a thousand stars ran through the rich crystal deposits, and through the two lovers, entwined within.

Davin chuckled as he imagined what this kind of energy must be doing all over the globe. The Earth would stand still— or at least its new inhabitants would—as the massive surge of wild energy flooded all nearby power sources, overwhelming the grid and causing spikes in Alvian cities and installations.

But Davin didn't care.

No, for once in his life, he cared only about the woman in his arms who made him whole. Callie seemed to be reveling in the energy flow as much as he did, calming his fears for her safety and reassuring him that she really was meant for him. She was incredible, this small human woman of his, and he would never let her go. Not now. Not ever.

He opened his mouth to speak, but Callie covered his lips with one finger, her eyes alight with humor. "I know you love me. I can feel it with every fiber of my being. And I love you. But I have one question."

He kissed her soft fingertip. "Ask me anything."

"What did we do to this chamber?" Her tone reflected the awe in her wide eyes.

"Our love made the crystal shine, Callie. It resonated with us as we resonated with each other." He began to realize what this could mean for their future and a smile lit his face. "I bet this entire chamber—perhaps the rest of this network of caves and crystal deposits is now tuned to us. We'll have to do a bit of exploring to find out the extent of the effect." He felt the twitch of her tight body around his cock and it roused in interest. "Later." He leaned down and kissed her neck, nipping gently and sucking. "Right now, I have some loving to make up to you. This time I promise it'll be better."

"I don't think it can get any better."

"Watch and learn, sweetheart." Davin began to move slowly, caressing her shoulders with his hands, her breasts with his chest. They were perfectly aligned in all ways. "I love the way you feel around me."

Callie's voice was pitched low with excitement. "I love the way you feel inside me."

It was a slow, sensuous loving, now that Davin was fully bonded with his mate. He was sure of her, the beast inside him sated as he pleasured his woman. She was pure magic to him and he wanted to bring a little bit of that to her. He stroked into her slowly, with greater care than he could have managed before. He regretted his loss of control, but she didn't complain. Her big heart encompassed all of him—his faults, his weaknesses, his *humanity*.

Davin had more in common with Callie's people than his own. But for his looks and lack of psychic skills, except those used in crystallography, he could be one of the survivors of humanity. If they'd have him, he'd be happy to make his home among them. For certain, he'd be using all that remained of his skill and position—if anything—to champion their cause.

But those thoughts percolated deep in the recesses of his mind as he loved his woman. She was young, to be sure, but she would grow and mature at his side. He'd nurture her. He'd give her everything in his power to give. He'd do anything for her.

Callie moaned under him as he sped his strokes. Reaching down, he played with the little nubbin at the apex of her thighs, gratified when she cried out. She was close now, and he couldn't hold back.

"Come for me now!" Davin's voice echoed through the chamber, amplified and reflected back in a chorus of love and need.

A strangled moan tore from Callie's lips as her body spasmed around him, drawing him over the edge. He spiraled over the cliff of pleasure with her, his body seizing as his seed splashed into her womb.

He had just enough energy to roll to his side, taking his weight off her softly curved body. He brought her with him, careful of her comfort, snuggling her into his body and wrapping her in his embrace.

"Rest now, my love." He kissed the softness of her hair as he held her small body against his. She felt so right in his arms, so perfect as she settled to sleep in his loving embrace.

He woke her several times in the night to gently make love to her, bringing her to a higher climax each time. And each time, the crystal chamber glowed and tuned even more to their energies as it welcomed their resonance with matching vibrations. It was a miracle of grand proportions. Not only did Davin claim his resonance mate and save himself from insanity, but an entire chamber of wild crystal had been tamed—a feat that otherwise would have taken years, if not lifetimes.

Callie woke sometime later and noticed immediately she was alone in the big bed. The crystals of the chamber glowed white, rose, gold and purple, the white breaking into rainbows here and there, spilling a comforting, almost magical illumination throughout the vast chamber. Callie sat up and tucked the blanket around her like a toga. She went searching for her lover and found him not far away, deep in thought as he studied a huge crystal that stood several feet off the floor of the cave.

"Davin?"

He spun when she spoke his name, echoing around the chamber in a chorus. A broad smile lit his face as he walked over to her and pulled her into his arms. The kiss he bestowed spoke of love, possession and joy in a way that made her breathless. He let her go much too soon, but kept one arm around her shoulders as he brought her over to the crystal he'd been studying.

"Look at this." He motioned to the giant crystal sticking up from the floor.

"What is it?"

"A near-perfect beacon. This single crystal could power an

entire city. Maybe even act as the focal for an entire power grid. It's a rare specimen, worth much to the Alvians. And it's tuned to us." His arm tightened as he sought her gaze.

"What does this mean?"

"It means we can pretty much write our own ticket." Davin gave her a smacking kiss, grinning widely. "I hoped things would work out something like this. I mean, I hoped you'd have some crystal talent we could barter with, but I didn't dare dream anything as big as this. For one thing, until we got here, I wasn't entirely certain you'd be able to withstand this chamber. Wild crystal can be very unpredictable. When I realized you were comfortable here, I began to hope. I thought if we could work together to retune a little bit of this deposit, we might have some leverage in bargaining for your safety."

"And your job," she reminded him, but he shook his head.

"Personally, I don't give a damn if I never see another Alvian ever again. I don't belong with them, Callie. More than ever, I realize I belong with your people. The only reason I'd go back to the Alvians is to help humans. They don't deserve the way they're being treated. I didn't have enough power before, but now, with you by my side, and this—" He gestured to the glowing crystal all around. "With this, our position has vastly improved. If they want these riches, they'll have to keep us happy. Both of us."

"This chamber is really that important?"

"It's not the chamber itself. It's the vast quantities of crystal—now tuned to us, Callie—and the power it represents. The Alvian race is expanding their hold on this planet. They need crystal to power all their technology. We've been having trouble meeting the increasing needs. There just aren't enough crystallographers, for one thing, and those we do have are swamped and can only handle the smaller tasks. Up 'til now, I've been handling all the bigger jobs personally. All the major crystals are tuned to me, so they need to keep me around—at least until the crystals settle and new engineers can be trained to resonate with them and keep them in tune."

"I didn't realize."

"Few people do. But the Council is well aware of how much they need me. I think that—" he looked pointedly at the beacon crystal, "—will point out how much they need you as well.

Maybe now they'll let me institute the plan I devised for training some of your people to work crystal."

"That's what I love about you, Davin." She reached up to peck his cheek. "You've got a sharp mind and a warm heart." She settled her head against his chest, snuggling in his arms. "Do you think they'll let you train people? I mean, they have no reason to trust that their prisoners won't turn around and sabotage the crystals once they know how to use them."

"True." Davin stroked her hair. "But Alvians won't realize that. They no longer understand the concept of holding a grudge or true anger and hatred. If they're too blind to see it, and change their behavior toward humans, then they deserve whatever they get for their shortsightedness."

She leaned back, looking up at him with concern in her expression. "Aren't you worried your students might turn on you?"

"No. If they don't realize pretty quick that I'm on their side, then I won't have been doing my job. Plus, you'll be with me. I can withstand anything, as long as you are by my side."

"You say the sweetest things." She sighed and rested her head under his chin. She fit so perfectly in his arms, he had little doubt she was made just for him.

Rick jumped when the lights flickered and went out. The entire city seemed to be without power. Was this his chance?

He'd planned for a situation like this for years, but still he hesitated. To escape with a large group, he'd need a few hours. He didn't want to leave anybody behind. The power outage would have to be a massive one. That was the only way they'd be able to get everyone out. They'd tried a number of times before, but were always recaptured before they even got above ground. This time the power was out. That might make all the difference.

"Do you think this is it?" one of his cellmates asked.

"Could be. The forcefields are off. Let's go out into the hall and see what's going on."

The scene in the common hallway connecting all the pens was chaotic. Emergency lighting gave the entire area an eerie golden glow, but the rest of the alien technology seemed nonfunctional.

When Rick stepped into the hall, people quieted, looking to him for leadership. It was a role he hadn't sought, but one he'd come to accept.

"Are we going?" a voice called out of the crowd.

There it was. Decision time. Rick quickly weighed the possibilities. Heaven knew, things couldn't get much worse. He grit his teeth and strode forward, toward the single exit. Only one guard stood watch over the narrow door, but he knew others would soon be on their way.

Rick faced down the big Alvian warrior.

"Get out of the way, friend."

The soldier bristled. "Go back to your cell."

"I can't," Rick said, moving into position for best advantage.

"You must comply." When the soldier went for his weapon, Rick acted. His foot smashed into the man's hand, sending the weapon flying even as his fist connected with the Alvian's temple, felling him like a tree. Rick didn't wait to see who followed. He knew everyone who was mobile would be right behind him as he sped out the door and headed upward—toward freedom.

It was a valiant attempt, but just as the ragged group of humans reached the perimeter of the city, the power kicked back on. Rick could see the green forest beyond the city's shield. It was so close—he could smell the loamy pine scent of the area.

But it wasn't meant to be. Rick went quietly with the platoon of soldiers that cornered them. It wasn't worth the fight. The shield was back up. They'd never get out of the city now.

Chapter Six

Callie and Davin made love repeatedly, in many different ways. She was an eager pupil and he loved teaching her every aspect of lovemaking he'd always longed to try. Callie was more adventurous than he would have imagined and even managed to surprise him a few times.

He pushed into her from behind, loving the feel of her tight sheath encasing him in warmth. She reached back and cupped his balls, teasing him with curious touches as she felt around the place where they were joined.

"Are you trying to kill me, sweetheart?" he asked, not entirely joking.

"Davin," she spoke hesitantly, "I've heard things I'm curious about." She seemed reluctant to go on as he slowed his pace, enjoying the feel of her and the shyness of her well-loved body. She was still new to loving, but by no means afraid. At times though, she managed to remind him that up until a few days ago, she'd been a virgin.

"What have you heard? You know you can ask me anything, don't you?" He leaned down to nip her shoulder, then placed wet kisses over the little love bite.

"Harry told me about some things an Alvian woman asked him to do to her. He said...he said she took him in her bottom."

Davin felt his heart stutter. Did she want him to try it? Did he dare? It was something he'd done before, with Alvian women, but he hadn't thought a newly broken-in virgin would even know of such things. Davin had thought to introduce the subject in a few months, perhaps, and see what she thought of the idea, but here she was, surprising him again.

"Did I shock you?" She pulled away from him, disengaging their bodies as she flipped over on the bed to look up at him. A sexy blush covered her cheeks and the tops of her breasts.

"Not at all." Davin sought for composure, but couldn't get the idea of coming in her ass out of his mind. Oh, yeah, he'd like to show her that dark pleasure.

"So, um, you've heard of it?"

Davin stalked forward on his hands and knees, crawling over her as she lay back on the bed. "Not only have I heard of it, I've done it. Many times, in fact. It's not for the faint of heart and it's said men like it more than women, but none of my partners ever seemed disappointed." He grinned, taking her mouth in a swift, hard kiss as the fires of passion revived within him.

When he let her up for air, she smiled at him. "Would you show me how it's done, Davin?"

"Would I?" Davin gave her a teasing, leering grin. "It would be my pleasure. Quite literally, in fact." He stopped teasing for a moment to see if she was really ready. "I'll try to prepare you as best I can, but if anything bothers you, I want you to tell me and I'll ease off. We don't have to do this. Do you understand?"

She lifted to kiss him quickly, her lips a thankful benediction, her tongue sweeping over his once in promise. "I love you, Davin. More than that, I trust you. I'm curious." She shrugged, lying back. "I want to know everything there is to know about loving you. In every way possible."

"Well, then." He moved back and flipped her onto her stomach once again. "Let the lessons begin."

She had the most beautiful ass. Davin had spent more than a few hours dreaming of the pert, rounded cheeks. And now it was his.

Davin bent to trail kisses down her spine, nibbling as he went, his hands kneading the fleshy globes of her ass, spreading them apart as he left his saliva there to mix with her own syrupy fluids. Dipping inside her dripping pussy, he moved the lubrication where it was needed, sliding one finger inside her to see how easy or difficult the task ahead might prove.

Davin was pleased with the way she relaxed around him, taking him in. He pulsed his finger in and out a few times,

103

letting her get the feel of it.

"How's this, love?"

"Mmm. Feels good. Weird, but good." She squirmed a bit in a way he now recognized meant her passion was rising. He withdrew and added another finger, stretching this time, going slow, doing his best not to cause pain. "Oh!" She gasped as he slid farther in.

"All right? I'll stop if you don't like it."

"No, I like it. Don't stop." Her words came on panting breaths as he began to stroke within her. She was a natural at loving. He should have known she'd take to this unconventional method as easily as she'd done the rest.

Using his other hand, he added more lubrication. He really should have some kind of cream, he realized, pulling away to search through the bag of belongings he'd salvaged from the ship. There was something there he could use. A tube of cream meant for first aid. True, this use was a little unconventional, but it wouldn't harm her if used internally and the viscous liquid would definitely make his invasion easier.

Callie leaned up on her elbows to watch him and he'd never seen a sexier sight.

"I hope you're planning on coming back," she said in a sultry tone of voice that set his cock to twitching. "It was just starting to get interesting."

"Never fear." Davin held up the tube he'd just recovered. Rising, he stalked back to the bed, noting the way she watched him—or rather, his cock. She seemed fascinated by it.

"What's that for?" She tore her attention away from his cock and nodded toward the tube in his hand.

"Normally it's for disinfecting wounds, but for us, today, it's going to serve as lubricant." He grinned as he opened the tube. "Give me your hand. I want you to put this on me first, so you'll know how it feels." She held out her hand and he squeezed a large dollop of the fluid into her palm.

"It's warm."

"The gel heats when it comes into contact with flesh. Very therapeutic." He moved to present her with his cock and she didn't hesitate to reach out and slide her slick palm over him, again and again. "That feels almost too good." He stepped away before he let his instincts overcome his sense. There was more work to do to prepare her.

"Now what?" The saucy grin she gave him told him she knew damn well what came next, but she liked to tease him into giving orders. And he found he liked giving the orders as much as she enjoyed taking them.

"On your elbows and knees. Stick that pretty ass up in the air for me like a good girl."

"Yes, Davin," she agreed with a secretive little smile that lit fires in his system that only she could contain.

Davin didn't waste any time. He squeezed a dollop of the gel into the crack of her ass, sliding it around with his fingers and right up into her, paving the way for what would come next.

"Not only will this be the most hygienic fuck I've ever given, but no doubt the hottest." He could feel the warmth of the gel against his fingers and could only imagine what it must feel like for her. Taking the final precaution, he pushed three fingers into her tight hole, going slow so as not to hurt her. "Do you like it so far?"

She writhed, but he noted she was careful not to dislodge him. "I love it. Come into me now, Davin. Please!"

"As you command, my love." Davin pulled his fingers away and rose up on the bed, positioning his cock at her rosy entrance.

With great care, he pushed within, going slow. His cock was a lot thicker than his fingers, but she seemed well able to take him. The lubricant helped enormously, but Callie's willingness counted for a lot too. She relaxed and pushed out at the right moment, all without being told what to do. It was as if she were born to take him any way he chose—or any way she could dream up.

When he was seated fully, she whimpered and started to push back. She wanted him to move, and she wanted to come. He could read all that from the small sounds and movements he'd learned over the past few days. She was expressive in a non-verbal way, though she did speak her mind when they made love as well. Quite different from what he was used to in Alvian women, this miracle girl was everything he'd ever hoped for in a woman—in a mate.

"Oh, Davin!" she panted. "This feels so good. I never dreamed..."

He rounded his back, moving over her for better leverage, enjoying the heat of her skin against his belly and chest. "I never dreamed I'd find anyone as perfect as you, Callie. Never."

"Davin!" Her body began to clench as her orgasm drew near. Davin pulsed faster into her, feeling his balls tighten in readiness for release. And this was going to be a big release. He could feel it.

He reached around with one hand to tease her clit and she cried out at the overload of sensation. "Now, Callie. Come for me now, my love."

She screamed his name as she came harder than he'd ever seen her come before. A heartbeat later, he followed her over the edge into blissful oblivion as he shot inside of her again and again.

He had just enough presence of mind to pull out and move to her side before falling unconscious from the pleasure. He woke a short time later to find her snuggled into his arms. They hadn't moved far, both wearing the silly smiles of the well pleasured.

"Are you all right, my love?" He squeezed her closer and placed a kiss on the crown of her head.

"Never better, Davin. That was better than anything I could have imagined. Thank you for showing me."

"It's I who should be thanking you. Not one man in a thousand is blessed with such an adventurous and willing mate. You continue to amaze and delight me, Callie. I love you so much and so deeply. Now that I have you in my life, I could never exist without you."

She reached up to stroke his cheek, a smile curving her lips and tears of joy shining in her eyes as she looked up at him. "I feel the same, Davin. I love you, so much. And no matter how this all turns out, I wouldn't trade a single moment we've shared for anything."

They slept, then woke to love again and Callie couldn't believe how perfect Davin was in every way. Sure, he had his idiosyncrasies, as all people do, but the ways they complimented each other were far greater than the ways in which they conflicted. All in all, Callie thought she was a very lucky woman to have such a loving, thoughtful and sexy resonance mate.

She still wasn't sure she understood all the ramifications of resonance mating, but Davin believed in it, and she respected his beliefs. She couldn't hear the Hum, but her skin tingled every time they touched and her empathic senses were bathed in the most amazing mix of love, caring and desire. In short, he was good for her. And she would spend the rest of her life being good to him.

The sex was out of this world too. She'd known what to expect from frank discussions with her brother, but he'd never explained how incredible it could feel to share something so intimate with someone you loved. Davin made it special. He cared so deeply and devoted so much effort to her pleasure, she was moved to do the same for him.

She'd stretched her own boundaries further than she ever would have believed and Davin had been right there with her, teaching her and never pushing for more than she was willing to give. Of course, for him, she'd do just about anything.

And he'd be certain to make her enjoy every last minute of it.

They stayed hidden in their little lovenest for a few days, but Davin knew after the energy disturbances they'd caused— and kept causing with their wild lovemaking—they'd be found sooner or later. Then they'd be taken before the Council. He thought it better to arrive before that unforgiving group on their own initiative.

He laid out the options, describing each of the Councilors and their views to Callie before they ever set foot outside the resonance chamber. He also packed up the beacon crystal and a few other specimens as insurance. They wouldn't harm him or gainsay his wishes while they carried such a dangerous and valuable artifact in their ship.

The beacon crystal came in handy when they were intercepted shortly after leaving the cover of the trees. All he had to do was send an image of the crystal to the warships that ordered them down and hold it up to the window so they could see it wasn't a ruse. The soldiers backed off, escorting them directly to the Council compound.

Callie sat behind him in the two-person ship. She was handling this so well, he was proud of his young mate. She had poise and intellect to match any of the Council. They were all in for a surprise when they finally met one of the Breeds they so disdained.

"How dare you defy the will of the Council?" Councilor Troyan's words were haughty, and as close to anger as one of the modern Alvians could come. Davin stood with Callie at his side, in front of the full Council, already in session. He'd timed their appearance to the weekly meeting he knew would be taking place. No sense having to wait to get them together when he needed their full attention as soon as possible. Best to take them by surprise before any of the troublemakers had time to work through the possible countermoves in their devious minds.

The Council Chamber held the Council Crystal, a large beacon of superior lines that sat in a place of honor behind the U-shaped Council table. It powered all the workings of the Council Compound and surrounding city.

The Councilors themselves were arranged along the two sides of the table, with their nominal leader, presently Councilor Hearn, at the center of the gently sloping U. Eight other Councilors sat at intervals on each side of the table, four to a side. Some were male, some female, each representing a different branch of Alvian society. There was a female crystallographer, Councilor Beyan, who oversaw all of the engineering facilities planet-wide. There were representatives of the various scientific fields, Councilor Gildereth from the military, Councilor Troyan representing the clerical workers, Councilor Hearn for the medical workers, Councilor Orin for those employed in language professions and the arts, and so on. Each represented their own interests and the interests of those who worked in their fields.

The new beacon crystal had gained all of their attention. All Alvians understood the nature of crystals and knew how rare the larger ones were. Though the big crystal rested far back in the gallery, they could all see it, and watch it respond to Davin's every breath—tuned so closely to him and his mate. He let the crystal glow and flux, drawing the Councilors' eyes in a small demonstration of his power that was not lost on any of them.

While they were glad of the new beacon crystal—it was, after all, a much-needed resource—some of them were being stubborn about Callie's presence. Troyan was perhaps the worst of them, but others frowned at them as well from around the large chamber.

But Davin stood firm. "I'll defy anyone who tries to come between me and my lawful mate." He produced a data crystal and fed it into the display unit at his table, projecting highlighted historical documents for all to see. "The law is on my side in this instance, Councilors. You will see here, very clearly, the ancient Alvian Code states that resonance mates, once Joined, cannot be forcibly separated for any reason. I have Joined with my proven mate. The crystals themselves prove that our Joining is a true one. So my question to you is: How *dare* you try to take my resonance mate from me?"

Grumbles were heard among the Council and the gallery of spectators until finally Councilor Orin raised his amethyst wand for silence.

"I say we cease our interference in this matter, since I do believe young Davin has the law on his side."

"It is an old law. Outdated," Councilor Beyan pointed out in her quiet way.

Orin nodded. "Perhaps, but we have never changed the ancient laws. We have never yet created any new law that was inconsistent with the ancient texts. I, for one, do not believe now is the time to do so. We have lost Alvia and have come to a new world. Let us not lose more of our heritage by disregarding the ancient wisdom and laws of our forefathers."

The debate went on for some time but eventually a vote was taken and most of the Councilors recognized Davin's legal right to keep his proven resonance mate, even if she was a Breed. They debated for a while on whether or not to grant her full rights of citizenship, but held off on that decision until some future date.

Davin didn't care. As long as he and Callie were free to live together as mates, that was all that mattered. She was safe and should be forever now, as his legally recognized mate. Even if something happened to him, she would still have the rights of his resonance mate, regardless of what the Council finally decided about her status as a citizen. He moved back from the table, and gathered Callie into his arms, uncaring of what the Council or gallery would make of their display of emotion. Perhaps, he thought, it was time his people saw firsthand what an emotionally bonded couple could feel for each other. Maybe it would make them think about what they'd given up in the search for genetic perfection. Maybe hearing the Hum of their skin touching and seeing their Kiss produce a glow like no other from every crystal in the vicinity would be enough to make them realize they'd turned down the wrong path.

Davin Kissed Callie, momentarily bringing a stunned silence to the entire Council Chamber as every crystal within began to glow. Callie pulled back and laughed when she saw the shocked faces, a becoming flush pinking her cheeks as she looped her arms about Davin's neck.

"I love you, my heart," Davin said in a whisper loud enough for all to hear in the silent chamber, lit with the light of their passion.

"Oh, Davin, I love you too!"

Councilor Beyan watched them with interest in her eyes. "Davin." She spoke softly, but garnered everyone's attention. She, of all the Council, understood him perhaps the best, since she too had a strong crystal gift. "Is your mate gifted?"

Davin held Callie's hand, addressing the Councilor's question with a firm nod. "Yes, she is very gifted. On par with a level eight novitiate, at least, and growing daily." Murmurs sounded throughout the chamber. Davin knew the idea that a Breed could have one of their most precious—and dangerous— abilities was unsettling to them. Good, he'd rock their boats just a little further. "It is my belief that all Breeds may have some level of the crystal gift. As we produce less and less gifted Alvian children in each generation, but require more and more crystal power, I've toyed with the idea of testing some of the Breeds."

"Outrageous!" Troyan exclaimed again. Davin wasn't really surprised. Troyan hated throwbacks as much as any modern Alvian could hate.

"Do you really think that's wise?" Councilor Beyan's soft voice challenged him.

"I believe it is necessary, Councilor. We need more staff to keep the new grid up and running. I propose testing and training acceptable Breeds to manage the small, day-to-day tasks that level one, two and three novitiates usually handle. Surely they couldn't do much damage with such simple tasks." None of the Alvians recognized the snide irony in his tone, but Callie squeezed his hand and when he looked back at her, the devil danced in her eyes. It was all he could do to keep from kissing her again, but this moment was too important.

Davin hadn't intended to broach this topic until the Council was more comfortable with Callie, but he was glad in a way that it had come up today. Each day they waited was a day longer in captivity for humanity. If Davin could gather just a few humans from the worst of the pens and give them a decent place to live in his engineering facility, it was a start. But he needed the Council's permission to begin such a daring program.

"It is true we have fewer crystallographers in each generation and we need more." Councilor Beyan sounded thoughtful. It was a good sign. "May I test your mate, Davin? Her name is Callie, right?" Beyan pasted on a smile, though it wasn't convincing on a woman who had no feelings. Still, that she would make the effort to put a human at ease meant something extraordinary. Davin tugged Callie forward. She shot him a worried look but he squeezed her hand to reassure her before he let her go, motioning her toward the Councilor who sat behind the high Council table.

Beyan removed a crystal from the pocket of her white robe and placed it on the table. Callie stood about eye level with the crystal, a lovely amethyst with regular edges. She could see the crystal was flawless on the surface, and could feel the resonances Davin had taught her to seek. Although it looked perfect on the outside, something was slightly off inside the crystal matrix that made the resonance a little harsh and jagged, not flowing smoothly as it should be.

"May I touch the amethyst, ma'am?" Callie asked politely, earning raised eyebrows from the Councilors. Apparently they all thought humans were impolite barbarians.

"Before you do," the Councilor countered, "can you tell me anything about this crystal without touching it?"

Callie nodded. "It looks perfect, but something's wrong. The resonances aren't aligned properly. There is a slight disharmony in the matrix and it's growing worse. If not aligned, I believe it will eventually crack near the center of the stone."

More raised eyebrows met Callie's words and the Councilor radiated a faint feeling of surprise mixed with respect. Of course, these Alvians had so little emotion, it was hard to read much, even for an empath as strong as she was.

"Can you do anything about it?" the Councilor challenged.

Callie tilted her head, considering. "I don't know. I've been able to retune smaller crystals with Davin's guidance, but I'm not certain I can handle as delicate a problem as this one seems to have. I would have to examine it first, by touching it and studying the disharmony."

Beyan nodded. "A wise answer. Truly, Davin, your mate speaks well."

"Let her try her abilities on your amethyst, Councilor. I believe she is up to the challenge you have placed before her."

"Truly?" Beyan looked back at Callie. "Then proceed, by all means."

Callie reached out and took the amethyst into her hand. It was even worse than she'd thought. The disharmony was a cacophony of warring resonances that she imagined she could almost hear, though such frequencies were well out of human hearing range. But the power was strong. If tuned properly, this crystal would be very powerful indeed. A light touch would be called for to do this work, lest it blow up in her face.

Callie concentrated, closing her eyes and focusing on the stone alone. She could feel Davin's reassuring presence behind her. She knew he had absolute faith she could meet this challenge and that made her stronger. There was no one on Earth who knew crystals the way Davin did. If he thought she could do it, there was no doubt in her mind she could.

She also had some idea of what was riding on this. The fate of many humans rested on convincing the Council that Davin's idea of testing and training humans had some merit. They needed power and they had few crystallographers to run their power grid. If she could prove humans could step into such an important role, she would be saving at least a few of her brethren from life—or death—in the pens.

Marshalling her strength, Callie tried to think of the quiet stream by the farm. All the currents running together helped her imagine the currents of energy focused in the crystal. Throw a stone in the stream and disrupt the current, much like the unseen flaw in the crystal threw off its harmony. But it could be fixed. Strength of will and suitable application of her psi energy could retune the crystal so its energy flowed freely like the stream.

Thinking peaceful thoughts and seeing that vision of harmony in her mind, Callie applied her power. She felt resistance at first, but then the power of the stone yielded and turned, redirected into a more harmonious flow. With what she knew was a smile of triumph lighting her face, she opened her eyes and placed the retuned amethyst on the table in front of the Councilor.

"It's done."

Callie walked back to Davin's side and reveled in the pride she could feel emanating from him for her. His love and his respect were two things she craved and he gave her both, swamping her empathic senses in what amounted to a body hug as she rejoined him.

Councilor Beyan touched the crystal tentatively at first, then picked it up and stared into its perfect facets. "Remarkable," she said softly as the other Councilors watched with varying degrees of interest. "She did a very nice job retuning this piece." Beyan's gaze rested on Davin. "I agree with your level eight ranking and would put her at seer status." Callie didn't know what that meant, but she could feel Davin's surprise, then the burst of pride that filled him, and the joy. "My friends," Beyan addressed the other Councilors now, "I believe young Davin has proven the sense of his proposal. If he can find a few well-behaved candidates with a gift even half as good as his mate's, it should end our grid shortages. I believe we should allow him to try."

"Are you certain, Beyan?" Orin, as head of the Council, asked for them all.

Beyan nodded. "I believe it is a sound plan."

Orin sighed and turned to Davin. "You have the Council's permission to test and appropriate such Breeds as you need for a pilot program."

Davin bowed and Callie followed suit. "It shall be done. You have my thanks." They left the chamber shortly thereafter and the next supplicant came before the Council.

Mara 12 had arrived at a crucial decision. It was a radical idea indeed, but she had always believed in taking bold steps to further scientific endeavor. She presented her facts to the Council, unsurprised by the barrage of questions she received, but she'd prepared well and had displays ready to answer each of their points.

After several hours of discussion, Mara 12 was granted permission for a very special project of her own. This time, Mara wanted to test volunteers from her own race with a DNA-altering concoction that might—just might—improve on Alvian genetics.

But it also just might have surprising consequences for them all...

One of the benefits of having the blessing of the Council was that Callie could communicate freely with Harry and Caleb. Of course they had to be somewhat circumspect in what they said because all their communications were monitored, but they could at least talk as often as they wished.

Harry was able to communicate telepathically with the family back at the farm, but the Alvians couldn't know Davin had given them a communication crystal. Callie could use that illicit crystal to access the rest of her family as well and spoke to them often.

It was good for Callie to talk with her family and it made her feel somehow safer, even as she struggled to help Davin set up his training program in the Southern Engineering Facility. It was slow going, but within a few weeks they had nice quarters and equipment ready for the humans Davin was finding and rescuing from the various settlements and cities.

Callie was also learning the Alvian alphabet and how to work their comm systems and other devices. Each day, Davin would show her a little more. She had a hard time wrapping her tongue around their spoken language, but the written form was a little easier. Not much, but a little.

One night, Davin sat her down at a comm console with a very serious look on his face.

"What I'm going to show you now, nobody else knows. Nobody, Callie, but you and me." He brought up what she recognized as a subroutine on the comm panel. "It's important that you commit this operation to memory. You can't write it down anywhere. It's too dangerous for anyone else to know and I don't want any spies finding out I've created this backdoor, or it will be useless if we ever need it."

"What is it?" She watched in wonder as he brought up an innocuous display that she knew could be accessed from even the most rudimentary comm panels in the facility. Even the airships could bring up this particular subroutine that had to do with simple system diagnostics.

"It's something I created in case of emergency. A way to disable communications over a wide area. I thought—" He halted, shaking his head as he turned to look at her. "I thought when I finally went crazy and they were going to put me down, I'd use it to buy enough time to go out my own way. I didn't want to be at their mercy when I breathed my last. I wanted to die free, by my own choice."

"Oh, Davin." She covered his hand with hers, imparting her love with a slight squeeze.

"Well," he cleared his throat, continuing, "now that insanity is no longer an issue, I still want to keep this little trick for emergencies. We're not the Council's favorite people, in case you hadn't noticed." He tapped out a string of commands that brought up something she'd never seen before. "This," he pointed to the sequence, "is a special code that will douse the crystals of every comm panel connected to this one and cause a cascading failure throughout the system. It will cripple the military and Council alike, at least for a few minutes."

115

"Wow."

"Yeah." He smiled as she leaned in to study the sequence of characters. "I want you to know this, in case something should happen to me, or if you ever need to create a diversion to get away. I don't know what kind of situations we might face in the future, but I want you to have this insurance against my people, should the worst happen. I don't want them to ever hurt you, Callie." He stroked her cheek with one big hand and she relished the caring in his touch.

"I love you too, Davin."

Rick St. John hadn't yet found the right time or opportunity to escape, but he was by no means resigned to his fate. But even so, he almost didn't recognize the opening when it was handed to him.

When the Chief Engineer for the Alvians on planet Earth came to call on the prison beneath the city, Rick was at first as hostile toward the stranger as he was toward all Alvians with whom he didn't work. He kept up a constant stream of veiled remarks to the soldiers and most of the caretakers of the jail, refraining only when Mara 36 or one of the other scientists who had the power to change how the humans were treated came by.

So when the Chief Engineer peered into his cell, Rick was his usual, impolite self. Not that it mattered to Alvians. They couldn't appreciate a good insult. They just didn't have it in them.

"What do you want?" Rick challenged the man who stood outside the forcefield that kept Rick and the other men contained in the large barrack-style cell.

"I've come seeking volunteers to be tested for the crystallography program." The strange alien was tall, but not as massively built as some of the soldiers. He was pale and blond, elven-looking like all the aliens, but this one had something different about him that Rick couldn't quite place.

"Why would any of us want to cooperate with one of you?" Rick didn't hide his sneer.

An eyebrow quirked upward on the patrician face. "Acceptance into my pilot program would mean a significant improvement in your circumstances, including a move to the Southern Engineering Facility and accommodations above ground, which I understand is preferable to most humans."

Rick was immediately struck by this Alvian's words. "You called us human."

The Chief Engineer gave him a knowing nod. "I did." Their gaze met and held, sizing each other up. With a slight nod, the Chief Engineer disabled the forcefield and stepped into the cell. "I'm Davin. What's your name?" He accompanied the startling words with a very human gesture. Davin held out his hand for a shake.

Rick knew then there was something odd going on. He shook the man's hand, startled when he felt echoes of feeling—true feeling—from this Alvian. Rick's weak empathy required him to touch a person, skin to skin, in order to get any kind of read on their emotions.

"No numbers? Just Davin?" Rick asked the most obvious question first.

An amazing smile lit the Chief Engineer's face. "Just Davin. I'm a throwback. That means, unlike other Alvians, I experience emotion, much like you."

"I've never heard of such a thing."

"Well, now you have." Davin ended the business-like handshake and turned to the men standing behind Rick, addressing them all. "I'm starting up a new training program. If accepted, you'll move to my engineering facility and train to work with our crystal power sources. You'll have to be tested to see if you have the ability to work with raw crystal before I can invite anyone to join the program, but I'm not forcing the test on anybody. If you want to take the test, step forward now. If not, no harm done."

"What does the test involve? Is it harmful?" Rick wanted to know. Nobody moved, though Rick could sense some were willing to try almost anything to get out of this damp cell.

"No, not harmful. I just want each of you to hold a raw crystal and concentrate. If you do well with the first, I may ask you to try a harder one, to roughly gauge your level of ability."

Davin turned to Rick with a grin. "And I never did get your name."

Rick took his words as a challenge and stepped forward. "Rick St. John, at your service," he said, with his usual sarcasm around the Alvians. "I'll take the test first, just so we know you're telling us the truth."

"Ah, a leader willing to put himself before his men." Davin reached into his pocket and pulled out a small crystal point. "I think I like you already, Rick St. John." Davin dropped the quartz crystal into Rick's open palm and gave him a friendly smile—such an alien thing to see on an Alvian's face. "Now I want you to listen to the song of the crystal. Shut your eyes if it helps. Concentrate on the tone."

Rick shut his eyes, aware of heat coming from the quartz rock in his hand like he'd never felt before. It wasn't uncomfortable, but it was startling. After a few seconds, he was able to hear a tone—actually a series of tones playing together in harmony—though one note was slightly off.

"I hear a chord, but it's not quite right," he said, his eyes still shut. The sound of the crystal in his mind was entrancing.

"Good." Rick could hear the encouragement in the alien's voice, but he still didn't want to open his eyes and possibly lose the beauty of this experience. He heard Davin's words as if from far away. "You can make the chord true, Rick. Think it and it can be so. Concentrate on the crystal and bring your will to bear on it."

Rick didn't quite know what he did, but he felt a touch of his healing power rise to encounter the rough crystal in his palm, healing the rift that made the chord sour and producing a trilling descant above the new, perfect harmony of the stone. The act brought a rush of pleasure that felt almost like sexual completion, but more sacred than any he'd ever experienced. It was as if this tiny piece of the Earth itself sang to him. It was awe-inspiring.

Rick opened his eyes and noted the crystal was now giving off a bright white glow in the palm of his hand. He looked up and saw the pleased smile on Davin's alien face and the skepticism and surprise on the faces of the men gathered around.

"You have a strong and very peculiar crystal gift, Rick St.

John. With that performance, you've earned a spot in my program, if you'll have it. Unlike the other experiments you've no doubt been made to participate in, this one is truly voluntary, but I can tell you right now, I'd be pleased if you accepted the position."

Rick handed the crystal back, though if he were honest, he really didn't want to let it go, and stepped back. "Test the others. I'll give you my decision before you leave."

Davin nodded and turned to the waiting men. All of them were willing to try the test now that they'd seen it wasn't dangerous. They had varying degrees of success with the crystals Davin handed out and Rick watched each carefully. He could hear the tones, and the failures and successes, as each man tried his best to do what he'd done. Many failed, but a few managed passable results. Nobody else produced the pure white glow Rick had but several others were invited to join the program and Rick was torn.

He wanted to get the hell out of this cell, but he also felt a responsibility toward the people he'd come to lead. Davin turned to him, a raised brow questioning his decision, but Rick truly didn't know what to say. His indecision must have shown on his face because Davin's gaze filled with understanding.

"Come with us to the meeting room," Davin said, pulling Rick aside. "There is someone you should talk to before you make your decision."

Rick followed the Chief Engineer and the men who'd already accepted positions in the program out of the cell and into a large meeting room. There were perhaps twenty humans there, with an Alvian soldier posted outside the door, keeping guard.

Rick stopped short in the doorway as he beheld the most beautiful woman he'd ever seen, standing at the front of the room, using an Alvian datapad to record names and the numbers that had been assigned to each human prisoner. She had a lovely smile and an understanding expression as she worked with each prisoner individually.

"Callie?" Davin called to the vision and she smiled when she spotted him. "Can you spare a minute?"

Callie made her excuses to the person she'd been talking to and made her way across the room to where Davin stood, just inside the door. Rick moved a pace forward, into the room, allowing the man behind him to enter and take a seat toward the back, but his gaze was glued to the radiant woman heading their way.

She stopped in front of Davin and smiled so beautifully at the alien, Rick's heart hurt. Never before had he been so taken by a female at first sight, but it was becoming clear, she was already claimed. Rick did his best to tamp down his attraction, lest she see it and pity him. Rick didn't want or need anyone's pity.

"Callie, my love, this is Rick St. John. He hasn't decided whether to join us yet or not, but he's very gifted and I think he'd be an asset to the program."

The woman named Callie turned her luminous blue eyes on Rick and he caught his breath. "You're hard to read, Rick, but I do sense some conflict in you."

"You're an empath?"

She nodded, making an amused yet curious expression as she no doubt tried to feel what he was feeling. Rick redoubled his shielding. He'd be damned if he'd let her read him so easily.

"Believe it or not, I'm a very strong empath, but you're a tough nut to crack, Rick. Why such strong shields?"

"It's pretty miserable where we live. It's become second nature to block." Rick grabbed at the most likely excuse he could find.

"You have some empathy?" Callie stopped concentrating and looked up at him with an open, friendly expression.

"Some, but not strong."

"Telepathy?" she asked in his mind.

He liked the feel of her thoughts in the intimacy of his mind all too much. *"Some. But not over great distances."*

"Me either. My range is limited to two or three miles."

"Yeah, that's about it for me too."

"So what has you so conflicted about joining Davin's program? I can assure you he's not like the other Alvians."

"Yeah, I get that, though it's the weirdest thing I've ever seen. I never thought an Alvian could have emotion."

"It's rare. But it gives him a unique understanding of what

our people are going through. He chose to come here first to test because he knew of all the Alvian settlements, this one treated us the worst."

Rick was surprised by the statement, but felt an odd flare of hope kindle inside him. He looked around the room, glad to see Sadie among those chosen for the program.

Watching the dear older lady, Rick spoke more candidly than he otherwise would have. *"I've been doing my best to help them. That's why I don't know if I should leave. Who will take care of the rest?"*

A soft hand covered Rick's and shocked his gaze back to the beautiful young woman standing in front of him. *"You've done all you can here, Rick, and you can continue to work toward better conditions for humans even more effectively if you come with us. That's what Davin wants. It's what he's working toward—freedom for us all to live in peace."*

"How do you know we can trust him?"

Callie's smile lit the universe as she turned back to Davin and took his hand. *"That's easy, Rick. Davin is my husband. He has a vested interest in helping humans. If he hadn't fought for me in front of the Alvian Council I'd be dead already."*

Rick was floored by the revelation. Here wasn't just a dalliance between the odd alien and a gorgeous human woman, but a marriage. Callie glowed when she was near the man and was obviously deeply in love. Rick felt his own hopes of catching her eye dwindle, while his hope for humanity rose. Davin was special. He had to be to marry such a special woman. Rick would envy him for that, but he'd also work with the alien if it meant better treatment for the people in this room.

Rick stepped up to Davin and held out his hand. "I'm in."

Davin shook his hand with strength and a smile of welcome on his face. Rick felt no malice in the other man, dropping his shield just a tiny bit to read what he could of the alien throwback's character. What he found was steadfast determination and a residual pain so deep, it touched something deep inside Rick as well.

Chapter Seven

Davin chose Rick as his new assistant. It was unprecedented, but warranted when Rick displayed a crystal gift unlike any Davin had ever seen. Rick was proving gifted in a way that could rival Davin's own ability, with proper training. Davin wanted to keep an eye on such a strong crystal gift, and having such a potentially powerful assistant, in addition to Callie, might mean he could finally get some of the pressing work done that needed to be accomplished before the Earth could stabilize.

But Rick was a hard case. He was enormously talented with the crystals and learned quickly, but was very quiet, watchful and kept mostly to himself. Davin decided to try to crack his armor with a challenge.

He brought in a badly damaged, large crystal. Whole, this crystal would have been an excellent conduit for large loads of energy, but flawed as it was, it would shatter should even a small amount of power be channeled into it. There was a deep gouge running the length of the crystal along one side, and flaws within. Davin wanted to see if Rick could realign the inner flaws. It was something Davin could do—with great difficulty. This would be a major test of his abilities, though Rick had no idea and Davin didn't let on.

"Try this," Davin said casually, producing the crystal. He handed it to Rick across the work table. They were finishing up work for the day with a little one-on-one training.

"Damn." Rick whistled through his teeth. "This one's in bad shape. What do you want me to do here?"

Davin shrugged. "Whatever you can. Consider it a little

test."

"I'm not promising anything, but I'll give it a whirl." Rick looked doubtfully at the crystal as he studied it, turning it this way and that before laying his hands directly over the gouge. Davin wouldn't have chosen that plane to start with, but he refrained from correcting Rick. He wanted this test to be completely unimpeded.

Rick's eyes glazed as the resonances built. Davin could feel something happening—something unexpected—but he didn't understand it. A new energy rose to counter the disharmonies in the stone and it seemed to be coming from Rick himself. Davin knew that during great crystal workings, ancient crystallographers had been reported to become tuned to the crystals, giving of their own energies to create masterworks. But such knowledge and abilities were beyond all but the most powerful crystallographers today. Even Davin had never fully tapped into his own personal energy while attempting a difficult tuning. It was hard to do, for one thing. It was instinctive and Davin wasn't even sure he knew how.

But here was this human, doing it as naturally as breathing. Davin was stunned and more than a little awed.

"Man," Rick panted as he worked, a grim smile on his face, "this is a stubborn little guy."

The crystal was one of the larger natural formations, so the word little was a massive understatement. Davin could hear the inner turmoil of the stone realigning successfully, drawing together the discordant notes into a more harmonious tone and overtones.

"You've almost got it," Davin said, unable to hide the approval in his voice.

"Not quite." Rick redoubled his efforts and more of his own power went into the crystal to be refracted, refined and multiplied.

Davin couldn't believe his eyes as Rick lifted his hands away from the now-smooth surface of the quartz. The gouge was gone. Healed completely.

This was *not* something Davin would have been able to do. At best, he'd hoped to shear off the gouged plane of the crystal and salvage the remaining structure, but Rick had managed a miracle of sorts. He'd repaired the thing completely.

Davin didn't know how to react. Rick was already one of the most gifted students and he knew it. Would the knowledge that he had even stronger gifts than his teachers be a good thing or not?

Davin decided to tread carefully. He needed to seek Callie's opinion before he moved forward, but even she had trouble reading Rick's emotions. A plan began to form in Davin's mind. They were due to start a new class next week where teams would work together on crystallographic projects. Perhaps he'd pair Callie with Rick. Working together on difficult projects, he might reveal more of his inner self than he would in normal everyday interaction.

So Callie joined the small class Davin taught, and paired up with Rick for the team experiments and assignments. She was doing well, her own crystal gift emerging strongly, and as a team, she and Rick were at the head of the class, surpassing their classmates easily.

Davin hypothesized that Callie's progress was due in part to their mating. His innate knowledge had merged with her own fledgling gift to propel her ahead. But Rick was just plain gifted.

Callie and Rick were closely matched in ability, but Callie confided to Davin privately that the silent man scared her a little. When pressed, she couldn't say exactly what it was about Rick that frightened her, but Davin watched him closely and could see his gaze following Callie when he thought no one was looking.

Jealousy sparked inside him. It subsided as he realized Rick might be attracted to Callie, but he wouldn't act on it. It was clear Callie and Davin were mated and Rick appeared to have some respect for that. Among this group there were a surprising number of women and Davin didn't mind that several of them had paired off with men they found attractive for one reason or another. In fact, Davin observed the pairs that were bonded in some way often worked better together than singlets.

So Davin shouldn't have been surprised when he first noticed the Hum coming from one of the newer pairs as they held hands surreptitiously during one of his longer lectures. Their human ears couldn't hear it, but Davin decided to explain to the budding human crystallographers some of his theories about Breeds and the history of Alvian resonance mates.

They were interested, he could tell, and as he demonstrated the way a Kiss could make the crystal glow with his own resonance mate, he was glad to see the Humming pair could do the same. The lesson turned humorous after that and Davin felt he'd finally found some way to break the ice between himself and these people who had been through so much.

The small class of human trainees was working with large pieces of untuned crystal for the first time when disaster struck. The pair next to Callie and Rick moved a little too carelessly. The crystal they'd tried to tackle was too strong for them and their untried abilities. Davin rushed in, but it was too late to avoid a shattering explosion of crystal shards that shot out all over the room.

The two who had been working on the crystal had the sense to duck, but Callie, standing with her back to them, hadn't even seen the danger coming. She was hit from behind by the full force of sharp shards scattering everywhere. She screamed and fell to the floor. Davin's heart shot up into his throat from across the large room. He was running before she ever hit the ground.

But she didn't hit hard. Rick was there to break her fall, gathering her in his strong arms and checking her injuries. Davin reached for his mate, but Rick stopped him.

"She's hurt bad. I can help her. I'm a healer." His words were gruff as both men fought with the bloody clothes hampering their ability to see where she was hurt. She'd fallen unconscious with pain, luckily for her, but the paleness of her face struck fear into Davin's heart.

They turned her over and his heart plummeted as he saw the sharp shard of crystal sticking out from her side. She was bleeding profusely and he doubted medical help would get there in time to save her.

"Do what you can," Davin said in a low voice as he helped Rick hold her steady.

Rick met his eyes briefly and a flash of respect lit them before he turned back to Callie and the sharp crystal slicing through her flesh. Rick grasped it, his crystal gift tuning the small shard to his energies almost absently as he pulled it from her skin. Blood welled up, spilling over the deep wound, but Rick placed his palm over the gash, closing his eyes in concentration as Davin heard the increase in resonances around them.

He thought he even saw a glow of energy around Rick's hand, pressing into the wound as the bleeding miraculously slowed to a stop. Rick let up on the pressure as he opened his eyes, watching the reaction of the deep wound to his application of energy. Davin was fascinated as he heard the crystal Rick still held in his hand vibrate with the man's reflected and amplified energy.

"It's working," Davin gasped, watching as the angry red flesh knitted itself together before his eyes.

"Get the rest of this off her," Rick said between clenched teeth as he moved on to the next, somewhat smaller wound in her side. He tugged at the remnants of her shirt and Davin helped him pull it away so they could find the worst of her injuries.

Rick continued to pour his healing energy into her wounds without regard for himself. The crystal still clutched in one hand seemed to help him focus and was feeding him what felt like limitless energy, but he knew all too soon he would run out of gas. He only hoped she was fully healed before he passed out.

He hadn't used his gift in such a dire situation in a long time, but he knew from prior experience, he would give until he collapsed. He might even come close to death himself, but he'd gladly trade his life for Callie O'Hara. She was that special to him.

Of course, she'd never know it. She was with Davin, and it was obvious they were deeply in love. Rick wouldn't intrude on that, but he couldn't help the feelings that nearly overcame him each time she smiled at him, or touched his hand as they worked together on the crystals. He enjoyed every moment spent in her presence, but he guarded against letting her feel it. She was an empath, he knew, and he didn't want to burden her with the emotions he couldn't seem to control.

As a healer, he had a natural ability to keep his thoughts

and emotions from affecting those around him and he'd only strengthened those natural shields since coming into his power as a teen. It had served him well in the past, but never more than when he'd first met Callie O'Hara and been broadsided with the most impossible case of love at first sight that had ever occurred in the history of man. Rick never would have believed it if it hadn't happened to him, but he'd loved her deeply from the moment he'd first laid eyes on her.

The healing was nearly done. Rick had used his own energies to stop the flow of blood from all of her many cuts and knew her internal injuries were healed. She would survive, that's all that mattered to him as he passed out. He felt Davin's arms catch him around the shoulders as he slumped, but he remembered nothing after that.

Harry called not long after Callie woke up. She wasn't surprised. Harry always seemed to know things.

"Are you okay?"

"I'm fine now. Just a little mishap." She didn't want to worry him, but she should've known he'd be able to read her tone.

"Come on, Cal, what happened?"

"I got hit by some flying crystal. One of the raw ones exploded. Davin says that happens sometimes."

"Jeez, Cal! Don't you know how to duck?"

She chuckled. "It was behind me. But you can be sure I'll be on the lookout from now on."

"Damn straight you will, or I'll be having some words with that guy who's supposed to be taking care of you."

"Oh, Harry, he already feels bad enough. And please don't tell the family. I don't want to worry them."

Harry seemed to hesitate. "Are you sure you're okay?"

"Right as rain. Turns out Rick is an honest-to-goodness healer." Callie had told her brother all about Rick during their frequent calls.

"Really? Healers are rare, Cal. You're lucky he was there. Or maybe luck had nothing to do with it."

Callie felt the import of his words. "What are you saying?"

"Nothing, Cal." Harry sighed. "I don't know what I'm saying. Papa Caleb's the oracle in the family, not me. The important thing is, you're okay."

They talked for a few more minutes before Callie went to check on Rick. She didn't like that he'd overextended himself and the worry she felt surprised her. Rick had wiggled his way into her heart and she hadn't even realized it.

When he woke, Rick was in a luxurious bed, in a private suite. The soft linen was very different from that in the barracks where he was used to sleeping. But even those barracks were a major step up in the world from the accommodations he'd been subject to as a prisoner in the pens. As promised, Davin had brought him and the others here and given them a fair shake. They lived above ground now, in sunny, well-supplied buildings, though they were still under guard.

Davin truly wasn't like the other Alvians. He had feelings and was closer to human than anyone would have guessed. Little by little Rick was coming to respect the alien man who'd stepped in and helped quite a few humans and never treated them badly, but Rick also realized the limitations put on the Chief Engineer. Davin could only do so much. He was watched just as closely—maybe even more closely—than the human prisoners. The guards were a fact of life and even as Rick kept up his insulting barrage, the Alvian soldiers never reacted, just did their jobs like good little unfeeling robots.

"How are you feeling?" Callie's soft voice floated to Rick out of the darkness at his side. A moment later, she flicked on a bedside lamp and he could see her sitting in an old rocker next to his bed. Suddenly it all came back to him.

"You should be resting." He tried to sit up, but the effort required was beyond him. He was too weak.

Callie placed her hand on his shoulder, stilling his movement. "I'm fine. You gave me too much of your energy when you healed me, Rick. You're the one who needs looking after now. Not me." Her gentle smile touched him deep inside. He fought against the pull he felt—had always felt—for this special woman. "Thank you for saving me. I didn't know you were a healer, but it explains a lot."

He scowled up at her. It was either that or pull her into his arms for the kiss he so desperately wanted. "How so?"

She sat on the side of his bed, watching him with an almost tender expression he'd never seen from a woman before. "It explains why I can't read you. You're very adept at hiding your emotions from me and I'm a strong empath. But I've heard healers can develop a sort of emotional camouflage. Who taught you that, Rick?"

"My dad. He had a gift too. He was a doctor...before."

She touched his hand, taking it in her own and squeezing softly. "I was born after the cataclysm, but my parents told me what it was like before. Do you remember any of it?"

Rick shook his head just once, watching her carefully. "I was young. We had a nice house. I was in school with other kids, then all hell broke loose. My mother died in the initial attack and my dad took me into the mountains. We lived off the land for a long time and he taught me as I grew." He tried to pull his hand free. His energy was at its lowest ebb. He wasn't sure he could continue to hide his attraction much longer. "Callie, you shouldn't be here. You need to go."

She smiled and shrugged. "I would, but you're in my bed."

"Oh, God." He groaned and tugged his hand free. "Where's Davin?"

"Just outside. He's sleeping on the couch, I think."

"Damn." He nearly whistled through his teeth, but couldn't work up the energy. "He brought me here? To his private apartment?"

She nodded with an angelic smile. "He carried you. I wanted to make sure you were all right. You gave so much of your energy to me, Rick. I was worried."

He tried to look away, but her pull was too strong. "I'm fine, Callie. Go get some rest. I just need to sleep it off. My energy will return in a day or two."

"You've done this before." Her tone was accusatory and he had to suppress a smile.

"Once or twice."

"Never again, Rick. You need to draw back before you give too much. Promise me you'll never drain yourself like this again."

The intensity in her eyes confounded him. "I can't promise that, Callie. But I can tell you I didn't do it lightly. I've only gone this far a few times before. Only when it was important."

"You shouldn't have done it this time, Rick. I'm not that important."

"I beg to differ." Davin's voice floated out of the darkness of the doorway as he walked into the room. "Thank you, Rick, from the bottom of my heart." Davin placed one broad hand over Callie's shoulder in a possessive gesture. Rick understood the other man's prior claim and respected it. Slowly, he nodded, using what little energy he had.

"You're welcome."

"Callie," Davin bent down to speak by her ear, "why don't we let Rick get some rest?"

She stood, smiling at both men. "Try to sleep, Rick. If you need anything, we'll be right outside in the living room."

Rick nearly died when Callie leaned forward and kissed him on the cheek. He couldn't help but inhale her delicate scent and a wave of lust hit him before he could control it. She pulled back, her expression startled, searching his eyes, but he kept them carefully blank. He hoped she'd just shrug off the momentary lapse in his control. It was late. She was tired. Maybe he could convince her that jolt of desire she'd undoubtedly felt coming from him was all in her imagination.

Yeah, right.

"Good night, Rick."

"Night, Callie."

She lingered by the door, looking toward Davin. "Are you coming?"

Davin sent her a smile. "In a minute. I just want to talk with Rick for a moment."

She left, her expression troubled.

Davin ran a hand through his hair, a sure sign of the other man's frustration. "I'll be blunt. I'm pretty sure you're attracted to Callie."

Rick hated this. He had no intention of coming between Callie and the man she loved—the man who'd done so much good for the human prisoners he'd given shelter. Rick owed Davin his loyalty and the truth, at least. He decided to level with the Chief Engineer.

"Look, I have no intention of poaching, Davin. It's clear she's yours."

"She is." Davin's piercing alien eyes bore into Rick and he felt like an amoeba under a microscope. Then Davin relented, sighing deeply as he sank into the chair at Rick's bedside. "But she might also be yours."

"Come again?" Confusion clouded his thoughts.

"Remember the things I told the class about resonance mating among my kind? Callie is my true resonance mate. But she also Hums with you. I hear it every time you touch her."

Rick was shocked, but granted the idea was conceivable. "I don't hear anything."

"You wouldn't. It isn't audible to most humans. But to Alvians it's clear as a bell."

"But you told us there was only one mate for every Alvian."

"That's true. Or at least it was in the old tales." Davin sighed again. "There is some precedent for there being more than one true mate in my people's history and on this planet as well. Callie's parents, for example. Her mother is true mate to three men." Davin stared into the distance. "I have my theories as to why this is so. I think our attack on your planet and the resulting shortage of females has a lot to do with it, but it's only a theory."

"Look, Davin, I'm not here to steal your woman. She loves you. It's obvious to everyone. And you love her in return. I won't mess with that. I'm old enough to remember how things are supposed to be. My folks were happily married. I remember how they looked at each other—just the way Callie looks at you. You have nothing to fear from me."

"I don't fear you, human." In that moment Rick remembered he was talking to an alien who literally held the power of life or death over him. Davin was so human sometimes it was hard to remember he was one of them. The enemy. "I feel sorry for you. And I feel deep guilt for what I helped my people do to your planet." The hard edge was gone from Davin's voice, just like that, and Rick relaxed a tiny bit. "I don't deserve the happiness I have with Callie, but without her I would have descended into madness. She is my sanity."

"I didn't realize." The tormented look on Davin's face couldn't be faked. Rick was getting a harsh look at the reality of this man's—alien's—existence, and it wasn't pretty.

"Few do, but you needed to know. I can't give her up. Without her, I truly don't know what I'd do. Or rather, I'm afraid of what I'd do."

"I told you, Davin. I'm not here to mess with that."

"But you could. And I wouldn't blame you. If Callie is your true mate, it would be criminal of me to keep you apart."

"But—"

Davin held up one hand. "Like I said, there is some precedent for a multi-partner union."

"You mean *share* her?" The thought both tantalized and outraged. Rick never would have even considered such a thing before meeting Callie. Hell, he knew better than to listen to the little devil on his shoulder, tempting him with something that just wasn't right. If he really cared for her, he'd leave her in peace with Davin. Rick had to be strong. Treating Callie like so many other human women would be as wrong for her as it was for those other women.

Davin sat forward in the chair and his expression wasn't happy, but rather, resigned. "I've done a lot of research on the matter. Under extraordinary circumstances, males have had to share females before in my people's past. Before they bred emotion out of us, Alvian males had to find their resonance mate or lose their sanity—like I almost did. I think by doing what we did to your planet, we've unwittingly created the same circumstances here on Earth."

"But we're human, Davin. We're not like you. I won't go crazy without a mate."

The look Davin shot him was almost frightening. The man *knew* something. Rick could almost taste it. "Are you so sure about that?"

"What are you not telling me?"

Davin sat back, watching him like a bug. "Your last name

is St. John, right? Sometimes pronounced Sinjin?"

"Yeah, so what?"

"What if I told you that among the first Alvian explorers lost here on Earth a few centuries ago, there was a rather highly ranked warrior called Sinjin? The leader of the expedition was named Hara. There was a biologist named Mara, an explorer named Riley, a cartographer named Roarke, and many others who seem to share common names with many of the human survivors of our retuning."

Rick was floored by what Davin was implying. "You mean to tell me you think I've got alien blood in me?"

Davin nodded, completely serious, stunning Rick further. "It's not generally known, but Harry O'Hara's existence and abilities pretty much confirmed the theory that our exploration team settled here and bred with humans. The Breeds—those who survived—all have psychic abilities like you, Callie and Harry, and I believe must have some Alvian DNA. That's why we call you Breeds—or half-breeds, to be more formal about it."

"Holy shit." Rick closed his eyes and tried to absorb all this information. "So if I'm part Alvian, then you think this resonance mate stuff could apply to me?"

Rick opened his eyes to see the resignation back on Davin's face as he nodded again. "It definitely applies to Breeds, but I'm not certain if not finding your mate will cause a descent into madness as it would have caused me. Chances are, your human side evens you out a bit emotionally. Alvians—before the scientists changed us—were given to more emotional extremes than I've observed in humans."

Silence reigned for a long moment before Rick spoke again. "You've given me a lot to think about, Davin. Thank you for your honesty."

Davin stood, looking down at Rick. "I won't give her up for anything, but I will consider other options if she should happen to discover another true mate." The alien man sighed, looking like a heavy weight had settled around his shoulders. "It's only fair. I helped my people steal your entire planet, though I didn't realize the enormity of the crime I was committing at the time. That I found Callie at all is a miracle. I can't deny that same miracle to another when I'm the cause of such misery for your people."

Rick's jaw firmed. "Your guilt is misplaced, Davin. You've been better to us than any of your people, but the fact remains, I won't poach on another man's territory. It isn't right. Callie is yours. You need her way more than I do." Davin would never know how hard it was for Rick to say those words, but it was the right thing to do.

"You're tired." Davin's shoulders slumped. The poor guy looked defeated, which Rick had never seen in him before. It was humbling, and a bit alarming. "We'll discuss this when you're better." Davin paused at the door, one hand on the frame as he faced away from Rick. "I can never thank you enough for what you did. Without Callie..." Davin's voice broke, giving Rick a glimpse into the man's deep emotions. "Without her, I'm lost. Your sacrifice to save her means more than I can ever say, and will never be forgotten."

"You don't owe me a thing, Davin. I'd do it again. I was born a healer, it's what I am. I couldn't let her die." Rick wanted to ease Davin's burden. The man looked so beat down, even Rick's hard heart went out to him. He was learning a great deal here and the emotions riding him were more turbulent than anything he'd felt in years. He'd kept himself free of emotional entanglements for the most part. Life was easier that way.

But Callie and this enigmatic alien had sucked him in and now he felt concern for them both creeping into his mind even as he fought against it. He had to stay out of their lives as much as possible. They were a couple. He had no right to expect to be let in on the happiness they'd found with each other. Perhaps happiness wasn't for him. Rick wouldn't be surprised if that was his lot in life.

Davin left without another word and Rick was relieved. He had a lot to think about, but for right now, he needed sleep more than anything. His problems would still be there when he woke and had more energy to deal with them.

Councilor Troyan turned to his colleague. "Davin must be dealt with."

"I'm afraid you're right. The way he defied the Council

cannot be tolerated."

"I agree." Troyan's mouth firmed into a line that was almost angry. "He must be eliminated."

"But what about the grid? Half the major crystals on this planet are tuned to him."

"The problem will only grow worse the longer we wait. We must be prepared for initial power interruptions. In time, the grid will stabilize with new caretakers. With Davin out of the way, more suitable crystallographers will be forced to step up and do the job."

"If we proceed, we must do it in a clandestine way. He has many supporters, though they are quiet about it. Most of the crystallographers are in awe of the man. They just might rebel if we act outright."

"Then assassination is called for. Discrete, clean and final." Troyan made a slicing motion with one hand.

"I concur."

"I'll set someone on it. He'll be dead within the week."

"Good. It can't be too soon for me. The throwback has been a thorn in the side of the Council for too long."

Rick woke to comfort. A comfortable bed, soft linens and a soft, decidedly feminine touch on his face. If he were dreaming, he wanted to stay asleep, but daylight tugged at his eyelids until he opened them.

"Good morning." Callie's voice floated to him as she sat on his bedside, her hand touching his cheek gently. The look on her face nearly stilled his heart. No woman had ever looked at him in just that way.

"What time is it?" He had to stop thinking about dragging her down so he could kiss her lips the way he'd dreamed of doing since the first moment they met.

"A little after noon. I just came to check on you and see if you were up for some lunch." At that moment his stomach rumbled and she laughed. "I'll take that as a yes." She stood from the bedside and picked up a tray from the dresser near the door.

Callie stopped a few feet away from the bed, the tray still in her hand, and just watched him, her head tilted to the side, her eyes narrowed in concentration. Rick started to sweat under her scrutiny. She was so beautiful and she'd never looked at him quite that way before, concentrating on him, on his comfort.

"Something's different."

Rick sat up and rested back against a pile of pillows. "I don't know what you mean."

Callie placed the tray on the bedside table. She sat on the edge of the bed and stared at him as Rick tried to stay calm. He'd always been careful to school his thoughts around this woman.

She reached out to touch his face, but he shied away. Immediately he regretted the move when he saw hurt cross her face.

"You know I'm empathic." He nodded, not liking where this conversation was heading but helpless to stop it. "Well, you've always been blank to me, Rick." She spoke in a low voice, her hands cradled in her lap. "But you're not anymore. I'm starting to pick up...things...from you." She blushed and looked down at her hands.

Rick swore under his breath. "Ignore it, Callie. Just forget all about it."

She looked up until her gaze met his. "What if I don't want to forget it? What if I can't?"

"Dammit, Callie." Rick looked away in frustration, but she drew him like a magnet and he found himself staring deep into her eyes as his emotions bubbled over. "You belong to Davin."

She nodded. "We're mates. I'm his and he's mine." Her expression turned shy, but determined. "But...what if..."

"Forget it." He took her hand. "It's not right."

She laughed in his face. "If you only knew my family, you wouldn't say that. Besides—" she took his hand and pressed it to her heart, "—I know what you're feeling, Rick. I feel your conflict, your desire to protect, and your attraction. I feel it too."

He pulled away, shaking his head. "It isn't right, Callie."

She stood, looking down at him until he met her gaze. "My mother has three resonance mates. My biological father is

Justin O'Hara, but his brothers Caleb and Mick are every bit my fathers as well. They raised me and they all love my mother. If you truly are my resonance mate, we could have that, Rick. You, me and Davin could share our happiness and love for the rest of our lives. Give it some thought."

Leaving him speechless, she turned and walked away.

Rick ate his breakfast mechanically, but her words haunted him.

Chapter Eight

Sinclair Prime was the Council's best assassin. Retired now to participate in an experimental treatment program, he'd been called back for one last mission. He had never questioned the Council's orders before, but since taking the treatment—which consisted of a concentrated dose of DNA-altering substances administered through a skinpatch—he was beginning to feel...things.

Startling, really, for an Alvian.

Sinclair had applied the skinpatch two nights ago, just before retiring for sleep. The next morning the top secret call had come in and he'd been activated. Bad timing, but the Council was well aware of his participation in the program. He knew it had to be very serious for them to call him out of retirement for one last job with his physical status at all in question.

So far, approximately thirty-seven hours since applying the patch, he was feeling only slight physical differences. He had a bit of a headache. That was all. The emotional component was much more worrying.

Sinclair Prime had never had emotions bother him much at all, though he was of warrior stock. The warrior DNA made him just a little more animalistic than the rest of the Alvian population, but the genetic designers who'd bred all emotion out of his people let the imperfection remain, since it made for more aggressive soldiers. As an assassin, he'd trained to suppress even the vestigial emotion that sometimes allowed him to feel echoes of pleasure, anger, anxiety and the like.

Problem was, he could no longer suppress it. Since

applying the skinpatch, those vague echoes of emotion were no longer vague. They were becoming sharper with each passing minute and he was starting to long for things he'd thought dead and buried.

As a soldier, he'd never had a family except for the men he served with. When he'd been chosen as an assassin, even those loose ties to others of his kind had been severed. He found himself remembering the men he'd come up through the ranks with and laughing at odd memories of the things they'd done in their youth. He felt genuine fondness for some of those people in his past that he knew they would never understand.

Well, maybe soldiers would understand such things better than regular Alvians. His kind at least felt *something*, where the rest of the population had no emotions left at all.

Mixed emotions were not something to be brought on an assassination op, but Sinclair Prime couldn't help it. The Council called and he answered. This would be the last time. As the hours wore on, the emotions were getting stronger and stronger. He was feeling happy emotions and frightening emotions he didn't know how to deal with. He started thinking back over his career as he headed south in his personal transport, and didn't like what he remembered—or felt—at all.

Guilt hit him out of nowhere for the lives he'd taken. No longer did he feel an efficient sort of vague pride about the cleanness of his kills. No, now he was feeling horror at the thought of how many lives he'd snuffed out without a second thought and it sickened him.

And now he was going to do it again. One last time.

He wasn't sure if he could, but he knew it was either do this last job, or be the next target on the Council's hit list. It was his life or Davin's.

Rick recovered over the next day and a half. Callie brought him food and chastised him when he overtaxed himself walking to the bathroom and back to the bed, but he sort of enjoyed it. He'd never had anyone look after him. Well, not since before the cataclysm, but he'd only been a kid when his mother died.

Callie mothered him a bit, but with her, there was also the attraction. Rick loved to watch her move. He liked to make her smile and inwardly he basked in her attention, though he'd never let her know it.

Davin was a background presence, there constantly, watching with troubled eyes. Rick used the tall alien's presence to keep himself on track, and Davin left him in peace...until he was healed and it was time to go back to his own quarters.

Preparing to leave the Chief Engineer's suite, Davin blocked Rick's path.

"We need to talk about Callie before you leave."

"I've already said all I'm going to say on the subject." Rick tried to push past, but Davin blocked him again.

"Don't be a fool." Davin's voice was low, urgent. "You could be her resonance mate! It'd be a crime to throw that away."

Rick's reply was cut off as Callie walked in from the other room, her brow furrowed. She undoubtedly felt the emotion crowding the room and zinging back and forth between the two men in a standoff by the door.

Rick kept his voice pitched low. "Look, we don't even know if I could be this resonance thing you keep going on about." Rick was fed up.

"There's one sure way to find out," Davin's words and stance dared Rick. The alien didn't bother to keep his voice down. "Kiss her."

Silence reigned for a long moment while Rick stood, tempted beyond reason. Then Callie pushed him too far, simply by moving to stand altogether too close. She reached up and placed her hand on his shoulder.

"What's this about?" she asked.

Rick's fingers formed fists as he fought against his baser instincts that said to grab her and kiss her like she'd never been kissed before. Instead, he backed off, moving back into the room, leaving Davin facing his woman.

"Callie, you and Rick Hum. He could be another resonance mate, but he's too stubborn to find out."

Callie actually blushed as Rick watched. "Davin, I..." She moved into the alien man's arms, hugging him. "I didn't realize.

I'm so sorry, my love. There's something there, but I..."

"It's all right," Davin brushed her hair back with one hand as he stepped away from her. "We need to know if he is your resonance mate or not. Otherwise, the uncertainty will drive me mad."

"I don't want to hurt you." Her voice was shatteringly gentle.

Davin leaned down to kiss her, just once. "Hurting you, hurts me. Your joy could never bring me pain."

"You're a generous man, Davin, and much too good for me." Callie kissed him once, with palpable tenderness and love, then turned to face Rick. She walked right up to him and Rick felt frozen in place like a deer in a spotlight. Callie crowded him until they stood toe to toe, then she angled her sweet face upward in invitation.

"Just one kiss, Rick. I know you want to." Her voice was that of the siren, tempting men to their deaths. Rick was powerless against this, the final test. He'd been strong for weeks, but he could be strong no longer.

He jumped in headfirst, his arms snaking around her waist as his head dipped to claim her lips with his. He'd been wanting to taste her delicate flavor for a long time. Hunger rode him as she responded to his demanding kiss. He knew he was going too fast, but he couldn't help himself. Callie O'Hara was in his arms and his body knew no respite from the yearning he'd too long denied.

She gasped as he moved closer, pulling her unresisting body against his, conforming her curves to the hard planes of his chest, his abdomen and his aching cock. She felt so good, he never wanted to let go.

But this was wrong. A niggling voice in the back of his mind insisted that she wasn't his to keep. He had to let her go.

With Herculean effort, he eased off, bit by bit, though his body protested every millimeter he put between them. At length he lifted his lips, allowing one final caressing sweep of his lips against hers, over her cheek and down into her soft neck.

"We can't do this, Callie."

"I think we just did." Amusement filled her breathless voice, stunning him. How could she see humor in his utter failure of

141

control? Rick stepped back, heat rising to his cheeks in an angry flush as he broke the contact between their bodies completely. Opening his eyes at last, he was blinded by the shining crystals all around the room. His heart sank and soared simultaneously as he understood what it meant. Callie was his resonance mate.

Rick looked beyond her, searching for Davin, but the Alvian was gone from the room.

"I'm sorry, Callie." Rick stepped away, heading for the door. "I can't do this. It isn't fair to Davin and it isn't fair to you. You're not living in the Waste with no choices. You chose Davin long before I arrived. I respect that choice."

He left before she could speak, but he still heard the faint echo of her voice in his mind as she 'pathed just one sentence to him.

"What if you're both my choice?"

That one sentence haunted Rick's sleep for days, but he did his best to act as if nothing were changed between them when he went back to work. He was still partnered with Callie for the bigger experiments and he treated her professionally. He was torn inside, knowing how she tasted now, how she responded, but it was all wrong. She deserved more than to be shared between two men. She deserved his respect. The respect that grew out of the love hidden deep in his heart for her.

Sinclair Prime looked through his scope, lining up Chief Engineer Davin in his crosshairs. With one squeeze of the trigger, Davin would be gone and Sinclair Prime would be officially retired. He'd turn down any further missions, no matter what they said. He couldn't do this anymore. He was beginning to feel things that made it impossible for him to kill anyone in cold blood ever again.

But that's all he was good at.

Sinclair Prime didn't know where that left him. An Alvian with uncontrollable emotions was unstable. He'd probably end in madness sooner rather than later if the way he felt was any indication. An assassin with a brand new conscience, who could no longer kill, was a liability. The Council would mark him next.

Either way he was a dead man.

Much like Davin, who even now moved around his training hall, not knowing death waited a nerve impulse away. Sinclair Prime studied the man. A throwback, Davin was a rather famous oddity among his people. Sadly, Sinclair hadn't given the Chief Engineer much thought before today.

Now that Sinclair Prime had some idea of the emotional storm the Chief Engineer had to deal with every day of his life, he had new respect for the man. And envy.

Sinclair Prime watched through the scope as Davin put his arm around a pretty Breed female and walked out of the room. A few minutes later they reappeared in his private quarters, several floors above the training area, locked in an embrace. The passion Sinclair saw between the resonance mates was astounding, and humbling.

Sinclair had to pull the trigger now, before his new emotions unmanned him. He had to do it. Had to. It was Davin or him. Simple as that.

Sinclair took careful aim, lining up the shot, but at the last possible moment, he moved just a millimeter to the right.

Glass broke and a second later, a red stain erupted on Davin's sleeve. Confusion reigned as he looked around in bewilderment. He'd been shot.

As the thought registered, Davin pulled Callie down with him, behind a metal screen. Someone had shot at them!

"We've got to get to the hallway. Whoever it is, they're outdoors, shooting in. We need to get away from the windows."

"But you're hurt!" Callie tried to see his wound, but he pushed her away with some force, toward the door that led to the hall.

"Get to safety first! Whoever shot me is still out there. I'm fine for now. It only hit my arm." Davin knew there was something odd about that. Any assassin worthy of the title

143

wouldn't have missed when he'd been standing out in the open like that. Davin hadn't moved suddenly to throw off the shot. No, he'd been standing quite still, making all too easy a target. The assassin shouldn't have missed.

So why had he? Was it a warning shot? Some kind of game? Davin didn't know, but he did realize he had to be suspicious of everything now. The stakes had just been raised once again.

They crawled on their bellies to the door and out into the windowless hallway without further incident. Davin sent a message on the hall comm for security and med help, but Callie called Rick as well. Davin would have argued—Rick had kept his distance from them in the past weeks—but he couldn't be sure of the Alvian med team. They might yet kill him in the guise of treatment if they were somehow part of the plot to get rid of him. Rick's observation of their work couldn't hurt.

Rick arrived before the med team and applied pressure to the flowing wound, his face grim. Davin felt a tingle of heat and realized Rick was using his healing abilities to stop the flow of blood. Things were more dire than he realized, then, since Callie made no protest.

Davin looked from his beautiful mate's worried eyes to the grim face of the man who also loved her. He knew what he had to do.

"If I don't make it," Davin gasped as pain hit him anew, "take care of Callie. Promise me, Rick." Davin grabbed on to Rick's arm, digging deep with his fingers.

Rick knew Davin was in bad shape the moment he arrived on the scene. The shot had hit an artery, though there was no way a sniper could have aimed for such a thing. No, more likely, the sniper had missed the juicier targets and hit Davin's arm, the projectile hitting just the right spot more out of luck than any skill on the shooter's part. Rick used a burst of his healing energy to repair the nick to the artery, but Davin had already lost a lot of blood. Still, he'd pull through if Rick had anything to say about it—and if the Alvian med team could pump him up with fluids or a blood transfusion—but they hadn't made the scene yet.

Now Davin was demanding a promise to take care of Callie and Rick couldn't say no. Suddenly, everything was clear. He loved Callie, but he cared for Davin too, like a brother in arms, an older, wiser sibling who looked out for his family. Rick was part of that family now. Had been ever since Davin convinced him to take part in the crystallography program. Davin had been looking out for him, and for many others, for quite a long time and Rick not only respected him, but also felt affection for the other man. Davin had done so much to help Rick and the others, he'd do anything he could to help Davin now.

"I promise. I'll look after her, but you're going to be all right. I stopped the bleeding and if your med team gets here reasonably soon, they can pump you up again. You'll make it."

Davin was about to speak when the medical team arrived and Rick moved back so they could work on his patient.

"Watch them, Rick." Callie's voice entered his mind. *"We probably shouldn't trust anyone right now."*

"Wise thinking. I'll keep an eye out."

Rick took stock of the situation as he watched the med team. Someone had tried to kill Davin—either tried and failed, which he didn't think likely, or made a token attempt by way of warning. The security contingent that arrived a few seconds later agreed, after Davin told them what happened, and sent teams out to investigate. Frankly, Rick didn't expect them to find anything, but when they came back with a prisoner, he was surprised to say the least.

The med team did their job well as Rick watched. The projectile hadn't been poisoned and he'd fixed the nick in Davin's artery, though he wouldn't be able to use his arm fully for a few days, given standard Alvian healing techniques. Rick figured he could speed that up some more, but he'd wait to offer his assistance until the other Alvians cleared off.

"I want to talk to the prisoner," Davin insisted. Callie held his hand as Rick watched everyone—the med team, the guards, and the couple—from a few feet away where he had a clear view.

"That's not wise, Chief Engineer. The man tried to kill you." The head of security, a fellow named Rilan 3, said. He wasn't bad, for an Alvian, Rick thought. At least he'd never dealt badly with him.

"Do you know who he is?" Davin asked.

"Sinclair Prime." Rilan answered with a slight inflection of dismay in his voice. Rick understood the Primes were the top of their genetic lines—both the most experienced and the most gifted. He wasn't sure what having a Prime attempt murder would do to the Alvian social order, but from the tight looks on the alien faces, it wasn't good.

Silence filled the room.

"Sinclair is a warrior line," Davin observed. Rick recognized the cunning look in his eyes, though it was probably lost on the Alvians attending him.

"Yes, Chief Engineer," Rilan answered.

"Covert operations, if I'm not mistaken," Davin went on.

Rilan stiffened. "I'm not at liberty to say, Chief Engineer."

"No matter. Have you already made your report on this incident, Rilan?"

"I will transmit it when I leave this room," he responded.

"I see." Davin's gaze went to Callie. She nodded and moved back, toward Rick. "I know you have your duty, Rilan, but can I ask you to delay your report until I can get my mate to safety? Given the identity of my attacker, I believe both she and I have been targeted by a rogue member of the Council. Knowing that Sinclair Prime failed will bring even more trouble. They'll send someone else and I plan to have my lady secure before they get the chance."

Rilan looked as uncomfortable as an Alvian could. As a soldier, he had more emotion than most, but still lacked a basic understanding of human feeling. Still, he had to understand the duty to protect. His gaze cut to his lieutenant, standing by the door, then back to Davin.

"As long as the comm system is operational, it is my duty to file my report at the earliest opportunity once order has been established."

Rick caught the rather deliberate phrasing of the soldier's words, as did Davin. The Chief Engineer nodded. "I understand your position, Rilan. Thank you." Davin winked at Callie and Rick saw her turn to the comm panel next to him and input a few commands. The status of the panel went from blue to yellow, then to red as the system went down. She'd disabled the comms.

Rick didn't know how they'd done it, but he was glad they'd thought ahead. They had bought themselves a little time. Not much, but perhaps it would be enough to get out of Dodge before another assassin showed up to blow them away.

"I still want to talk to the prisoner," Davin insisted.

Rilan voiced his reluctance yet again, but was eventually convinced to bring the prisoner to them. Rick and Callie stood off to one side while Davin confronted the man who'd shot him. The Alvian guards were vigilant, protecting the Chief Engineer against any possible threat. They paid little attention to the two humans in the room, so only Rick noticed Callie's reaction. She swayed, off balance when the man was brought in. Rick moved to her side, steadying her with one hand when she tried to brace herself on a nearby console. He could feel her trembling and moved closer in case she needed...something. He didn't know what, but the way she clung to his hand made him realize she needed his support.

"What is it?" he whispered.

"He's—" Callie breathed deep, as if looking for words. "I need to talk to him, Rick."

"Are you sure?" Rick came around in front of her to search her expression.

She nodded, clinging to his arm. "He feels." She breathed the words, mouthing them more than actually speaking them, out of view of the Alvians. Rick realized she didn't want them to know and he understood her caution. If this guy—this assassin—had emotions, it would explain a lot about why he missed, but it would also stir up a whole new batch of questions.

"Wait here for a minute." Rick left her as she nodded and moved to confront the Alvian contingent. He eyed the restraints on the assassin's wrists and feet before taking the next step.

"Chief Engineer, do we really need all the guards?"

Davin wasn't unaware of Callie's reaction, or her words, except those last few spoken too low for his hearing. Something was strange about their prisoner, but the man refused to speak. Bound hand and foot, he couldn't hurt anyone, and judging

147

from his demeanor, he already knew he was powerless to carry out his mission.

"Chief Rilan." Davin turned to the ranking officer. "Please take your men and wait outside. I wish to speak to the prisoner alone."

Rilan objected once more, but Davin outranked him. With a last, almost puzzled look, Rilan cleared the room, taking his men and the Alvian med team with him. It was just Davin, Rick, Callie and the prisoner now and Davin intended to get some answers.

But before he could ask a single question, Callie spoke.

"You feel emotion." That bombshell statement landed in the middle of the room, aimed, to Davin's astonishment, at the prisoner, Sinclair Prime. "Don't worry. Comms are down all over the facility and this room is fully shielded. Nothing can eavesdrop here. You're safe for the moment."

Sinclair Prime's eyes dilated as his shoulders seemed to relax a small fraction. "I didn't understand what empathy was until recently. Can you really feel what I'm feeling?" His tone held a curious mix of dismay, wonder and resignation as his expression pled with Callie, looking to her for profound answers.

She nodded, holding Sinclair's gaze. "I feel your confusion and turmoil. I feel your guilt and pain. And I feel your wonder at this." She grasped Davin's hand as the comforting Hum sounded to Davin's ears. "I love Davin and he loves me."

"I don't understand love," Sinclair admitted, pain in his eyes.

Callie gave Sinclair a compassionate smile. "It's not a simple concept, to be learned in a few days. For most of us, it takes a lifetime."

"How do you know it's only been days for me?" Sinclair's eyes shuttered, suspicion filling his stance.

"It stands to reason. You're not a throwback. There's no way you could've hidden such a perceived flaw and rise to the level of Prime. So these emotions have to be something new. From the level of your confusion, you can't have been feeling long."

Sinclair crumpled then, his knees giving out as he leaned

against the edge of the console behind him. "It's been two days since the worst hit. I tried to control it, but it's...it's overwhelming. I don't know how you Breeds do it day in and day out."

Davin put his arm around Callie's shoulders, drawing her to his side. She'd gotten through to the assassin. Perhaps now they would get some real answers.

"How did this happen?" Davin asked.

"The emotion, you mean?" Sinclair gave a short, bitter laugh. "I was approached a few weeks ago by one of the Maras. They've cooked up a potion to alter us on a genetic level. I don't know all the particulars, but I agreed to be part of their study. A few days ago, at their direction, I applied a skinpatch with a gene-altering agent. The effects were slow to arrive at first, and I fear I'm not completely done with them."

Callie stepped toward the man, but Davin held her out of the assassin's reach. "There's nothing to fear in unlocking emotion, Sinclair Prime. I understand your confusion, but I think you'll discover living this way is better than your prior existence."

"But there's so much pain." His eyes were a study of agony that was hard for even Davin to watch.

"And joy too, once you get past the hurt. Give it time. After the dark comes the dawn, and after you work through the pain, you'll discover things to inspire happiness, amusement, wonder and perhaps even love."

Sinclair seemed to think about it, but his gaze didn't clear. "You don't know the things I've done, Lady. Only now am I beginning to understand the impact of my actions and I feel hatred for the first time."

"For the ones who made you kill?" Davin asked, curious.

Sinclair turned to him. "For myself, Chief Engineer. I loathe what I am."

"What you *were*." Callie's voice was firm. "You are reborn. A new entity."

"I can't erase the memories of what I've done." Sinclair's tone was bleak as a winter day.

"Nor should you," Callie agreed. "But you can learn from the past and overcome it to be a better man from this moment forward."

Sinclair's mouth quirked up at one corner. "I begin to understand the concept of optimism, Lady, thanks to you, but I do not feel it."

Callie smiled at the man who'd killed so many. "That's okay. I have enough for all of us."

Davin was amazed by the turn of events. The Maras were experimenting with returning emotion to the Alvian race and doing it successfully, if Sinclair Prime was any indication. This was something to investigate, but there was one more pressing matter to look into.

"Why did you try to kill me? Or perhaps," Davin tilted his head, "the better question is, why did you miss?"

The expression on Sinclair's face was again tortured when he raised his gaze to Davin. "I watched you interact with your mate for hours before taking the shot. I could've bagged you any time, Chief Engineer, but at the final moment...I couldn't. I can't be the man I was before. Everything's changed. I've changed. I feel things. Things I can't control and don't understand. I saw you with your mate and finally understood what I was looking at—happiness. True happiness and joy. My eyes were wet and I knew I could not take the shot. What you've found is a miracle. It's not for me or the Council to take that away when all you've known in life to this point must've been fear and pain." Tears wound down the tough soldier's face, unheeded. "I'm feeling now what you must've felt your entire life." Sinclair's eyes unfocused. "How you must have suffered. I cannot comprehend how you survived it." He shook his head and returned his full attention to Davin. "You're a stronger man than I, Chief Engineer. Stronger and more courageous than any member of the Council. They have no right to sit in judgment of you or your mate. That realization made me miss when the imperative trained into me from my earliest days told me to take the shot. I am deeply ashamed. My career is over, as is my life."

"It doesn't have to be." Rick sauntered over to face the assassin. He shot a questioning look over his shoulder at Davin, continuing at his nod. "You don't have to go back to the Alvians. You have emotions now. You could be of great help to the pockets of humanity trying to survive all over this planet. Hell, you might even find a mate among our women—the few that are left."

"You would allow this?" Sinclair's wide eyes searched Davin's.

Davin leaned back, watching the assassin. "It's not up to me, but if you help the humans, they're likely to help you in return. They are a generous people."

"You'd let me go, knowing I was sent here to kill you?"

"You're a different man now than you were just a day ago." Davin saw Callie nod in agreement at his side. "I can imagine what you're going through—I've been through it myself, as you pointed out. You deserve the right to explore the man you are now, the man you could've been had the geneticists not tampered with our DNA generations ago."

Sinclair dropped his head back against the wall, watching them with pain in his eyes. "You are too forgiving of my sins, Chief Engineer."

Callie spoke up. "In time, you'll learn to forgive yourself, Sinclair Prime."

"I am Prime no more, Lady. Please don't call me that."

Callie smiled and nodded. "You know, on this world, Sinclair used to be a common surname."

"Indeed? One of my ancestors was part of the expedition that never returned to Alvia."

"Well, start thinking about a new name, my friend." Rick walked over to stand beside Callie. "If you want to leave your old life behind, you have an opportunity to reinvent yourself, starting with your name. Sinclair is a respectable, human-sounding surname, but you can choose a new first name, if you want. For now, I'm going to call you Bill."

Callie giggled as Sinclair Prime started, coming completely to his feet. "Bill?" He said it as if tasting the name. "This is not an Alvian name."

"Great," Rick said, moving toward the prisoner. He stopped opposite Sinclair Prime and faced him down. The men were about the same height, and both had that wiry musculature that indicated coiled strength. "Time is short, Bill. Do you really want to do this? Do you want to go with Callie and Davin and live, or return to the Alvians and almost certain death?"

Sinclair took a deep breath. His mouth firmed as his body seemed to gain strength where before he'd been the picture of defeat. His posture straightened and his eyes shone with a new light.

"I want to live. I want time to figure out these emotions."

Callie smiled but didn't move any closer, much to Davin's relief. "You'll have help. I'm not the only empath on this planet. There are quite a few others, including most of my siblings. Speaking of which," she swirled and placed her hands against Davin's chest, "we need to call my family."

Davin reached into his pocket for the private comm crystal he always kept on him, but it was gone. Lost in the shuffle of the assassination attempt, probably.

"Do you have your secure comm?" Davin asked her. "Mine's gone."

She bit her lip, making him want to bend down and kiss her, but time was of the essence, so he refrained. "It's back in our room."

"All right. I can bring power back to this console in isolation, but it won't be secure." Davin moved toward the comm station Callie had used to disable the entire system. He could bring back power selectively, but it wouldn't be easy. It'd take some maneuvering. "Rick, watch the door. They should leave us alone for a little longer before Rilan's men check on us. If necessary, I can buy us some more time. Leave Sinclair in the cuffs for now, until we know how much time we really have."

Davin worked his magic and Callie called the most knowledgeable member of her family first. Caleb would know, if anyone could, what was coming. He was also the leader of their family, the one they all went to when there was trouble. Just hearing his voice made her feel better.

"Callie, baby, how are they?" Caleb O'Hara's strong voice sounded in Callie's ear.

"Papa Caleb! This is an open channel."

"Doesn't matter anymore, sweetheart. I saw what happened. You have to listen to me. Things will start moving fast from here. You need to take them all home."

"Are you sure it's safe?"

"Trust me. Your mother can help the new one while you see to your mates."

"Then Rick—?"

"Definitely yours, sweetheart. Congratulations. But he'll still need some convincing. Get him to talk to my brothers. That'll do it."

Callie chuckled despite the desperate turn of events. "Yeah, that ought to do it. Now why didn't I think of that?"

"Get going, munchkin. You don't have much time, but once you get to the ranch, you'll be safe. They won't dare send someone there. Not after I've had a little talk with Mara about the future. Harry's going to stay here with me and see what he can find out."

Callie trusted her farseeing father to know what was coming. He'd never steered a single person wrong yet and every member of the family trusted him with their lives. This time, she trusted him and his visions to steer a safe path for not only herself, but Davin and Rick too.

"I love you, Papa Caleb."

"Love you too, munchkin. We'll talk soon. Call me when you get where you're going."

Chapter Nine

A few hours later, the four of them arrived at the O'Hara ranch, nestled in a protected valley in what was once known as the Canadian Rockies. The weather was much colder up here and the air was dryer, but the scenery was every bit as majestic and beautiful as the jungle-rich mountain range they'd left below the equator. Only here, instead of jungle, the white of snow covered the mountain peaks and an invigorating chill permeated the air.

Jane and Justin were there to greet them. Callie raced straight into her mother's arms and was enveloped in Justin's arms a moment later. Davin envied the family and tried to imagine how it must feel to be part of an extended familial unit. His people had been that way in the distant past, but now most Alvians were bred in a lab and raised as one of many other children, in the collective.

He was so lost in his thoughts, he didn't feel Rick sidle up beside him.

"Nice family," Rick said, leaning back against the side of the small transport, next to Davin. Rick's gaze was on Callie and her parents, standing some yards distant.

"Did you have a family like that, Rick?" Davin felt unreasonably isolated by the idea.

Rick shrugged, but wouldn't meet Davin's eyes. "For a while. I remember my mother, but she died in the first wave of crystal attacks. I had my dad longer, but we were separated by your people a few years back. Still, he raised me and taught me everything I know. He was a good man."

Davin both envied and pitied Rick in that moment. "What

happened to him?"

Rick straightened away from the hull of the craft and stared out over the horizon. "I don't know." His voice grew fainter. "But I always figured he'd been captured or killed. Otherwise he would've found me. Or I would've found him. As it is, I never caught a trace of him."

Davin didn't know what to say to the pain he could hear in Rick's voice. He said, "I'm sorry," but knew it was inadequate.

Sinclair stood silent on Davin's other side, watching all with a painful mix of emotions on his pale face. Davin turned to him as Rick moved a short distance away.

"You'll have to remain locked up for now."

Sinclair glanced down at the cuffs manacling his wrists together, then shrugged. "It's what I would do. For what it's worth, I'm sorry I shot you."

Davin sighed. "I can only imagine how difficult this time is for you. Callie told me a little on the trip here of the massive fluctuations she feels in your emotional field. Perhaps it will even out over time, but for now, we're going to ask Justin to keep an eye on you. Perhaps Jane will take pity and work with you on the emotional upheavals you must be feeling."

"What can she do?" A note of despair colored the other man's tone.

"Jane O'Hara is an even stronger empath than Callie. She helped me a lot, just by understanding. She is a great woman."

Sinclair turned to face him, surprise in his light eyes. "You really mean that."

Davin nodded. "I do. You'll find these humans have much more to them than we've been led to expect. I believe, had we any understanding of emotion left in our people, we could have come to them in peace and been allies. Instead, we've committed unspeakable crimes against them by taking their planet and killing so many innocent beings. It is a guilt all Alvians will bear for the rest of our days. Give the humans a chance. I guarantee, they will astound you."

Mick joined the group, swooping down to pull Callie into an exuberant hug. When he caught sight of Davin leaning against the vehicle, he suggested the group move to his medical office.

He took a look at Davin's injury with professional eyes and used some of the topical antibiotics the Alvians had given him in trade for his continuing medical observations of the O'Hara family. It was a deal they'd struck years before and only a small part of the complex compromise that kept most of the family safe on the ranch.

Justin took charge of Sinclair Prime and escorted him to an outlying barn where he could question the man, with Jane and her empathy to assist. So Mick was left with Callie, Davin and Rick.

"Looks like the guy who shot you either didn't know how to aim at all or knew his business very well, and didn't intend to do much damage. You should regain full use of the arm after it heals a bit." Mick wiped his hands on a cloth, then threw the used bandages in a trash bin at the foot of his exam table.

"Sinclair Prime is the Council's top assassin—or was— before he retired." Davin grimaced as Mick began cleansing the area around the wound.

"Crazy thing that. We've heard rumors of a new experiment, but even Harry couldn't find out what the goal was. If your people really want to restore emotion, well, I'd be amazed," Mick said, concentrating on his work as he applied the fast-acting antibiotics.

"They're not my people." Davin was adamant on that point. "After this, they'll be lucky if I don't sabotage every crystal on this whole damned planet." The fire in his blood belied the low rumble of his voice. Davin was pissed and only just starting to realize the full implications of the past few hours. His people— or the Council at least—wanted him dead. Sinclair could have just as easily shot Callie. They'd been sitting ducks. Just the thought of it made his blood boil.

Mick stopped working and looked up at him until Davin met the man's eyes.

"Point taken." Mick nodded significantly. "Didn't mean to insult you. You're nothing like them, and thank God for that." Mick finished applying the dressing and sat back on his rolling chair. "If you want to discuss strategy, I'm thinking you should wait to hear what Justin and Jane get out of our visitor. And we'll want to see what Harry knows. No sense going off half-cocked."

Davin could see the sense in Mick's words, but he ached to retaliate. Nobody put his mate in danger. Nobody.

Davin bowed his head in respect as Mick rose. "Thank you." It was clear, from the way he held Davin's gaze, that Mick understood the words referred to more than just the medical treatment.

Mick walked to the sink as Callie stepped close to place her arm around Davin's waist. She reached for his hand and the soothing Hum of their compatibility sent tingling waves of warmth through him. Thank the stars for her. She was his entire world. Mick walked back and ruffled her hair, smiling at them both.

"The Alvian med team did a good job on your arm. They, at least, meant you no harm. Actually, they must've used something on the wound that sped healing beyond what I'd normally expect out of the supplies they've given me. Lousy holdouts." Mick snickered as Callie laughed. "I never thought they'd given us the best of what they had anyway, but this confirms my suspicions. Unless..."

"Unless what?" Callie asked.

"Well, aside from Harry, I don't have any experience treating Alvians. I don't know much about full-blooded Alvian physiology. Maybe they heal faster than we do. I know Harry has a slight immune boost compared to the rest of the kids." Mick's eyes turned thoughtful as his scientific mind worked on the problem.

Davin recognized the look. "It's not my specialty, but from what I understand, we do have some advantages over humans. I didn't realize you were unaware of them, Mick. I'd be happy to answer any questions you have and if I can get to a dataport, I'll hack in and give you a copy of the entire Alvian medical database."

A cunning light gleamed in Mick's eyes. He, of all the O'Haras, had a thirst for knowledge not easily quenched.

Rick watched from the edge of the room. He'd gotten a good look at the wound before the Alvian med team arrived, but hadn't been able to talk to any of them or find out what they'd administered to replace Davin's lost blood.

Rick was very impressed with Mick O'Hara's laboratory and his doctoring skills. Here was a man he could learn from—if he ever got the chance. The way things were, Rick wasn't sure sticking around would be a good idea.

He had to be certain of Callie's safety. He'd stay until the immediate problems were resolved, but then he'd probably have to go his own way. He could be free now. Davin wouldn't stop him, and neither would Callie's human kin. The only threat that remained was the one he'd always faced—capture by Alvians—but Rick thought he knew enough to keep himself hidden and free from now on.

Still, leaving Callie would be difficult. He knew it was wrong to want her—to want to share her the way Davin had suggested—but it was all he could think about. He wanted her like he wanted his next breath. She was fast becoming the center of his universe and he knew that walking away from her would be one of the hardest things he'd ever do.

But it still had to be done.

Maybe not today or even tomorrow, but soon, he'd have to leave her to Davin and try to get on with his life. In the meantime, it wouldn't hurt to make friends with Callie's family. Mick, in particular, seemed like the kind of man his father would have respected. Justin, too, for that matter. Zach St. John had been both warrior and healer, and had passed both those skills down to his son. The O'Hara brothers were cut from the same cloth as Rick's dad, and he already liked them both, though they'd only just met.

Callie looked up and pinned him with a glance. Her beautiful green eyes lit as she smiled at him and Rick almost forgot to breathe. A single finger beckoned him closer and he was powerless to resist.

"I'm going to out you, if that's okay," she told him in the privacy of their minds. Her voice felt like a caress in his head.

"What? Out me how?"

"Papa Mick is a good doctor, but you're a healer. He'll want to talk to you about that. If you don't mind." Big green eyes beseeched him.

Rick weighed his options. He didn't go around telling folks about his abilities as a general rule. He liked to remain a mystery. But he couldn't see the harm in telling Mick—and by extension the rest of the O'Hara clan. In fact, it might just help him build a rapport with the older man, which Rick found he wanted.

It's okay, Callie. I don't mind your family knowing.

Great! Callie held out her hand to him and he went like a lemming over a cliff. "Papa Mick," she said, "Rick might also have something to do with Davin's speedy recovery. He stopped Davin's bleeding before the Alvian med team got there. There was so much blood." Her smile dimmed as she remembered, but she shook it off. "Rick has a really powerful healing gift. He saved my life too, as a matter of fact, when I got hit by a crystal shard a while back."

Mick's gaze pinned him. There was no doubt the elder O'Hara was interested. Callie knew her family well.

"No kidding? I've always wanted to meet a healer, but they're rare." Mick looked him over minutely, his eyes narrowing. "And what's this about saving my girl?"

"It was a silly accident," Callie jumped in, probably to deflect the storm clouds Rick saw gathering in Mick's expression. "I was facing the wrong way and didn't know the crystal was about to explode. A big chunk flew off and hit me right about here." She stood away from the exam table and Davin, lifting her shirt to expose the area on her side where newly knitted flesh marked her injury. The area was still a little pink, but otherwise healthy and showed no sign of the life-threatening trauma.

Mick moved closer to inspect the site himself. "Darnit, girl, you could've lost your spleen."

"I almost did. But Rick fixed everything inside and out with his amazing gift. It left him flat on his back and drained for a day or two." She reached for Rick's hand again, tugging him forward to stand at her side, facing Mick. Davin watched from the side and knowing he was there made Rick uncomfortable. He'd never been one to seek the limelight. "Whatever you did to stop Davin's bleeding, Rick, it didn't drain you as much this time."

"It was just a nick to the side of the blood vessel." Rick tried to shrug it off. "It only took a small zap, but made a big difference."

159

"Well then." Mick faced him. "We all owe you a great debt of gratitude, and I for one, would love to hear the details. I didn't see any evidence of that kind of trauma when I examined the wound."

Callie smiled at them both, retreating to Davin's side. "We're going to the house. I'll help make lunch and we'll expect you both within the hour." Her teasing tone made Rick aware that this was something of a habit with the family.

"Don't worry. We'll be along," Mick assured her before turning back to Rick. "I sometimes forget to go in for meals, which is why we installed the intercom. Janie will ping us when it's time for lunch."

Rick was touched by the easy way he'd been incorporated into the family's little rituals. Davin left with Callie, and Rick couldn't help the wistful expression that must've crossed his face as he watched them go.

"So you're in love with our little girl, eh?" Mick surprised the hell out of Rick with the blunt question. He stuttered for an answer, but Mick forestalled him. "Oh, it's obvious, boy. Don't try to hide it. Besides, my brother Caleb saw this coming. He always knew there were two for Callie, but we never expected the first to be a damned alien. I'll admit, I'm a bit more comfortable with you as her second. You're more what I'd expected, though this healing business is something special."

Mick moved to his desk and a small refrigeration unit that stood next to it. He reached in and grabbed two long-necked brown bottles, popping the caps and handing one to Rick. He took it and sampled the contents as Mick took a drink from his own bottle. It was surprisingly good beer. Something Rick had rarely had—and never since being captured.

"Jane brews this for us. She's a hell of a woman and Callie is made in her image. You couldn't find a finer girl if you searched the world over. But then, I'm probably a little biased." Mick winked as he downed another swallow of the cold brew.

Rick felt like he had to say something, but this conversation was beyond him. Still, he made an effort. "Callie is a special woman."

"You can say that again." Mick plopped down on the big rolling chair behind his desk. "Have a seat."

Rick took the chair in front of the desk. It was big and more comfortable than he'd expected. He relaxed back into it and savored his beer.

"I don't want you to think that I'm going to take advantage of Callie. She's Davin's mate. I respect their prior commitment and won't intrude on it." Rick felt his tongue running on as the alcohol mellowed his mind. "I remember how it was in the old days. I remember my mom." His words trailed off.

"It's good to remember, son," Mick's tone held the wisdom of age, though he wasn't all that much older than Rick. "But you can't let yesterday get in the way of tomorrow. I know. I felt much as you do at one time. Jane was married to my brother Caleb before the world exploded. He's got the gift of foresight and we came up here and set up this place well before the attacks began. We lived as we used to, with me and Justin single and Jane happily married to Caleb, but it was driving Justin and me crazy. We'd all loved Jane from the time we were kids. We all grew up together because her daddy owned the next ranch over." Mick sat back in his chair, a smile on his face. "When her father died, Caleb snatched her up before Justin or I had a chance to court her. But then the whole world changed almost overnight. We had to change with it or—according to Caleb's visions, which are never wrong—we all would have been dead long ago."

Rick didn't know what to say. Mick was much more than a simple doctor and just as fierce as his brothers.

"I was the last holdout. I was so stubborn. I knew that giving in to this strange way of life was wrong. It would never have happened in the old world and I was desperately clinging to those beliefs. But by doing so, I was sentencing my beautiful Janie, and my two brothers, to death. Faced with that certainty, well, you can see how simple the decision really was."

"But that's not the case here," Rick objected. "Nobody says Callie is going to die if I walk away."

Mick eyed him. "I wouldn't be too sure of that. For one thing, Caleb's not here. Getting his predictions is harder now, but we know for sure that he's seen you in Callie's future. Hell, you've already saved her life once. Maybe you're meant to be around to do it again. If you leave her, you might as well kill her yourself."

"That's one hell of a stretch." Rick started to get angry.

"All right. Maybe I was being too melodramatic." Mick shrugged. "But there's no denying that by leaving, you'll break her heart. I see the way she looks at you. She's already in love with you. You leave her, she'll suffer. Is that what you want?"

"What if I believe that by staying, she'll suffer more? This multiple-partner thing isn't the way it's supposed to be. We're not animals or barbarians to subjugate and share our women around. We're human beings with free will. My father taught me that and I'll always believe it."

"Your father sounds like a wise man," Mick agreed, his voice quite a bit lower than Rick's agitated tones. "But what if you've got the wrong end of the stick? I agree that women shouldn't be forced to accept men they neither want nor love, but what about when a woman wants more than one man? When she loves them, and they love her? Where's the harm in that?"

Rick was both confused and torn. "I don't know the answer."

"Don't you think you'd better figure it out? Seems to me, you're in just that situation with Callie, and your decision will impact not only your life, but Callie's and Davin's as well." Mick saluted him with the bottle before polishing it off. A few seconds later, the intercom buzzed. Lunch was served.

Justin had stashed Sinclair in one of the smaller hay barns, far away from the main house and livestock barns. He had secure rooms there, built with various purposes in mind. One of the chambers was close enough to a secure cell to suit their purposes. Sinclair hadn't put up any kind of resistance and Jane kept tabs on his emotional state—an upheaval so intense it made her knees buckle a few times as they'd walked their guest to the barn. Justin didn't like that, but it couldn't be helped. He needed Jane's empathic observations to gauge the man's state of mind.

There was some furniture in the room—an old cot and chair as well as a table and lamp. There was no electricity this far from the main house and the small generator they ran on biodiesel, but there was an oil lamp and lighter to get it going.

They left him there, locking him in with his consent, while they went for lunch. Justin figured if he was still there when they got back, Sinclair would play them straight. It was the first of many tests Justin would subject the man to before he began to trust him to any degree.

So it was with some satisfaction that Justin found their guest waiting for them when they returned with a plate of sandwiches for him. Rick, Davin and Callie came too, wanting to be present while Justin questioned the man more closely. They hadn't gotten very far before lunch. Jane had told him that Sinclair was in too stressful an emotional state, so they left him alone to settle down a bit. Callie was nearly as empathic as her mother, so she came along this time to gauge Sinclair's emotional response.

Sinclair was an assassin. That much they knew. But Justin could see this man was even more than that. A Prime, he was the top of his line on this planet, and his line was a warrior line. No doubt, if he didn't want to be held, he'd have been long gone before now. Which meant he wanted something from them. Justin didn't have to think too hard to realize what it was. The man—new to his emotions—was probably in a worse place than even Davin had been. He probably wanted acceptance and understanding. Maybe reassurance and guidance through the tough new emotions he was dealing with. Which was where Callie came in, though Justin might be able to help as well, and he certainly wouldn't leave Callie alone with this big brute.

"Look, I know you're a soldier. Believe it or not, I have a friend of sorts, among the Alvian warrior lines."

That caught Sinclair's interest. He looked over at Justin with suspicion. "Who?" he asked simply.

"Grady Prime comes out here every once in a while with Mara 12. We've talked a few times and of all the Alvians I've met, he actually seems to feel something. Not much, I grant you, but something. He's a little different than the others, in a subtle way."

Sinclair actually smiled. It looked rusty, as if he hadn't done much smiling in his life. "All warrior lines are more primitive than the rest of the population. Gradys even more so.

163

They are considered highly aggressive soldiers. Unpredictable and unstoppable."

"Yeah, that's Grady, all right," Justin agreed with a grin. "I like the bastard for all that."

"He cannot understand the concept of affection." Sinclair's expression was lost. "Neither could I until a few days ago. Now, I wonder that I could ever do half the things I did. I have a great number of transgressions on my soul."

"Do your people believe in the idea of an immortal soul?" Callie asked from near the door where they'd positioned her. They wanted her to be able to flee should their guest turn violent.

"There is little doubt the energy of one's being is not destroyed when the body ceases to function. We do not know where the energy goes, but we do live on. It is the one thought that gives me some solace for all the lives I've taken over the years." A tear leaked down the side of Sinclair's face, surprising Justin. He shot a questioning glance to Callie.

She nodded, using telepathy to communicate privately with her father. *"His sorrow is real and deep."* She turned to address the Alvian. "You're a new man now," she said aloud. "You can make up for what you've done and try to ease your burden of guilt through your future actions."

"For one thing," Justin pounced, "you could begin by telling us who ordered the hit on Davin and how badly they want him dead. Were you supposed to take out Callie as well? Rick? Anybody else?"

A tight muscle in Sinclair's cheek ticked as Justin fired questions at him, but he stood firm. The warrior had a backbone of steel.

"I was sent for Davin alone. He's the one with the power. He's the one they fear, though they do not recognize the emotion. Yet it is fear—in a sense. They fear his power as the single person who could interfere with their plans for this world and their desire for ultimate power over our people and this planet. Davin's grown too strong to confront openly. The whispers about his instability are for naught now that he has a mate to ground him. And many are beginning to study our old ways, intrigued by the idea of resonance mating. I wasn't instructed to target Davin's mate, but I believe Callie bears watching in case subsequent orders change."

Justin felt a knot form in the pit of his stomach. A quick look at Callie's face told him she'd already faced this idea and would fight for her man. Justin admired her grit, but feared for her safety.

"Who?" Davin's voice was deathly low and filled with malice. "Who ordered my death?"

"I don't know." Sinclair pinned Davin with his gaze. "I'd tell you if I could but I'm always activated by code and it could have come from any member of the Council. I haven't been paying close attention to their activities for months now. I'm officially retired and participating in Mara's new experiment. I was never supposed to be sent out again, but the code was my failsafe. I had to do this one last job. I tried." Sinclair's mouth tightened as his expression grew taut. "But I couldn't. Thank the Maker."

"He's telling the truth," Callie confirmed aloud, but her expression spoke of sympathy for the alien man. "I'm sorry for what you're going through, Sinclair," she said. "And I know you'd tell us if you knew more. As it stands, we'll have to puzzle this out on our own, though we'd appreciate any assistance you can offer."

"Anything I can do to help, Lady, I will do." Sinclair bowed his head in her direction, a sign of respect.

"And we'll help you." Callie stood and walked over to Sinclair while Justin, Davin and Rick bristled, watching the alien soldier closely. Callie took his hand and squeezed it. "The next few days will be rough, but you're a strong man. You'll come through this and be a better man for it. My family can help."

"Your help is much better than I deserve. I thank you."

Callie found herself alone in the kitchen with her mom after dinner as they put away a few dishes. The men had gone out to talk to Sinclair again and the rest of her brothers and sisters were seeing to the animals and finishing up evening chores. Callie had brewed a pot of tea and settled in for a nice talk with her mother.

"What's on your mind, sweetie?"

Callie should have realized. Her mom always knew when she needed to talk.

"It's Rick. And Davin too, though he doesn't think he's got an issue with Rick. Still, I sense it. There's a lot of conflict between them. I feel it every time I'm with them."

"I know. I felt it from the moment you three got here. You've got yourself a problem, my girl. No doubt about it." Jane wiped her hands on a towel and motioned Callie over to the table. It was clear now and the kitchen was back the way it had been. The other kids had helped clean up before they headed outdoors.

"So what do you think I should do?"

"You? Honey, this is something you might not have all that much control over. This is something your men have got to come to terms with on their own. I remember when Mick had me pretty much convinced he was okay with our new arrangement. Then he lost it and nearly got away before we could straighten things out. But he was the one who had to deal with his issues. I could sort of nudge him in the right direction, but ultimately, it was his decision."

"Yeah, I get that, but there's got to be something I can do." Frustration made her want to tear her hair out.

Jane smiled and Callie knew that grin. It often spelled trouble, or so the family joke went.

"Well, I think you should seduce him. That always works with your fathers."

Callie laughed and practically choked on her tea. Jane was known for her frank speaking, but Callie had never discussed her sex life with her mother before. It was a little embarrassing.

"Seduce who? I mean, which one?"

Jane shrugged, grinning. "Whichever one is handy. I know you and Davin have been together a while, but what about Rick? Have you made love with him yet?"

"Mother!" She felt a blush steal over her face.

"I'll take that as a no. Darn, girl, how can you let a man as good looking as that get away? I bet he'd be a great lover. I remember when your father was about Rick's age. He could go all night. Still can, come to think of it."

"Too much information, Mom." Callie jumped up to refill her teacup and busy her hands.

"Well, it's true. And I'm sure you understand what I mean, now that you've got Davin in your life. I know he's an alien, but he positively steams when he looks at you. And the emotion coming off him is explosive."

Callie thought about that for a moment and a dreamy smile tugged at the corners of her mouth. "Yeah, it is. He's something else, Mom. He feels so deeply. Rick does too, but he's better at hiding it. Half the time, I'm not sure what he's feeling."

"Sounds like Mick." Jane held up her cup for Callie to refill from the teapot. "I think there's something about medical training that helps them close off their emotions—sort of compartmentalize or something. It's hard to get past, but I hope you know passion is the easiest way to break down whatever mental barriers he can throw up. Seduce him. You'll learn a lot and get him thinking about what he could have and what he'd be missing if he decides to go lone wolf on you. Give him a taste of what could be between you. That's my advice, for what it's worth."

Callie decided to put her plan—nebulous as it was—into action the next day. She picked a time when all her siblings were off doing chores around the ranch and the adults were otherwise occupied. When she saw Rick head for the big horse barn, she followed.

She'd chosen her outfit carefully. A skirt with no panties for easy access and a stretchy top with no bra. Her nipples were already standing out, eager for a man's attention. As was Callie.

It was time to give Rick a taste of what he'd be missing.

Chapter Ten

Rick sought solace in the big horse barn. He'd learned how to care for animals from his dad, as he'd learned so many other things. Rick didn't share the special kinship with animals his father had, but he still loved them—horses in particular. The chance to bask in their uncomplicated presence was calming and something he hadn't experienced in far too long.

Callie almost snuck up on him while he was grooming a beautiful chestnut mare. Only the horse gave away her presence, whickering as she came into view. Rick put aside the brushes and escorted the animal back into her stall before turning to face Callie. He sensed confrontation in the air, which shouldn't have surprised him. Callie was as direct and straightforward as any person he'd ever known. He liked that about her. Being a simple man, Rick valued people who didn't play games but came straight out and spoke their mind. It was just one more way in which Callie was perfect for him—one more thing he had to ignore for the greater good.

"You know horses?" Callie began the conversation on a friendly, slightly curious note as she stepped into the light. Rick's mouth went dry when he caught sight of her outfit and the two perky nipples sticking out, begging for his touch.

"We didn't keep as many animals as you have here." Rick tried desperately to keep his mind on the conversation, but found his gaze drifting to the hem of her short, floaty skirt and the sexy legs flowing from it. "My father and I had one or two horses. He had a way with them, and with all animals."

"What happened to your dad?" Callie stepped closer, leaning against a saw horse next to him. The mare watched them from over the half door to her stall. Rick watched Callie's legs cross at the ankle. She wore dainty little boots, but her tanned skin shone in the dim light from the middle of her shapely calves to mid-thigh.

"I don't know." Rick concentrated on her question and felt the tightening in his chest he always felt when thinking of those last days with his father. "The Alvians came one night. We took off in different directions as we'd planned, but Dad never showed up at the rendezvous. I waited and waited. I spent a month camped out in the woods near where we'd planned to meet up, but he didn't come. Eventually, I had to move to lower ground because winter was coming on and the Alvians started patrolling the area more heavily from the air. I can only assume they captured my dad. Or killed him. I tried searching for him in the Alvian computers once I got to the engineering facility, but I didn't find anything."

"We should get Davin to try. He's got backdoors and trapdoors into almost every one of their systems. I bet he could find out what happened."

Rick felt his heart clench with that familiar pain and a burgeoning hope he didn't dare let get out of hand. "I'd like that. If I'm still around."

"What do you mean, still around?" Callie faced him.

"I was considering heading out in the morning."

"No!" Her exclamation startled the mare, who backed up into her stall. "I mean, that's not smart, Rick. They know where Davin fled to. The ranch is the only safe place for miles around because of Harry's mother. If you set foot off this ranch, chances are they'll pick you up again."

"That's a chance I'm willing to take. Callie, I wasn't born to live in a cell. A man can't live that way. I need to be free."

"But what about all those others you've helped? If Davin can salvage this situation, you might be able to help hundreds more. Isn't it worth sticking around to see how this all plays out?"

"I would if I could, but this is just getting too hard, Callie." Rick felt every one of his muscles tighten at the thought of never seeing her again. "I can't do this." He turned away, but she followed.

"Can't do what? Rick, I love you."

"Oh, God." He shut his eyes against the look on her face, but she stepped right into his space, looping her arms over his shoulders. He could feel the warm press of her breasts against his chest, the brush of her thighs against his. His cock stood at attention at the first hint of her caress on the sensitive skin at the back of his neck.

"Rick?"

Steeling himself, he opened his eyes, ready to push her away, but one look at her face and he couldn't. His resolve began to disintegrate.

"You belong with Davin, sweetheart."

"Yes," she agreed. "But I also belong with you. You're every bit as important to me as he is."

"That's crazy, Callie. You and Davin have a solid relationship. You've known each other a long time. I don't want to come between you. It's not right."

Callie moved closer. "What if I was the one between you and Davin?" Her big eyes turned sexy and she licked her lips. "Lately I've been fantasizing a lot about being the filling in a Davin-and-Rick sandwich. I've never been with two men at once but my mom says it's like nothing else."

"Good God, woman. Are you trying to kill me?" Rick tried hard to move away, but he was caught in the magnetic field that was Callie O'Hara. She pulled him in like nothing he'd ever experienced before. She was a force of nature.

"Only with pleasure," she answered on a sigh. "And I haven't even started *that* yet." She smiled up at him and he knew he was a goner.

"Don't do this, Callie."

"I must." She reached up and pulled his head downward. He didn't put up much of a fight. His head knew he should stop, but his heart wanted nothing more than to taste Callie's kisses again. "Can't you tell how much I want you, Rick?" Her whispered words against his lips nearly stopped his heart.

Then there was no talking as she kissed him, wild and deep. It wasn't tentative or gentle. It was pure passionate fire and it burned through both of them.

Rick backed her up against the barn wall, reaching between them to lift the skirt she'd chosen to wear that day.

When he encountered nothing but bare, womanly skin, he nearly lost it.

"Where are your panties?" His brain wasn't working very well or the question wouldn't have slipped out.

"I left them off this morning in your honor." She smiled up at him. "But it's a bit chilly. I think you need to warm me up, Rick. Give me some of your heat between my legs where I need it."

"Damn, woman." Rick had never been so aroused. Would it be so wrong to taste her this one time? Just once, and then he'd go his way, never to see her again. Just one perfect fantasy fuck to remember through all the lonely years ahead. He was only human, after all.

Decision made, he pressed her into the wall. There was no more time to think. No time to reason. His brain was out of the equation now and he was acting purely on instinct. And all his instincts were clamoring for him to get his cock into this woman as fast and hard and deep as possible and fuck her 'til they both came in wild, gasping passion.

There was no reason. No thought-out plan. Just the urgency of the male animal needing its mate.

His fingers went straight to her pussy, pleased by the warm wetness that coated his hand as she gasped. Rick pulled back a short distance to lift her top with his other hand, stretching the knit fabric up past her taut nipples. His head dipped as he captured one hard peak in his mouth, plying the other with the tips of his fingers, twisting and pinching as she writhed under him.

"Rick!" Her gasping cry was music to his ears. She was as hot for him as he was for her. There would be no stopping him now. No need to wait any longer.

He licked her nipple, switching to the other one after placing a delicate bite on her soft skin. She tasted like heaven and responded like his very own personal she-demon, molten fire in his arms. He'd never had a woman who reacted as quickly as this one—this perfect one—his mate, though he refused to think weighty thoughts at this moment. Right now there was only bliss and the urgent hunger that demanded to be fulfilled.

Rick slid two fingers up into her core, stroking deep in an ancient rhythm that made her whimper. She was more than ready for him. He wanted to stretch this moment out, but he couldn't wait. He needed her too badly.

He pulled his fingers out, raising them to his lips so he could taste and smell the sweet, salty taste of her as he held her gaze. Her eyes flared with passion as he sucked her essence into his mouth. She tasted sublime, but he had no time to spare.

Before he could get to it, Callie's small hands made short work of the fastening of his pants, freeing his cock. Her touch sent shivers down his spine and when she grasped him and squeezed, he nearly came in her hand.

"Stop that, baby, or I'll come without you." He moved forward as she dropped her hand. He caught her around the waist and lifted her off the floor. He was too tall to take her with her feet on the floor, but there were ways. He leaned her against the smooth wall of the barn and trapped her between his body and the unyielding wall. She obliged by wrapping her legs around his hips. Her smile let him know she was ready as she faced him, by all appearances eager for his possession. "It's going to be hard and fast, baby."

"Good." She licked his lips as he moved closer. "I like it hard and fast. I especially like *you* hard, Rick. I can't wait to feel that big cock of yours inside me."

"No need to wait." He lifted her again and aligned their positions before setting her down a few inches onto his waiting cock. She stretched around him beautifully, as if made just for him.

"More, Rick." She gasped. "Do it now!"

Unable to wait, even to savor the moment, Rick pushed deep into her in one long movement. She cried out, but he could tell it wasn't in pain. He felt the little contractions of her sheath around his cock, letting him know she'd gained a small completion at the moment he pushed inside. Well, wasn't that interesting?

He began to move, shoving her against the wall, but she didn't complain. Her breath panted across his neck and he bent to take her little cries into his mouth. Pulling back, he watched her tits bounce. They were bigger than he'd thought and perfectly shaped with big, ripe nipples that begged him to suck. He'd do more of that...later. But first he had to come and bring her with him. He was a desperate man.

Rick's pace increased along with her little moans. As her cries grew in volume, his balls tightened, ready to explode.

"Now, baby. Come for me now," he coached her as one hand slipped between them to rub her distended clit. Callie screamed as she came, her body clamping on his cock like a milking hand, only twice as warm and slippery. He erupted in a torrent, emptying himself into her welcoming womb. He'd never come so hard with any woman ever before. Callie was special. Special and utterly loveable.

Rick pulsed one final time and Callie felt the most incredible bliss. Her mother had been right. Seducing Rick was one of the better ideas she'd had in a long, long time. She'd like to do it all again, as soon as possible.

But her bliss was shattered by the soft whine of approaching engines.

"Oh, no!"

They both heard it at the same time. Callie scrambled down and straightened her shirt as Rick shored up his pants. Alvians were about to land. The distinctive nearly silent purr of their technologically advanced engines was unmistakable.

Before they had a chance to get their clothes completely in order, the barn door flew open. Davin stood on the other side, his expression tense.

Callie felt the mixture of emotions running through her first mate with some confusion. There was an uncomfortable hint of jealousy as his eyes swept over them both, followed by anxiety, fear and love in rapid succession, ending with a sort of agonized hope.

"What is it?" she asked.

"Your brother Harry sent a message. He said something about an unlikely ally. Mick sent me out to tell you he wants us to all stay put here for the moment. Caleb sent word through Harry that we might find a way out of this, if we just hear them out."

"Who's in the ship?" Rick asked as he tucked his shirt in

and stepped forward.

But Davin shook his head. "I don't know. I had to run over here and duck out of sight before Mick could relay everything."

Rick's eyes narrowed as he tried to communicate with the O'Hara brothers, but they weren't responding. Likely they were too busy attending to their own preparations for Alvian visitors, or maybe Rick's telepathy was just too weak after the traumatic events of the past few days. His psychic energy was at a low ebb with all the emotional turmoil. Uncertainty had always had a detrimental effect on his psychic abilities, ever since he was a kid.

Callie brushed past him and though he wanted to pull her back into his arms, he let her go. A pang of conscience hit him when she reached for Davin's hand and let the alien sweep her into a hug. It was so clear to Rick that Davin and Callie loved each other deeply. As much as Rick loved her, he still didn't feel worthy. But that was another battle for another day. Right now, they had even bigger fish to fry.

The three of them stared at each other as the ground trembled. The craft had set down. Close by.

"Harry's mother usually lands in the pasture," Callie whispered.

"I doubt Mara 12 would have any interest in our problems," Davin said.

"Now there, you might be surprised." A man's voice spoke from the other side of the barn door. "Callie, are you in there?"

Rick wanted to stop her when Callie straightened out of Davin's arms and headed for the door. She squared her shoulders and spoke, but didn't open the latch.

"I'm here, Grady. Davin and Rick are with me."

"All right then," came the strange male voice, with an almost friendly edge, if such a thing were possible from an Alvian. "Open up, little one. I'm not here to fight. Mara 12 wants to talk with the Chief Engineer."

Callie opened the door and allowed a huge Alvian warrior into the barn. His weapons were holstered, but Rick knew that didn't mean much. The man was obviously prepared for just about anything.

"Greetings, Chief Engineer." The stranger nodded toward Davin.

"Grady Prime. It's...troubling, to see you here," Davin responded.

"I've accompanied Mara 12 on many of her visits to the O'Haras over the years. I have known Callie since she was a newborn." The soldier had a curious expression on his face as he looked at Callie. Rick stepped forward to protect her. Hell if he knew what he could do against a bruiser like this Grady Prime guy, but something about him woke all of Rick's protective instincts.

But Callie actually smiled at the alien. "All my siblings think of Grady as a sort of uncle. We used to see him a lot when we were younger. Mara 12 used to come out here a few times a year to check our progress and Grady was almost always with her."

"Protecting those in authority is one of my duties," Grady agreed, then turned back to Davin. "Chief Engineer, Mara 12 requests your presence."

"Of course." Davin would have left with the alien soldier, but Callie followed right behind. Davin stopped her, taking her by the shoulders.

"I want you to stay here," Davin said, a sense of urgency clear in the tone of his voice.

"I'm going with you. I know Mara." Rick could see the stubborn set of her jaw and feared this was one argument Davin would not win, though Rick had to agree with Davin's plan. Callie might be a little safer here, away from the aliens. Sometimes the old adage was true—out of sight, out of mind.

"Which is all the more reason you should stay in the barn. She's not to be trusted, Callie. I know what she's done to your family in the past. She doesn't understand us." Davin's voice held a pleading note.

"Please, Davin, don't ask me to stay behind. Whatever happens, we should be together." She clutched his arms, the tension thick in the air.

Rick saw Grady shift his stance, almost as if he were uncomfortable as he watched Davin and Callie, but why should their obvious feelings for each other affect this Alvian? Grady couldn't possibly understand the emotional upheaval going on here. Or could he?

Davin lowered his head so his forehead rested against Callie's. "All right. You're my resonance mate. We'll do this together." Davin raised his head and sought Rick's eyes. "You should come too."

Rick was shocked by the inclusion, but glad of it. He wanted to see what this new development would bring as much as they did. Davin let go of Callie's arms and let her precede him, pulling Rick aside before they left the barn.

"If anything goes wrong," Davin said in a low tone for Rick's ears only, "I want you to get her to safety. It's me they want. You might have a chance to get clear if I put up a fight."

Rick didn't have a chance to reply before they were out in the sunlight, facing a tall Alvian woman. She was beautiful, in that Alvian way, but her expression was cold.

"Chief Engineer." Mara 12 had a musical voice, like most Alvians.

Davin strode forward to meet her, taking the lead. Rick noticed that Grady hung back near Callie, watching all. Rick brought up the rear, his eyes wide and senses alert. He saw Mick off to one side. He'd been standing with Mara when they came out, but was quickly forgotten by the alien woman when her true quarry came into sight. Justin was nowhere to be seen, but Rick suspected he was watching from cover, a little extra insurance against things going bad, and Jane was most likely watching over the other children.

"Mara 12," Davin greeted the scientist. "What brings you here?"

"We must talk. The power situation is unacceptable." Demanding and cold, Mara was like most Alvians.

"Your inconvenience is unfortunate." Davin didn't give an inch and Rick admired his cool.

"You must return to your duties, Chief Engineer," Mara insisted.

"I cannot," Davin replied. "As you may know, an attempt was made on my life. I cannot return to work until that matter is cleared up."

Mick moved closer. "Might I suggest we discuss this inside?

I have a few chairs in my office and it's warmer in there."

Rick saw the wisdom in herding the aliens to Mick's outbuilding. It was closer to the barn than the big house, but on the other side, drawing the possible threat away from Jane and the other O'Haras.

The group started walking toward the outbuilding, Mick acting as escort with Mara and Davin. Callie and Grady followed behind and Rick walked a pace behind them, though he could tell Grady kept a wary eye on him over the scant twenty yards to the building.

They all trooped into Mick's small office, but there was enough room for them to sit. In short order, they were as comfortable as possible under the circumstances and ready to parley. Davin hadn't expected Mara 12 at all, but he would hear her out. He had precious few options left.

"Since you left, the power grid has been fluctuating. The power losses have interfered with my experiments in a very negative way." Davin could see Mara was as close to being annoyed as one like her could be.

"Unfortunate, but inevitable given the lack of skilled crystallographers. My reports to the Council over the past few decades detail the decline in crystal gift among new generations. It's not something I have control over, but something that troubles me greatly." Davin knew the woman didn't really understand what it meant to be troubled, but the wording was neutral enough not to remind her of his throwback status too much. He always had to tiptoe when conversing with Alvians—particularly scientists. They tended to analyze every little thing about him.

"I am trying to do something about that, Chief Engineer, which is why this disruption is so difficult."

"I understand the inconvenience it must pose, but I cannot help you at this time. I will not risk the safety of my resonance mate by returning to work." Davin looked at Callie and felt warmed by her smile. She was magic to him and he would never put her in danger.

"Things have changed," Mara broke into his thoughts. "By going after you, certain factions on the Council have brought their actions into question. I could help you expose those who ordered your death. Many of our people have been following your case with interest. It was thought that we could no longer mate as you have, with a true resonance match. Much research is now being conducted to correlate the loss of resonance mating with other losses, such as the crystal gift. Your case has reenergized the discussion of where we've been and where we wish to go with our genetic selection program."

"That's a good result, but not one I intentionally sought." Davin was at a loss. He had no idea this kind of interest had been generated by his and Callie's mating. He'd been too busy setting up his new programs and enjoying his mate to really take notice. This could work out in their favor, but he wasn't sure quite how to utilize it...yet.

"I am aware of that," Mara said. "The fact remains, there is great interest in you and your mate on many fronts. Whoever ordered your death was acting without sanction from the full Council."

"How can you be certain of this?" Davin fired back, angered still by the attempt that had been made on his life.

"I have spoken to three of the Councilors, with whom I communicate regularly. Each claimed no knowledge of the events leading up to your flight from the engineering facility. They were concerned that some of their number were going around the Council to order something as serious as the death of a highly ranked engineer, crucial to our success on this planet."

Davin was surprised and suspicious. "Why would you want to help me?"

"I want reliable power restored so I can move forward with my work unimpeded. You are the means to do so." She folded her hands in her lap, as if resting her case.

"There's got to be more in it for you than that. With all due respect." Davin didn't quite laugh in her face, but he came close.

"Very well." Her shoulders sagged the tiniest bit. "The operative they sent after you was part of my newest experiment, and as a result of his failure, is lost to me now. The member or members of the Council who activated him knew full well that he was part of my study, and therefore retired from fieldwork.

Blatant disregard for scientific precedence must be confronted."

That sounded more like it to Davin, though he was surprised she didn't seem to realize Sinclair was here at the ranch. Still, Davin wouldn't give up Sinclair to this woman. Davin knew firsthand how it felt to live among Alvians like her. Being the only Alvian with emotions among so many who wanted to study you was a living hell. Davin would not willingly subject Sinclair to that—even if the man had been sent to kill him. Mara would just have to find another lab rat. And then maybe Davin would rescue that one too—if he were still alive after all the machinations of the Council.

"All right." Davin sat back, catching Callie's eye. She winked at him and he knew all was well. A warm feeling swept through him as he felt her approval and love in the small gesture. "What do you want me to do? I assume you have some sort of plan."

Surprisingly, Grady stepped forward. He had refused to sit, instead taking up a guard position by the door.

"I have been looking into this matter. I believe I could provide security to get you safely to the Council Chamber. Mara 12 is correct in stating that many people are avidly following your progress with your resonance mating." Grady included Callie as he addressed Davin. "When you appeared before the Council to declare your mated status, everyone was watching, and those who didn't see it as it happened, watched it later in rebroadcasts on the news feeds. If we can get the two of you in front of the Council again, you will be guaranteed a hearing. No Councilor wants to be seen as unwilling to listen to you speak, and many people are wondering what has gone wrong with the power grid. Few know that you were forced to flee. If you are seen before the Council, all will watch to see what you report."

"So you think public exposure is the way to handle this?"

Grady nodded. "Mara 12 and I have narrowed the suspects down to three. Troyan, Gildereth, and Hearn. I will continue to make inquiries. Once we have something to confront them with, we can arrange to get you to the Council Chamber."

Davin stood. "Give me time to discuss this privately with my resonance mate."

"Of course," Grady acknowledged.

Mara 12 stood. "We will leave you to discuss your options. Grady Prime will give you a secure comm crystal—Davin, you can check it to be certain it is untraceable—so you can contact us with your decision. I suggest you communicate directly with Grady Prime on this matter, since he will be arranging security and gathering further information. I'd also remind you that the reason you're safe here at the ranch is because of my intervention. The Council will probably not dare act against you here, where they risk incurring displeasure from the entire scientific community should harm befall any of the O'Haras." Davin didn't like the way she saved this sinister reminder for her parting shot. "You're safe here, but I cannot vouch for your continued good health should you venture off this property. Either way, it is in the best interests of all concerned to settle this matter quickly."

Mara 12 and Grady Prime left the office and headed for their ship. Everybody else followed with varying degrees of relief and consternation. Mick, Justin and Jane escorted Mara, while Davin and Callie walked next to Grady, and Rick brought up the rear. Davin stopped next to Grady to one side of the ship's ramp as Mara boarded without looking back. Jane, Mick and Justin were on the other side of the wide ramp.

"I understand Mara's reasons, but why are you helping us, Grady Prime?" Davin asked, confused by the elite soldier's actions.

Grady surprised him, looking to Callie with what could almost be termed fondness—for an Alvian. "I've watched Callie grow along with her siblings. I don't understand it, but I...care...what happens to her." It was clear the warrior had trouble relating his astounding feelings. "They say soldiers carry more primitive DNA than the rest. They claim we can sometimes feel echoes of things our ancestors felt. If so, I feel those things when I'm here, with the O'Haras. It's the main reason I always took escort duty myself, instead of relegating it to one of my subordinates, when I knew Mara 12 was coming out here."

Callie stepped forward and put her hand on Grady's shoulder. "It's faint, but I do feel your protective feelings toward me and my siblings. We've always looked on you as a sort of uncle." Davin saw tears fill her eyes. "I wish you could understand."

Grady surprised them both by taking her hand in his. "I wish I could too, sometimes. And I'm honored that you would think kindly on me at all, Callie."

She reached up and pecked his cheek, clearly shocking everyone, including Grady himself. He looked at her oddly before he turned to go, while Rick bristled and the elder O'Haras watched everything with silent interest.

The humans moved away from the ship as Grady boarded and sealed the hatch. With a purr of its engines, the ship lifted off vertically and shot out across the blue sky.

"Well what do you make of that, Janie?" Justin asked as they all headed toward the main house.

"She's always been hard to read, but I think she's sincere," Jane replied, her brow furrowed.

"I believe she is on the level," Davin put in, surprising Callie. She wasn't used to anyone else offering opinions or insight where her family was concerned. For so long it had always been her mother offering insight while her fathers made the decisions. But she was an adult now and Davin was her mate. Heck, he was probably older than any of her fathers, though Alvians aged differently. If anyone had insight into the motivations of an Alvian mind, it would be him.

"Do you trust her? She might be telling the truth about her goals, but who's to say she won't change the plan to suit her own needs? Mara has changed the terms of our agreements before." Mick's voice held ominous tones and Callie shivered as they reached the kitchen door.

"I think we should contact Harry and see what he knows," Callie said.

"Good idea." Mick agreed. He went silent as his gaze took on a faraway cast, even as he moved with the group. Callie knew he was communicating telepathically with her brother.

Davin tucked Callie close to his side as the group entered the cozy house, releasing her only long enough for them both to enter and walk through to the living room. Once there, he claimed her hand, guiding her to the overstuffed couch and settling her at his side, one arm around her shoulders. She felt warm and safe next to him, but noted Rick's closed expression as he followed behind to settle on a nearby chair.

Mick shook his head as he sat down. "Harry didn't know about her trip here, but he says she's been more secretive than usual of late. He'll do a little investigating, poke into the files he can hack and see what he can come up with."

"Good." Davin nodded. "I think I can trust her to a point. She is sincere in her wish to both restore power and discomfit the Council who deprived her of one of her special test subjects. She wants to remind them of her power. By guaranteeing our safety here on the ranch, she's begun that process, but a more dramatic show—such as getting me in front of the Council—will drive home the point."

"Is she really that powerful in your society?" Callie asked, curious.

"Not so much Mara 12 as an individual, but more the power she wields as leader of a good portion of our most important scientists. They follow her lead. She's strong and ambitious, willing to take risks and challenge those in authority. The scientists like their autonomy and look to her as their unofficial leader. The Council knows this and tread lightly around her pet projects. It's a wonder to me that whoever activated Sinclair Prime didn't take into account her reaction."

"And did you notice, she seems to have no clue you brought Sinclair here with you," Mick pointed out.

"Yeah." Callie turned to Davin. "Why didn't she think we had him? There had to be some kind of record of us taking him with us. Isn't there?"

Davin grinned. "Actually, there are no recordings of any kind still viable from my facility. I trashed them all when we left. As for the guardsmen, they know only that I requested to speak to Sinclair Prime before we took off. It wouldn't occur to them that we would bring my would-be assassin with us."

"Why not?" Mick asked.

"Because it's not logical," Davin explained. "Bringing him with us was an emotional decision based on pity. Alvians do not understand the concept."

"Brilliant." Jane beamed at Davin, pride in her expression. "So we can keep him here and help him, without any of your people realizing."

"For a while, at least," Davin agreed. "I think he'll understand, if you don't want him here, around the children. He has dangerous skills you might want to consider before letting him run tame around the place."

"Already thought of that," Justin answered. "I got his agreement to stay out in the old barn on the edge of the property, and we've got it rigged so we'll know if he steps foot outside the place."

Davin looked worried. "As I said, he has advanced skills. Are you sure your precautions are sufficient?"

"It's low-tech stuff, Davin, don't worry. Your boy has mostly hi-tech training—and we do have some of that around the place so he knows we have some grasp of technology." Justin grinned as if he enjoyed the challenge. "Plus it'll divert him from the real warning systems I've put in place. Earth tech. Human stuff that few Alvians have ever seen."

They spent an hour discussing plans before the group broke up. Callie was worried when Rick spoke not one word in all that time. She felt his gaze on her from time to time, but he always looked away when she focused on him. His emotions were masked as well, so she couldn't read him. The frustration was starting to get to her and she realized she had to talk to him. She had to try to set things right. They'd had no time to figure out their new relationship. No time to even bask in the afterglow.

She knew Davin was feeling possessive, but at the same time he gave off pleased vibrations. She could only surmise that he was both gladdened and saddened by what he'd walked in on in the horse barn.

Callie stood when Rick left the room without a backward glance. His stride was terse and his shoulders stiff. Trouble was most definitely brewing.

She felt Davin's hand touching hers and looked back to find a faint, understanding smile on his angular face. She read the compassion in his heart and the almost painful sympathy he felt for Rick.

"Go to him," Davin said as he squeezed her fingers with a light touch.

Callie felt tears gather in her eyes as she bent and placed a tender kiss on Davin's lips. He was such a good man. She loved him more than life.

But right now another man she loved needed her help. That Davin understood and approved meant more to her than anything.

Chapter Eleven

Callie followed Rick outside and cornered him near the corral fence. He stood alone, with one boot propped up on the rail, his arms folded over the top as he stared out across the sunset-lit land.

"Rick, we need to talk about what happened before, in the barn."

His spine straightened with obvious tension. "Leave it alone, Callie."

"I can't. Rick—" she touched his arm, emboldened when he didn't shrug her off, "—I loved what we did. I want to do it again. I want you to love me and *make love* to me again."

Rick was silent a long moment, and Callie worried that she'd said entirely the wrong thing.

"That's the problem. I *do* love you. So help me, I do." Rick's voice was a bare whisper, as filled with emotion as the vibrating energy that bathed her empathic senses. "But it's wrong, Callie." He turned to face her, his jaw clenched with tension. "I can't help but believe it's wrong."

She stepped closer. "Do you really, truly, honestly believe that something so beautiful could be wrong?"

"I banged you against the barn wall, for God's sake." A harsh laugh mocked his own actions. "That's not right, Callie. I acted like a barbarian, just like those who call themselves men I saw in my travels. Their women prisoners. Toys to be passed around or bartered like cattle. That's not the way it should be."

"I agree." She had to stand firm in the swirling wash of his conflicted emotions. It was like a storm around her, trying to shake her from her beliefs, but she would not be swayed. She couldn't be swayed. This was too important. *Rick* was too important.

"Don't you see?" she asked him. "That's not what we have. We made *love*, Rick. Sure, it was fast and hot, and maybe a little too eager, but at the same time, it was perfect. Pure, unadulterated feeling. Deep and true love. And you can be sure I know the difference. I'm an empath, after all. Emotions are my bread and butter."

"I'm a healer, Callie. I have a little empathy too, so don't ask me to believe you're not conflicted over this whole thing. I think it would be a lot easier if I just left you and Davin alone. I'm causing the problems here. You two were happy together before I turned up."

She moved closer to him, holding his gaze. "You're right. There has been a lot of uncertainty between us all. I know you've been picking up on that, but your guess as to the reason for it is all wrong. Rick, I want you. And I want Davin to be okay with that and for the most part, I believe he is, though I'll admit, I have been feeling some anxiety over how it will all work out. Still, Davin's taking it better than I expected. He's seen how my family works. He can hear the evidence of our Humming every time we touch skin to skin. He knows we're resonance mates and that means something to him according to his people's ancient teachings. It's you and me that have to get used to the phenomenon." She reached out, pleading with both her words and emotions.

"I was born after the cataclysm, but I know you remember the old world. You remember monogamy and everything you've seen of how women are treated today has made you believe certain things, but you have to acknowledge that my family is different. You have to have felt the happiness my mother found with my father and his brothers. Their way isn't the way of the other people you've seen in your travels. Theirs is the way of love." Callie reached for Rick's hand. "My mother isn't mistreated and she loves each and every one of the O'Hara men equally. It would kill her to have to choose between them. Just as it would kill me to have to lose either you or Davin. I'm in love with you both. Just as I know you're both in love with me. The dark feelings you've picked up on stem from my worries that somehow, even after all we've shared, you're going to leave me. I'll never be happy without you, Rick. Just as I'll never be happy without Davin. I need you both."

"Dammit, Callie. You're not making it easy to do the right thing." He surprised her, pulling her into his arms and she felt his resistance fall before the driving need and desire he felt.

"The right thing is to come to bed and make love to me all night long." She reached up and stroked his stubbly face. "You know you want to."

He stared at her for a long moment, but she felt his passion, his giving in to the moment. "God help me, I can't say no to you, Callie."

She knew he wasn't fully convinced as she led him toward the spare bed in Papa Mick's medical office that was used for guests. Callie knew Davin would find them there later. It was, after all, the room Davin used whenever he stayed at the ranch, but Rick didn't know that.

By the time they closed the door behind them, the only thing Rick cared about was getting Callie naked as soon as possible. He noted a massive, wooden four-poster bed with a vague sort of awareness before he bent to take Callie's lips in a bruising kiss. He hungered for her so deeply, he was aware of little while she was in his arms.

Clothing flew in all directions as they gasped, kissing almost continuously as Rick's fever climbed higher. Seams ripped under impatient hands until finally, they were both naked. Rick tumbled her onto the bed, following her down seconds later to cover her soft skin with kisses and long, languid strokes.

He had to slow down. He had to regain control or this would be a repeat of last time. Yet, he was ready to be inside her this very moment. No way could she be ready so fast.

Rick's hand stole down between her thighs and found incredible warmth, wetness and welcome. It seemed impossible, but she *was* ready to take him. Rick pushed two fingers inside her, testing further, gratified when she made a whimpering sound of pleasure and grabbed at his hair, dragging his head downward for a lingering kiss.

He stroked into her, knowing he couldn't wait long, but she

was right there with him. The first time they'd made love, he'd nearly pounded her into the barn wall. This time he had the presence of mind to let her be in control. He withdrew his fingers and flipped them over so she sat astride his hips.

"Put it in, Callie. Take me deep into your body." Rick watched the place where they met, licking his lips in anticipation as Callie lifted up, giving him a perfect view of her luscious cunt. When she reached for him, he gritted his teeth against the pleasure of her fingers surrounding his cock. And when she fit him to her opening and pushed downward, he groaned with the need to pound into her hard and fast.

This time would be different. He'd let her steer. He owed her that much. But the next bout would be his.

"Ride me, Callie. Squeeze my cock with that pretty pussy."

He pushed down on her hips, lifting upward at the same time until he was seated fully in her hot depths. It was like nothing he'd ever felt before. Callie was sheer bliss to his starved senses. She began to rock slowly at first, and he encouraged her with his hands on her full hips. She had the body of a goddess and he loved each and every curve. Smoothing his palms upward, he cupped her full breasts, pinching her nipples until she squeaked and contracted around his cock. She liked that. He'd remember.

"That's it, baby. A little faster now. Fuck me deep." He whispered encouragement as her eyes dilated in pleasure and her inner muscles contracted around his eager cock. She was on the brink and he wanted to push her over and feel her body milking him.

Rick tugged on her nipples in time with her rocking motions, thrusting up into her as she descended on each stroke. Gauging her readiness, he pulled hard on her nipples and felt her teetering on the edge. He knew how to bring her over. One hand snaked down her body, his fingers zeroing in on her distended clit. He brushed over it once, twice, three times, each movement eliciting a little cry from her swollen lips.

Rick pinched her clit between his fingers, tugging and rubbing as she climaxed over him. She slammed down on his cock, taking him deeper than before as she spasmed around him, climaxing hard. He didn't mean to, but he came with her, allowing her to pull him into the vortex of pleasure where their bodies met and completed each other.

She screamed at the last. He heard his name, like music to his ears, as he pulsed into her. She wrung him out, her inner contractions welcoming him and challenging him to give her all he had...and then some.

When their bodies started to calm after the perfect storm of loving, he pulled her downward to lie atop his body. His softening cock still lodged up inside her, happy there in the place it felt most at home. Rick felt a little goofy in the aftermath of such amazing pleasure, but he refused to think about the consequences. He'd face whatever came tomorrow, but for tonight, he had plans. The four-poster bed was giving him ideas and as soon as he had a little time to recover, he wanted to try them all out.

Callie must have dozed after that most amazing orgasm because the next thing she knew, she found herself spread-eagled on the bed, her hands tied to the upper posts with strips of bandaging Rick must have pilfered from Papa Mick's office next door.

"Hey," she said with a smile for Rick as he stood over her, looking down. "What is this?"

His grin warmed her as his gaze devoured her naked body. "I've always wanted to try this," he said. "Having a willing woman tied up for my amusement. How does it feel?"

She licked her lips. "Decadent."

Rick sat at her side, his fingers brushing over her abdomen, then up to her nipple. "Do you trust me?"

"Oh, yeah." Her words came out on a purr as he played with her nipple with those expert fingers.

"Good." Rick bent lower to kiss her, driving his tongue into her mouth and bringing forth an explosive response. His hand moved down to cup her pussy, one long finger pushing inward to glide up her wet channel. It was almost too much, but not enough.

"How does it feel now?"

She moaned as his fingers pulsed deeper.

"I'll take that as a compliment." He chuckled, feeling his

own temperature begin to rise. Their first bout had just whet his appetite and he was ready for more, but this time, he had more control. At least he hoped he did. He wanted to make this time unforgettable. "Bondage is a common fantasy." He pulled his fingers out and seated himself on the bed between her thighs. With the palms of both hands, he pushed her legs up and outward, exposing her utterly. "Did you ever dream of being tied up, exposed, held ready and waiting for your lover to take you?" He slid one finger along her folds. "Or not." He spread her inner lips wide as his head lowered. "Or to give you the most intimate kiss a lover can bestow?"

She writhed as his tongue laved over her clit, flicking over the sensitive flesh as she let loose a keening cry.

"I see you like that." Rick grinned as he sat up, positioning himself between her legs and wrapping them around his waist for added leverage.

So much for slow and easy. Things were about to get fast and hot once again. It appeared Rick had little control when it came to loving this woman, but thank God, she didn't seem to be complaining. No, on the contrary, her calves tightened on his butt, pulling him closer.

"Now, Rick! I need you inside me, now."

"I need it too. So help me," he panted as he slid into her, "I need you too, Callie." He groaned as he pushed deep, thrusting without delay or finesse, but Callie was with him. For long moments, he was lost in the feel of her, the magic that was Callie.

Dimly, Rick heard a door close. Feeling a presence over his shoulder, he looked up to find Davin staring down at the bed, a bemused expression on his face. Guilt flooded Rick, but it was overwhelmed by the passion still burning bright between Callie and him.

"Fuck! What are you doing here, man?"

Davin met his eyes. "This is where I always sleep when I stay at the ranch. I expected to find you here. You didn't expect me?" Davin's gaze went to Callie's. She had the grace to look sheepish.

"I guess I forgot to mention it." Callie tensed around Rick's cock, reminding him of the rather urgent business at hand.

"We're a little busy now," Rick said to Davin.

"That's okay," Davin said in an oddly strangled voice. "I have to admit, I like to watch."

"Holy shit!" Rick felt ready to explode at the alien's admission.

"You don't mind, do you? I mean, I know you were subject to constant supervision in the pens." Davin tilted his head in that very Alvian way that meant he was thinking something over. "I could fuck her mouth, if you like, to put us both on the same footing."

Rick fought hard against the climax building inside him. He didn't want to come now and cheat Callie out of an orgasm, but damn if Davin's ideas didn't excite him.

"He likes that," Callie spoke to Davin. "And so do I. Come over here, lover. I want to suck your cock."

"Fuck!" Rick fought for control, wondering how this situation had gotten so far out of his control so fast. Davin dropped his pants and fed a long, hard cock into Callie's mouth. She turned her head to take him deep and Rick felt a jump in his own libido as he watched them.

It seemed he and Davin shared the kink that made them both like to watch—and be watched in return. Exhibitionist voyeurs. That's what they were. But he'd be damned if he'd ever admit it outside this room.

Rick resumed his stroking deep inside Callie's womb, heartened when she started to moan. She definitely liked having two men fucking her at once, though Rick carefully monitored what he could of her feelings. So far, she was with them every step of the way.

She was an expert cock sucker. Rick watched with eager interest as she swallowed Davin's long cock down to the base. She had to be taking him down her throat at that rate. Rick wanted to feel some of that for himself.

He disengaged, motioning to Davin. "Untie her hands." He moved up to the other side of her head, releasing the knot that held one hand while Davin pulled out of her mouth and got the other. "Roll over, baby and get up on all fours." She moved to comply while Davin watched. Rick caught his eye and gestured with a jerk of his head. "Want some pussy?"

"I believe I do," Davin agreed with a sly grin as he moved down on the bed toward her rounded butt, sticking so beautifully up in the air. Davin positioned himself and pushed inward as Rick watched, stroking into Callie's pussy with practiced ease.

Rick stalked around to her head, presenting his cock. She didn't have to be asked, but swallowed him down deep without a word.

"Look at me, baby," Rick coaxed, tightening when those gorgeous eyes pinned him, her lips wrapped around him. It was the most electrifying sight he'd ever beheld and it shocked his balls with renewed energy. He felt them drawing up, getting ready to explode.

Davin set a pace that moved Callie's whole body in time with his thrusts into her pussy. Rick hadn't anticipated that, but it felt amazing. Then Davin stopped.

"What's up?" Rick asked, trying to see what Davin was doing.

"Just a second," Davin replied. His hands moved over Callie's ass and a moment later he was easing back in. Rick blinked, but he wasn't mistaken.

"Shit! Man, are you in her ass?" The very idea made Rick's nuts clench.

"Oh, yeah," Davin replied on a sigh. "She likes it. How are you, sweetheart? We haven't done this in a while."

Callie let go of Rick long enough to smile back at Davin. "I'm okay. It feels so good." She wiggled her butt as Davin settled deeper within. Rick could hardly believe his eyes. He'd had fantasies, but he'd never dared try that with a woman, and here was innocent little Callie, showing him a thing or two. She renewed her efforts on his cock as Davin started stroking inside again.

"You're nice and tight back here, love," Davin praised her. "You make me want to come. Are you ready, Callie? Are you ready to come for us?" Davin's gaze met Rick's in an uncommon moment of communion. They were in this together—for her. In that moment they were united in their purpose, to show Callie as much pleasure as they could.

Callie hummed agreement in her throat and the vibrations

blew the head off Rick's cock. He exploded in her mouth, and she surprised him yet again, swallowing his come as if it were the finest liqueur. She licked him and stroked him until he was completely wrung out, looking up at him with the eyes of love between every few pulses.

She came a second later as Davin rammed one last time into her. Rick was too far gone to see much, but he did feel the riot of emotion coming from Callie. His empathic sense told him how much she was enjoying all this male attention. If not for that, he thought later, he would've immediately regretted his actions. But feeling her acceptance—no, her *craving*—settled his mind about what they'd done, more than anything else could have.

The next morning, Callie served them breakfast on Mick's big desk, cleared and set with a tablecloth for the occasion. She'd fetched the food from the kitchen in the big house and brought it down to the office as a special treat. Rick appreciated the extra effort, tucking into the big breakfast as she ate daintily, seated between the two men.

"You know, Harry's mom has always been a factor in my life," Callie said as she finished eating, "but I begin to wonder if she can be trusted in a situation like this. I'm sorry to say that she never really does anything unless it furthers her own objectives. Poor Harry has said as much to me many times."

"Mara 12 is your brother's mom?" Rick was surprised by the relationship, though he'd known there was something different about the infamous Harry who didn't always live on the ranch.

Callie nodded as she sipped her coffee. "Mara 12 made a deal with my biological father a few days before I was conceived. Mara 12 wanted to be impregnated and in return, Papa Justin got her guarantee she'd put this ranch off limits for the roundups they were doing at the time."

"He bargained his son for the safety of the rest of his family." Rick couldn't quite grasp the enormity of such a decision.

"Yeah." Callie looked sad for a moment but then brightened. "But when Harry was a few months old, he let Mara 12 know that he wanted to live here, with us. He was a strong telepath, even then."

"He's a remarkable person," Davin agreed. "Did I tell you he was able to speak in my mind, even though I have no telepathic ability? Only one other person has ever been able to do that."

"Papa Mick, right?" Callie asked with a teasing smile. "He's a really strong telepath too. Taught Harry everything he knows."

Davin nodded. "Both of them are forces to be reckoned with. Especially where you're concerned."

Rick started to feel a little left out, realizing once again how far back the relationship between Callie and Davin went. Davin had known her and her family for years, They'd shared a lot and knew a great deal about each other. By contrast, Rick was a loner, unused to forming any kind of lasting friendships. He'd kept himself apart, even as he led the prisoners in standing up to the Alvians and brokering deals to help some of those who were in poor health or who needed other kinds of assistance.

"You've got that right. But the problem still remains, can we trust Mara 12?" Callie brought the conversation back to her original point.

"More importantly, can we trust Grady Prime?" Davin countered. "Grady's the one who'd be arranging our passage and performing the investigation. We'll have to double-check any evidence he comes up with. The last thing I want to do is put myself before the Council with incorrect data."

"You'd be a sitting duck, for sure," Callie agreed.

Rick finished his coffee and stood. "Look, you two have plans to discuss. I'll leave you to it." Rick would have walked away from the table, but Callie's words stopped him in his tracks.

"You can't leave, Rick," Callie said. "We need your help. Don't run out on me now. Not when the future is so uncertain."

She had him there. He couldn't leave until he knew for sure she'd be safe. That meant he had to stick around and see what happened with Davin's little assassination problem.

If the Chief Engineer couldn't get the price off his head, the situation could get even more complicated than it was already. If that were even possible. Still, he owed Davin a lot and he had a visceral need to be sure Callie was safe, well cared for and happy.

"I'll stay until this is sorted. I suppose you could use an extra hand on this." Rick nodded toward Davin.

"That we could," Davin agreed with a grim smile, but whether his expression reflected the dire circumstances or his displeasure at having Rick stay near Callie, he couldn't be certain. The alien had seemed to want to share Callie with Rick on a long-term basis, but after the scandalous night they'd all shared, Rick wasn't sure of anything anymore.

Their time together had shaken his belief that being together that way would be wrong for Callie. Once had been sublime, but Rick didn't think he could engage in a ménage relationship for any length of time. After a while, it *had* to be bad for the woman. He believed that deep in his heart. Once was a lark. Twice was fun, but as a lifestyle, Rick would need convincing it wouldn't be to Callie's detriment. Still, he cared for her deeply. He needed to know she was safe from the threat hounding Davin. Rick was resigned to stay until that problem was dealt with.

"All right then." Rick sat back down. "Where do we start?"

"Well—" Davin gestured with half of a buttered biscuit, "—we still need to decide whether or not we can trust Grady Prime and Mara 12. What do you both think?"

"Harry seems to think his mother is working this to her advantage and having Davin back is definitely her goal," Callie said. "She can be trusted to work toward that end, as far as it goes, but we'll all need to keep our eyes open."

"Always wise when dealing with a Mara, especially this one."

They talked over the pros and cons for an hour or more, running through various scenarios for the way this situation could be resolved. Ultimately, they decided to risk it and take Mara and Grady's offer of assistance.

Decision made, Davin used the secure crystal to place a call to Grady Prime. In short order, they discovered their options were better than before. Grady had managed to uncover comm records linking Councilor Troyan to the communications that had activated the retired assassin.

With that kind of evidence, they could confront the Council.

Davin also had documented instances from the past where Councilor Troyan had made very negative remarks about Davin and his proposals. In fact, there was a strong record of Troyan's disapproval of almost everything Davin had ever reported to the Council.

If Alvians could feel, Davin would have said that Troyan hated him. But as things stood, all Davin could prove was an uncommon ratio of disapprovals and negative lines of questioning. Coupled with the comm records, perhaps it would be enough.

"How did you come by the comm records, Grady? Are they reliable?" Davin had to ask, though he would check them himself before approaching the Council. Everything had to be just so in order to pass the Council's scrutiny.

"As a warrior Prime, I have access to all military networks. I had one of my comm experts search through all of Sinclair Prime's recent communications on the pretext of discovering what had happened to him. His disappearance has not gone unnoticed." Grady paused while that information sank in. "My tech noted the encoded signal and I asked her to trace it backward. It was tricky, but this tech is the best I've ever known. She was able to crack the encryption and trace the code signal directly to Troyan's personal-comm console and his personal access code. There is little doubt the communication originated with him."

"This is excellent news, Grady Prime. We're in your debt." Davin's tone was buoyant, but likely lost on the soldier.

"Just doing my job, Chief Engineer. I will transmit the information to your crystal. It should have sufficient capacity to store this data. You should familiarize yourself with the proof before you go before the Council to present it."

"I agree. Thanks." A slight elevation in the tone of the crystal he held indicated receipt of additional data. Davin would plug it into the reader in his ship later to verify its contents. "Now, as for travel arrangements, what do you have planned?"

They talked specifics of times and locations for the next few minutes, eventually agreeing that they'd meet Grady in the home pasture the next morning, just before noon. The Council was scheduled for open session all day tomorrow, so the vid feeds would be live and active and the gallery open to spectators. It was a perfect time to confront them.

Davin ended the call and went to his ship to verify the data, pleased with what he found. Grady hadn't been wrong. This evidence was the strongest they had against Troyan. Davin just hoped it would be enough.

Chapter Twelve

Callie felt Davin's triumph as he strode toward her. It was late, but she couldn't go in until he'd come back from the ship, so she'd talked Rick into sitting outside and looking at the stars. She stood from the comfortable, old, carved wooden bench that sat in front of Papa Mick's office and met Davin as he approached. She went right into his arms, loving the feeling of being loved that always met her when he held her.

Davin felt so good to her empathic senses. He felt like home, happiness and love all wrapped up in one. His feelings were so strong, so sure, they left her in no doubt whatsoever. Rick, on the other hand, was still clouded and mostly hard to read, but little by little she was overcoming his barriers.

Rick was a hard case, but she'd felt his powerful desire, his depthless love. She knew he needed her as much as she needed him and the struggle going on inside him had more to do with his belief that somehow getting involved with her—and Davin, by association—would be wrong for her. He still rejected the idea of a future together because he loved her. It was convoluted reasoning, but it was sweet, in a way, if frustrating.

"Grady Prime is as good as his word," Davin said as he hugged her close.

"Then the evidence is good?" Rick stood and moved closer.

"Better than good. It'll do the trick." Davin spoke to Rick over her head. "Now what are you two doing out here in the cold? I thought you'd take better care of our girl, Rick." Davin's tone teased, including Rick naturally in a way that warmed her heart. She knew very well even such a casual comment could set Rick off, but she only felt amusement through the small cracks in his natural shield.

"She wouldn't go in until you came back." Rick reached over and ruffled her hair, even as she stood in Davin's embrace. She turned to face him, keeping Davin's arms around her middle.

"I never said that." She liked this easy camaraderie between them. It was a glimpse of how it could be.

Rick nodded, conceding her point. "No, darlin', you never *said* it. But you forget you're not the only one with a little empathy around here. The minute I touched your hand, I knew you were anxious. Didn't take much to figure out why."

She stepped out of Davin's arms and into Rick's, surprising him with a gentle hug. "You're a good man, Rick St. John."

Callie felt the armor around his feelings crack a little more as she hugged him. He gave her such warmth and tenderness in return for her care. Their empathic abilities met and reflected back, bathing them both in a sweet kind of euphoria.

"We should all go inside." Davin stepped up behind her, reminding them of his presence. "It's getting cold out here."

For a brief moment, Callie regretted that Davin could never be part of the empathic sharing she'd discovered with Rick, but Davin had no real extrasensory abilities. No Alvians did, as far as they knew, though the mixture of Alvian DNA with human DNA produced psychic wonders like Harry and all those humans left alive after the cataclysm. It was something for the scientists to figure out.

"I'll go," Rick said in her mind, using the telepathy he rarely instigated with her. It felt even more intimate than making love, in some ways, to be able to share thoughts and feelings so quickly and privately. *"I feel your regret and pain. I see his confusion. I don't want to be the cause of any of it."*

She clutched his shoulders. *"My regret is that Davin will never know the intimacy of sharing thoughts or feelings, Rick. You read me wrong. I love him, but he can't share this connection. I felt sad for him. Still, I guess what he never knew, he can't miss, but I'll miss it if you leave. I want you to stay, Rick."*

Rick stepped back, turning toward the doorway. *"For now, sweetheart. I'll stay until this mess with the Alvians is straightened out. After that, we'll see."*

She'd expected as much, but to know he was still so uncertain was tough. He hadn't been definite about his future plans. Maybe they were starting to convince him there could be some kind of a future for the three of them. That thought gave her hope, though she felt him pulling away. She stilled him with a hand on his arm as they neared the bedroom. She felt his intention to keep walking, toward the other room, probably intending to bed down there.

She dug her fingers into his arm as she spoke aloud so Davin could hear. "Don't go. Rick, I need you to make love to me tonight. With Davin. Like we did before. You can't understand how amazing it was to have you both with me, loving me. I want that again, especially if tonight is the last night we'll ever have together." They all knew tomorrow they'd face the Council.

"Callie—"

She could feel he was going to refuse, but she'd have none of that. She cut him off. "Please don't say no. I love you, Rick, as much as I love Davin. I want to experience something I've only dreamed about. I want you both to love me at the same time."

She pulled both men through the open bedroom door with her, holding onto their hands as they stopped in front of the wide bed.

"We did that last night, love," Davin reminded her.

She faced him, trying to repress a flush of embarrassment. She'd gained a lot of courage and knowledge about sex since meeting Davin, but she was still relatively new to it and embarrassed to speak of certain things.

"What we did last night was unforgettable, but what I want now isn't exactly like that, Davin." She dropped her gaze momentarily, trying to find the words to spell out exactly what she wanted. "I've heard things and dreamed of things...especially since you, uh, came in my bottom that first time. Davin, I want to be filled completely. By both of you at the same time." She looked from Davin to Rick, finding the same expression of awe and fire on each of their faces. She felt the passion rise in both of them. They liked the idea—almost as much as she did. She let go their hands and started slipping the buttons on her shirt free. "So, are you game?"

Davin moved first, taking over the task of releasing buttons on her shirt while Rick moved to her pants. Within moments, she was naked, facing them.

She put one hand on her hip. "You two are overdressed."

Rick stepped up, taking the hand that was propped on her hip and bringing it to cover his thick erection. "If you want it, you need to undress it."

"Just your cock? Or can I have the rest of you too?" She looked up into his eyes, pleased by the teasing, hot sparkle there.

"You can have any part of me you want, baby. But I want to feel your hands on me, undressing me. Can you handle it?"

She rose to his challenge, unbuttoning his pants and pushing them and his simple boxers downward with agonizing slowness. She took extra time lifting his heavy cock free of the fabric, touching him as much as possible and cupping and rubbing his balls with a light touch that made him groan. She smiled as his lips descended to claim hers. He shrugged out of the pants and underwear, stepping free as he kissed her. He still wore his shirt, but she sent her fingers on a quest for buttons, sliding them free as he explored her mouth with drugging intensity. He was a thorough kisser. She loved that about him. That, and so much more. He was such a great guy. She'd never dreamed she'd find a man like him—or like Davin, for that matter. They were so different from what she'd envisioned for her life, but each was perfect for her in their own way.

She pushed the shirt off over his shoulders and brushed her breasts against his lightly furred chest. The slight abrasion felt fantastic against her beading nipples. Rick stepped close, rubbing his entire length against her, making her moan softly.

A second later, she felt warmth at her back as Davin began rubbing her bottom with his long-fingered hands. He moved closer, enveloping her back with his hot body as he dipped his head to nuzzle her neck and shoulder. The feeling of being cocooned in male heat and strength was like nothing she could have anticipated. They were moving slow enough that she could savor these moments. Last night had been fast, but this time, she would revel in every little touch, every small caress. This was heaven, and they hadn't even started yet!

Rick raised his head, his lips leaving hers tingling for more. Davin's head lifted from her shoulder and she could sense they were looking at each other.

"You up for this, man?" Rick asked Davin.

"Oh, yeah." Davin's rumbling reply made her stomach clench. "Anything she wants."

"It's bound to get a little...close," Rick warned.

"You've done this before!" Callie accused him, a little jealous of whoever the other woman had been, but she felt Rick's sincere denial even before he spoke.

"No, sweetheart. I've never done it, but I've seen it done, and I'll admit, I wondered about it." He stroked her cheek with one big hand.

"Well, now's your chance to find out." She smiled up at him. "I've wondered too. I mean, my mom has three husbands and I know they all disappear together from time to time. Just how does that work?"

"Let's start small, sweetheart," Rick laughed. "There are only two men you need concern yourself with tonight. And hopefully, forever."

She felt the anxiety he tried to hide. Placing one palm on his chest, she stopped him. "You know, I feel whole right now. Davin—" she turned her head to include him, "—I never told you this before, but when I first met Rick, something clicked into place inside me. I didn't understand it at the time, but now I know. I'm complete. We're complete. There won't be any other men resonating with me. Just you two. Forever." She turned back to Rick. "I just wanted you both to know that. You're the only two lovers I'll ever have."

"How can you be so sure?" Rick's eyes darkened.

She shook her head. "I don't know, but it's something that grows in certainty the more we're together. You two are it for me. Just as I hope I'm it for you." She sent them both teasing glances. Davin answered by lifting her around the waist and dumping her onto the bed.

"You know you're all I ever wanted and all I'll ever need, Callie." Davin's words filled her heart with warmth as he kissed her.

Rick just looked down at them, saying nothing, but she could feel further cracks in the protective wall around his feelings. He loved her. That she knew. But she also felt relief mixed in with the passion and desire. Both men were glad to have her reassurance there would be no others in her life but them. She was glad she'd told them now, before the complications of tomorrow. Tonight there would be no shadows...only love.

Davin hit a ticklish spot on her abdomen as he kissed his way down her torso. She smiled and squirmed, holding Rick's gaze.

"Come down here, Rick, and kiss me." She used the intimacy of their telepathy, though she didn't usually like to leave Davin out by speaking in a way he couldn't hear. She was still working on Rick, trying to convince him of the rightness of this relationship. Showing him how it could be between them using all their senses—the extrasensory ones included—might be helpful.

Rick put one knee on the bed, bending at the waist to match his lips to hers while Davin explored below. Rick's hand claimed one breast, Davin's the other. Rick kissed her senseless while Davin's exploring tongue circled her navel, leaving wet trails that made her shiver with delight.

Then he moved lower. Davin spread her legs and licked between, priming her for what she had no doubt would be one of the most amazing experiences of her life.

"You taste good, Callie," Davin said, his voice muffled against the skin of her inner thigh. The reverberations against her sensitive skin made her whimper as Davin chuckled in that wicked, sexy way he had. Rick lifted his lips from hers, his tongue lingering, his taste tantalizing. His gaze shifted down her body, eyes lighting as they landed on Davin's head bobbing between her thighs as he applied himself to her clit. Callie bit back a scream as Davin brought her to a small completion. Rick's hand tightened on her breast, squeezing gently toward the nipple as he lowered his head once more, aiming for her breasts.

Davin licked her clit while Rick took her nipples in hand, and into his mouth, sucking, laving and even nipping in a way that brought incredible pleasure.

She whimpered when Davin rose and left the bed. Her gaze followed his progress, but he left the room. A quick check with her empathic senses told her he was still aroused and eager to be with her, so he hadn't left for a bad reason. He felt some kind of determination tempered with a care so deep for her that it made her breath catch. Whatever he was doing out there in Papa Mick's office, it was something for her—for them. That thought gave her an idea what he might be about and a moment later, when he reappeared in the doorway, his sexy grin almost made her miss the small jar he held in one hand.

Rick's mouth trailed down her body, but he looked up when Davin settled on the other side of the bed, near Callie's head. Davin placed the jar on the bed.

"The last time we did this was spur of the moment and I was unprepared. Frankly, I'm amazed I didn't hurt you, but I was too far gone to think straight. This time, we're going to do this right." Davin's big hand stroked over her hair and the gentle tone of his voice made her feel humble. He loved her so much. She felt it freely from him. He gave her his deep and true, even violent, emotions with such open honesty, she didn't think she'd ever be the same.

"You could never hurt me, Davin. I loved what we did last night and I know I'll love this even more, but I love *you* for thinking of my comfort." She leaned up on one elbow, cupping his cheek to coax him down for a long, languorous kiss.

She was aware of Rick picking up the jar and heard the metallic tinkling as the lid unscrewed. Davin ended the kiss and Callie saw Rick sniff at the contents of the jar with a curious expression.

"Chamomile, calendula and something else, I think. In a glycerin base." He nodded at Davin. "Good choice."

"Truth be told, it is the one Mick recommended."

"You talked to him about this?" Callie was scandalized, but realized of all the O'Hara brothers, Papa Mick was the one with the most diagnostic mind. He *might* be able to let this slide without harassing her with questions or teasing comments. He also might refrain from lecturing Rick and Davin on her behalf. She hoped.

"Not in specific terms," Davin reassured her. "I merely inquired for a skin lubricant that would ease soreness and promote healing. Though I will admit, he gave me a rather probing look, but didn't ask too many questions."

Callie flopped back onto the bed. "Thank heaven for that. I mean, he's a doctor and all, but he's also my father, Davin. I don't want him knowing the details of my sex life."

"He's also a man in a four-way relationship. You think he has no idea what we're up to in here?" Rick countered, making her face flame. "He knows, Callie. The question is, are you ashamed of this? Because if so—" Rick made a move to stand and Callie could feel him beginning to shut her out.

"No!" She lunged for his hand, stilling him. "I'm not ashamed of anything we do together, but come on, Rick. This is all still pretty new to me. Would you have wanted your parents to know every intimate detail of your sex life? Tell me, honestly."

Rick's stiff shoulders relaxed and he sat back, the tempestuous fire returning to his dark eyes. "I guess you're right, sweetheart. There are certain things that should be kept private. This—" he gestured toward the large bed, including Davin, himself and Callie, "—is most definitely one of them." He surprised her, pulling her upward with one swift tug on her arm. He crushed her in his arms, lowering his lips to hers for a shockingly rough kiss. But it was just what she needed to bring back every bit of the fire that had raged between them. Within moments, she was writhing in his arms.

Davin came up behind her, coaxing her in to a kneeling position on the bed as he knelt behind her. She felt his hands kneading her ass cheeks, then delving between. Davin left momentarily, probably to pick up the jar of salve Rick had discarded on the bed because a minute later, he was back, but his fingers were slick with something that felt really good against her sensitive skin. She was a little sore from the night before, though she would never tell Davin that. She wanted this. She wanted them both before the uncertainty of tomorrow. If everything fell apart, at least she'd have this night, this memory to hold against the future.

Rick played with her nipples, ending the kiss as he drew back.

"Bend down," he ordered. "I want to feel those lips around my cock while Davin gets you ready."

His words brought her higher as she followed his

205

commands. She liked being ordered and he darned well knew it. She saw the spark in his eye as she lowered her head and made a teasing foray over the tip of his cock with her tongue. She loved the taste and masculine scent of him, loved the way he shuddered when she touched him just the right way. Unable to wait, she opened her mouth and took him deep. The groan he tried to stifle made her feel powerful and the pure passion bathing her empathic senses drove her even higher.

Davin wasn't still either. He had two fingers in her bottom and had begun a gentle rhythm that had her pulsing back toward him a fraction at a time. He prepared her gently, but the sensations were making things more urgent than she would have believed in a very short time. She moved back from Rick to look at Davin over her shoulder.

"Now," she panted. "I need you inside me now, Davin."

The two men shared a look as she split her attention between them. She could feel the restraint, the worry for her comfort, the unbridled passion and desire they both felt for her. The feelings coming from both of them were the sweetest kind of aphrodisiac. She felt the moment they both gave in to their desires and saw them share a nod of understanding before she took Rick's swollen cock into her mouth once more.

His hands tangled in her hair, guiding her and starting a rhythm as Davin shifted around on the bed to begin the gentle invasion of her ass with his cock. He was big and long, and he knew just how to please her. Moving slowly, he fed his cock into her tightest opening little by little, pulling out to push back in deeper as she whimpered around Rick's cock.

By the time he was fully seated inside her, she was ready to scream with pent-up desire. Rick moved back and helped Davin position her on her side. Davin lay behind her while Rick faced her, pulling her top leg over his hip, making Davin's cock fit even tighter in her ass.

"Damn," Davin breathed in her ear, "that feels so good. How are you doing, love?"

"Oh, Davin," she panted as Rick moved closer. "Feels so good!"

"Are you ready for more?" Rick's voice rumbled over her, making her shiver. She loved everything about both of these men.

"Mmm. Ready when you are." She gave Rick a little smile, hoping to entice him closer. He rewarded her with a hard, fast kiss as he settled deeper into her embrace, sliding his cock closer to where she most wanted it.

Rick pulled back and looked downward at the fit of their bodies as he positioned himself and began to ease inside. "How's that?" he asked when just the tip of him filled the empty mouth of her pussy.

"Good," she tried to catch her breath. "More. Please."

Rick chuckled and fed even more of his thick cock inside. "Damn, that's a tight fit. Feels weird."

"Good-weird, I hope," she joked, looking into his eyes as he moved even closer.

"Definitely good," he said, kissing her briefly as he pushed a little deeper. He backed up and pushed again, going even deeper this time, easing inside the incredibly tight place that felt so full and yet hungered for more. Callie was in heaven. She'd never thought to feel so incredibly loved and desired as she did at this moment.

Rick pulled halfway out then thrust back in, seating himself fully within her as she gasped.

"That's it," he said. "How do you feel?"

"Oh, God!" She was almost incoherent and he wanted her to answer questions?

Rick smiled over her shoulder, undoubtedly sharing some private joke with Davin at her expense, but she didn't mind. She liked that they'd become friends through her—and inside of her. The thought sent a shiver of wicked thrill up her spine.

Then they started moving.

Seeming in concert, one withdrew while the other plunged deep. They set up a slow, steady, driving rhythm that had her writhing between them in no time flat. She came hard after only a few thrusts, but they didn't let her go at that. No, they drove her higher still, pushing her beyond her limits and daring her to fly higher than she'd ever flown.

Davin's breath bathed her neck in heat as Rick's slick chest rubbed against her nipples. Their cocks worked in the intricate dance they'd made up on the spot, driving inside her with wicked intent and startling expertise. Rick claimed her fully from in front while Davin owned her ass. And she loved it.

Almost as much as she loved them.

That thought sent her spiraling upward yet again, but there was no fulfillment, only the need for more. She began to cry out with each thrust, her body straining toward something it had never felt before. She felt Rick and Davin doing the same as they increased their pace. It was so close now. Almost there...

Davin slammed into her ass and his body seized at her back as he came in rushing jets of come. A split second later, Rick came in her pussy with hot splashes of seed against her inner walls. Both eruptions triggered her own, sending her into the stratosphere as she reached a climax the likes of which she had never even contemplated.

She screamed both their names as she came, crying out, tears running down her face as they joined her in ecstasy. Rick kissed her deep as Davin sank his face into her neck and shoulder, part of them, as the three became one for a moment out of time.

Callie dozed, coming awake when a hard cock nudged into the crevice of her ass. She opened one eye to see Davin still snoozing in front of her, so that meant it was Rick nestling closer behind. She leaned back and turned her head to find him looking at her.

"Something I can help you with, Mr. St. John?" she teased.

Rick sent her a devilish smile. "I believe there is, Miss O'Hara. If you're up to it." Concern entered his tone, and she was touched by the care she felt coming from him.

"I'm up for it, Rick, but thanks for the consideration." She turned so she lay flat on the bed beneath him, reaching up to kiss his lips long and deep.

His muscular chest brushed over her erect nipples, making her squirm. Her body was on fire, just that easily. Rick was a gorgeous man and he knew a thing or two about how to ignite a flame. His hands moved over her skin with wicked intent as he trailed kisses down her neck to her breasts, stopping to nip and suck.

The bed shifted under her and she opened her eyes to find Davin watching them with interest. She smiled at him and he returned the gesture, his eyes languorous, his expression sleepy and aroused, though he seemed content to watch as Rick brought her to a quick, sharp peak with his hands and mouth.

"Will you take me in the ass, Callie? I've never done it before, but I promise to be gentle." Rick's impassioned whisper roused her senses even more.

"Get the cream, Rick. I want to feel you inside me."

She shifted on the bed, rolling to her stomach while she felt both men moving around her. Out of the corner of her eye, she saw Davin hand Rick the container with the salve. Davin coached Rick through preparing her. As he watched his cock rose to lie against his stomach and Callie wanted to reach out and stroke him, but he was too far away.

"Come here, Davin."

"Not just yet, Callie, my love. I want to see this."

Callie felt her hips bracketed by Rick's big hands, then raised so she was on her knees. With a gentle but firm motion, Rick positioned himself and pushed inside with small strokes, going up that tightest avenue. When he was seated fully, he groaned deep in his throat.

"Man, I can't believe how this feels." Rick lay over her, supporting himself on his hands as he rubbed along her back and nibbled on her neck. "Damn, woman, you're incredible."

Callie turned her head, but couldn't quite see him. "I'm glad you think so."

"Ready for more?" He kissed her cheek when she nodded and rolled them both carefully onto their sides, still tight within her. She came to rest facing Davin, who watched with hunger in his expression. "Want to join us, Davin?"

"You know I do." Rick lifted Callie's top leg in one hand, shifting forward until Davin moved into position, taking her calf and positioning her leg over his hip. She was stretched taut, but it wasn't uncomfortable. Rick groaned again as she moved on him.

"Damn that feels good. Move it along, friend, or I'll finish without you," he warned Davin in a strained, but teasing tone.

"Can't have that," Davin chided as he positioned his cock at Callie's opening.

He moved slowly, but with sure movements, filling her completely as he delved inside. Callie could feel the two cocks, rubbing against the thin flesh separating them, hitting each and every sensitive place in her body. She cried out as they began to move. The men had learned from their first go-round and knew just how to coordinate their motion to drive her crazy.

She let loose a keening cry as her orgasm swept closer, a hard, fast wave of blistering passion that was almost frightening in its intensity. She called their names as the wave crested and broke over her, registering faintly when Davin and then Rick came inside her spasming body. She heard Rick say her name and felt the emotion—the love—that filled both male hearts. That warm glow only made the overwhelming climax all the sweeter.

Callie roused sometime later in the center of the big bed. Someone had tucked her under the blankets and from the feel of her thighs, cleaned her up a bit too. Warmth flooded her as she remembered what they'd done. It was a memory she would hold with her for the rest of her days.

A quick check told her Davin was to her left, Rick on her right. Rick had a leg flung across hers as he slept on his stomach and Davin's hand rested on her breast as he lay on his side, facing her.

All was right with her world.

Callie woke again to sunlight shining weakly through the curtains. It was early dawn by her reckoning, but both Davin and Rick were gone from the bed. She got up to use the bathroom, then dressed quickly, curious as to what her men were up to this morning.

She entered the office to find they'd brought breakfast down from the big house for her this time. Satisfied smiles showed on both male faces as she teared up, overwhelmed for a moment by the love in the air. For the first time, Rick was open to her and she knew he'd given that to her as a gift. It was one she'd treasure for the rest of her life.

She sat at the desk at their urging and began to eat, joining them in a hearty breakfast. Her mother had prepared it, of course, but they'd boxed it up and carted it all here, keeping it warm and ready to serve. They'd gone to a lot of trouble on her behalf and she appreciated every minute of it.

Rick cleared his throat. "Callie, about last night." He seemed hesitant to speak. "Was it everything you wanted?"

She nearly choked on a piece of toast. "You have to ask?" She could tell her teasing went a long way toward reassuring him, but for some reason, he was feeling uncertain this morning. She leaned toward him and gave him a quick kiss. "It was everything I'd dreamed and more. I never expected it to be *that* good." She drew back. "Why do you ask? You said you'd seen it before and I'll admit, I'm curious how that came about. I never knew you were a voyeur."

The teasing brought a slight flush to his skin, but he was also conflicted. "There's little privacy in the pens. I saw a lot of things I wish I hadn't and some that made me curious. Up until I confronted him, our Mara—a male called Mara 36—liked to put a naked woman in a cell with multiple men. Most of the women were used to it by then and played along. Some screamed, but some seemed to enjoy it. That's where I saw double and triple penetration, as my father called it. He'd explained about sex to me while I was growing up, but I'd never seen that until I was put in the pens."

Callie put her arm around him. The memories of imprisonment were sad, but some of the images made him feel a sexual urge as well. She could feel the conflict in that and wanted to help him.

"If they enjoyed it, then there's nothing wrong in it. I bet you enjoyed watching too, right?" She smiled up at him.

"You know I did. I'm an open book to you this morning, baby." Rick leaned down to kiss her forehead. "I'm perverted enough to admit it. But I didn't enjoy it when the women were hurt."

"Mara 36 told me how you'd stood up to him," Davin interjected, surprising Callie and Rick both. "He told me how you'd protected a young girl they'd put in the cell with you and about ten other males. If Mara 36 could feel, I'd have said he felt admiration for the way you stood up to him and the soldiers who guarded you. As it is, he was interested in your defiance and your reasons for it and very disappointed when I requested you be transferred into my program."

"You saved a young girl?" Callie asked Rick, feeling his discomfort with the praise and approval in Davin's tone.

"She was twelve years old and they took her away from her family to be raped by a dozen grown men. What else could I do?"

Callie squeezed him. "I love you, Rick. You're a noble man, even if you are a voyeur." She giggled, glad when she felt the tension in him ease.

"In that case, I have a confession to make too." Davin surprised her with his words. "I used to hack into the observation vids from the pens. This was back before I met you, Callie. I wanted to know more about humans, so I spied on the scientists and watched what they watched. Some of it sickened me, but I remember this one couple that really seemed to enjoy each other." A fond smile lit his lips.

"Davin! You're a Peeping Tom." She laughed at his puzzled expression. "So I have two voyeurs on my hands, huh? Well, it's a good thing, because between the two of you, I've discovered I like to be watched."

"A fine trio of perverts we are," Rick agreed, laughing. It was the first time he'd spoken of them as a group and it gave Callie hope that he was softening toward the idea of a future with her—and Davin.

"I'd love nothing more than to take you back to bed right now, but we have an appointment with destiny this morning," Davin reminded them as he rose, beginning to clear the make-shift table. "Grady should be here within the hour."

And just like that, their mood darkened. Callie could feel her men girding for battle—figuratively, at least. They all knew the coming hours would be difficult and very, very dangerous.

Davin tried to convince Callie and Rick to stay behind, but Callie flat out refused and Rick would go wherever she went, to keep her safe. Grady landed with little fanfare and the three of them went out to meet him. Callie said her goodbyes to her family privately and carried their best wishes back to Davin as they boarded the small military craft. By flying in this kind of shielded transport with Grady Prime at the helm, they could go anywhere with few questions asked.

Grady Prime merely raised one eyebrow when Rick boarded right after Callie, but said not a word. Undoubtedly, they made a strange trio, but Davin didn't care what Grady Prime thought. He only cared about the battle ahead.

They took off and Davin sat near the helm by Grady Prime. Rick and Callie sat behind them.

"Chief Engineer," Grady spoke to Davin once they were airborne. "I believe I must warn you that the power fluctuations since you left have been worse than you might have anticipated."

"Can you be more specific?" Davin asked, not really caring what might've happened to the grid in his absence. There were more important things than powering the cities and research facilities. Love was more important than anything.

Grady grimaced. "I was ordered not to speak of the specifics. The damage is perceived as a weakness that could be exploited by...hostile entities."

"You mean humans?" Rick challenged the warrior. Davin was quick to get between them.

"I can't imagine anything that could be that serious, but I thank you for your warning, Grady Prime." Davin recaptured the soldier's attention. "We'll have to deal with whatever we find as it comes."

Grady nodded and concentrated on his flying. They were approaching the city in which the Council compound was located. It would take some finesse to set down close to the heavily guarded Council Chamber—finesse and the clout of being a Prime-level warrior. As Davin and company ducked out of sight, Grady obtained permissions to land and glided to a stop within the perimeter of the Council Chamber itself.

They'd planned to make a dash for the doors while Grady ran interference, but the number of guards was lower than anticipated. In fact, they encountered no resistance as soon as the guards saw Davin's familiar face. The Chief Engineer was apparently still welcome before the Council, even in the company of two Breeds.

Chapter Thirteen

The Council was in session and the gallery filled with spectators when Davin, Rick and Callie stormed the floor. Councilor Hearn tapped repeatedly on a crystal chime to gather attention and restore order, but murmurs followed their progress as Davin led the way to the main floor in front of the gently sloped U-shape of the Council table.

"What is the meaning of this interruption?" Hearn demanded in his regular, moderate tone. Even such a violent interruption was seen as nothing more than an oddity to be dealt with. A rudeness, at best. Rick still marveled at how little emotion touched these people.

The lights flickered and Rick's attention was snagged by the large crystal set in a place of honor at the far side of the room. It pulsed sickly with painful light, quite obviously cracked in a devastating way. Rick nudged Davin's arm, motioning to the far side of the room, but Davin had already seen it. His lips compressed in a thin line.

"So this is what Grady was warning us about." Callie's voice came to Rick in his mind, a warm, telepathic caress.

"Looks like the Council Crystal is in bad shape. No wonder he was worried. From what I've heard, that crystal powers all the defenses surrounding the Council compound and this city. It must be a huge drain on the rest of the grid, plus it makes their leaders very vulnerable. They'd need another really superior crystal to replace it. But wouldn't you know it? Their Chief Engineer is out of the picture because one of these idiots put a hit out on him. Not too bright, if you ask me."

Callie's mental chuckle echoed through his mind. *"You've*

been studying up on the big crystals, haven't you? I never realized how important some of them can be, though it was a beacon crystal that Davin used to gain my freedom the first time."

"Yeah, I heard about that. It was a gutsy move on his part, and on yours."

"Is that admiration I hear in your voice? Could it be you think Davin has some redeeming qualities?" Her tone teased him.

"One or two," he admitted with a lopsided grin. They came to a stop in front of the Council and the big chamber quieted in anticipation. "Look out," he warned her, "this circus is about to start."

"And look who just walked in."

Callie's gaze swiveled to Mara 12, who'd just taken a seat near the front of the audience section on the main floor of the multi-level chamber. The area was reserved for petitioners and highly ranked Alvians. Mara's seat had undoubtedly been reserved once she knew Grady's plan was set. She had a small entourage with her. One young man, in particular, caught Rick's attention.

"Isn't that your brother?"

"I wonder why Mara brought Harry with her," Callie said privately. "He's never been allowed near the Council compound before."

"I'm just here to see and be seen," Harry's voice sounded through both of their minds. "You're looking good, Cal."

"Oh, Harry!" Rick gripped her sleeve, squeezing her arm, helping her repress the response. It wouldn't do to let the watching Alvians know they were communicating, or that there was any connection between the Alvian-looking male with Mara 12 and the very human girl at the center of the storm.

"The Council knows all about me," Harry said. "Though most Alvians have no clue. My presence here is supposed to remind Mother's allies on the Council of her power. Subtle, huh?"

"As a sledgehammer." Callie's dry tone nearly made Rick laugh out loud. "Oh, Harry, no matter what, I'm glad you're here."

"To the bitter end, Cal. But I think you'll do all right. Davin's got a good shot at saving this. The Council needs him and that *damaged crystal is an ugly reminder of just how much. Watch out,"* Harry cautioned. *"It looks like you're on."*

"Councilors," Davin said in a strong voice. "I come before you today, unexpectedly, because of the assassination attempt made on me a few days ago. Since that time, I've been in hiding, healing, and assuring myself of the safety of my resonance mate."

"Assassination attempt?" Hearn asked with mild interest. "Can you prove this?"

"Yes, Councilor. Undoubtedly you already have the report from my security detail before I left the engineering facility. A highly ranked warrior was apprehended outside my living quarters with a sniper weapon that had been recently fired. Size and velocity matched the wound made in my arm and the prisoner admitted freely to shooting me. It is now apparent that the prisoner was a covert operator specializing in assassination."

"Surprising," Councilor Hearn commented, looking around at the other Councilors. Rick interpreted that look to mean Councilor Hearn had added two plus two and come up with the inevitable conclusion that one of his fellow Councilors had ordered the hit on Davin.

"As you might suspect, I grew concerned not only for my own safety, but for that of my resonance mate. She and I share living quarters. The projectile that hit me could just as easily have been used to injure or kill her and that is something I cannot allow." Davin deliberately took Callie's hand in his. Rick saw Alvian heads perk up all over the room as the Hum only they could hear undoubtedly filled the chamber. "Even if you cannot understand it, you should all be well versed enough in our people's history to understand the duty I have to keep my mate secure and protected from all that could harm her."

"And my duty to keep my mate safe as well," Callie chimed in, surprising them all. Rick bit back a smile at the Alvian reaction to her words. She was just the woman to teach them that humans would no longer be trifled with. She was firm, yet polite, something the Alvians could neither object to, nor fully understand coming from a supposedly inferior *Breed*.

Davin bent to place a gentle kiss on her lips and even the fractured crystal in the back of the hall began to glow yellow as the sun. Yet another reminder of the power Davin held and the energy he and his resonance mate could generate between them. Rick noted the expressions on the Councilors' faces. Though they showed no emotion, Rick could discern varying shades of interest, concern and dislike. From that he could gauge which of them might be on their side in all of this. The number was greater than he'd expected.

"Do you realize how much your absence has drained the grid, Chief Engineer?" Councilor Beyan asked, sounding merely curious. She made a gesture toward the fractured crystal mounted behind the Council table and her eyes narrowed with what might've been distaste.

"I have been away from all news and information since the attack and did not know the extent to which the grid has failed. For that I regret my absence, but I will not return to my duties until I am assured that no further attempts will be made to kill either myself or my resonance mate."

"What do you propose we do about it?" Councilor Hearn asked, bringing them back on track. "I suppose you have some idea you wish us to consider."

"Indeed I do, Councilors. Permit me to present you with the following data." Davin produced the crystal that contained Grady's information and placed it in the receptacle that would feed the information directly to the Councilors' workstations. They would see the incriminating data all at the same time, once Davin flicked the send key. Rick watched Davin time everything just so. He held his finger over the key, explaining further before he presented his most damning evidence. "It occurred to me right away that very few would have the power to activate such a highly ranked assassin. In fact, this particular warrior had to be reactivated out of retirement and assigned to this task. I'm certain his new employer had no knowledge of the covert mission to kill me, and that same employer would not have approved, had they been asked. It takes a position of great power to overcome such obstacles. In fact, only a Councilor is so highly placed."

"Do you accuse one of us?" Hearn asked, leaning forward with a slight raise of one eyebrow.

Davin nodded. "I do. As you will see from my evidence, the communication that activated the assassin traced directly back to Councilor Troyan." Davin pressed the send key and all nine Councilors studied the private displays hidden inside the table. Troyan went pale and rose to his feet.

"I object. None of this is true."

"So not only do you try to have me killed, but now you are calling me a liar and impugning the validity of certified records? Councilors, you will note the authentication timestamps and heightened security parameters on the evidence I have provided. You may have your experts examine it, of course, but I would not—in fact, could not—tamper with such evidence. Troyan ordered a hit on me, in defiance of the Council directive that I and my resonance mate should be allowed to live in peace at the Southern Engineering Facility in order to provide for the increasing power demands of our people as a whole. By ordering my death and causing my injury, which prompted me to flee my home and my work for my own safety as well as my mate's, he has brought about the power fluctuations that were even more severe than I anticipated." Davin stepped toward Troyan as his voice rose. "Your actions have caused grave damage to the Council Crystal itself."

"That was unanticipated," Troyan said without thinking.

The other Councilors rose and turned their backs on Troyan, using the age-old symbolism that told all without uttering a word. He was no longer welcome among them.

Guards strode forward and removed Troyan from his seat, bringing him around into the petitioner's position before the Council to hear their judgment. Rick, Davin and Callie moved to the left to make room for Troyan and the guards holding him by the arms, forcing him to face his former peers as they turned back around.

"Troyan 4," Councilor Hearn began, intentionally leaving off the honorific that would have indicated his status, and using his designation instead. "You will be held pending further inquiry and all your activities suspended. You will communicate with no one and not be allowed visitors. Any associates who might have been in collusion with you will be sought and tried for treason. It will go better for them, of course, if they turn themselves in at the earliest opportunity. Any and all threats to the well-being of Chief Engineer Davin or his resonance mate will not be tolerated." Hearn made a shooing motion and the guards dragged Troyan away.

"Thank you, Councilors," Davin said respectfully, but Rick could feel there was more in the air. "I will gladly return to work, but I have something more to show you all that has been a long time coming. Simply put, though I am the strongest Alvian crystallographer on this planet, even my skill is not enough to power our cities at their current rate of growth."

"What do you propose, Chief Engineer?" Council Beyan looked intrigued, which Rick took as a good sign. It was the most life he'd seen out of her yet.

"You all know I've been training certain gifted humans. I would like to take the program one step further and I think the merit of my idea is better proven by a demonstration. May I have your permission to approach the Council Crystal with my friend?"

Davin motioned to Rick, shocking the man into a slight jump of surprise he was quick to try to hide, but Davin saw it. He tried not to laugh. Rick was going to be more than surprised when he found out what Davin had in mind.

Councilor Beyan raised one eyebrow, then turned to Councilor Hearn and nodded her approval. One hurdle passed.

Councilor Hearn sat back in his chair, regarding them closely. "You could not do any more damage to it than has been done already. You have permission to approach."

"Thank you," Davin said and the irony of his tone was completely lost on them. He motioned to Rick and together, they rounded the left side of the U-shaped table and approached the crystal. It was worse than he'd thought. The poor thing had a crack as wide as his wrist and looked as if it had been gouged by an angry bear. It shone a sickly greenish color instead of the radiant gold and white is should have radiated.

Davin stopped a few yards from the crystal and Rick halted beside him. He turned to the Council, and saw all eyes were on them. The Councilors had swiveled in their chairs to watch their progress.

"Councilors, this man is my new assistant and perhaps the most crystal-gifted person I have ever encountered. His natural abilities not only rival my own, but surpass them in many ways." Murmurs rose in the audience part of the chamber, which was full to the highest gallery. "Though he has come to the training late in life, Rick can do things I and my fellow Alvian crystallographers can only dream of. I propose to let him try his hand at healing this crystal."

Rick started at his side, but Davin forged ahead. This was no time to be faint of heart. This was an opportunity.

"You really believe he can do such a thing?" Councilor Beyan asked doubtfully.

"I do," Davin replied in a strong voice, above the whispers in the room.

"And what do you hope to prove by such a demonstration?" Councilor Gildereth spoke for the first time.

"I hope to show you all that humans are more valuable than you believe." He let that sink in for a moment. "I also wish to secure Rick's place in my facility. I want your guarantee that he will not be targeted for assassination as I was, nor removed from my custody—ever. This is very important to me, Councilors, and I will have your pledges of honor on all points."

"First prove to us that he is worth such an outlay of trust," Councilor Olin spoke from the farthest seat on the right. "Show us what he can truly do."

Davin bowed his head in mocking respect that was again lost on the Alvians. "As you command." He turned to Rick, finding a nervous smile quirking one corner of the human's mouth.

"Are you sure about this, man?" Rick asked.

"I've never been more sure about anything, except maybe Callie, and you know how well that worked out." The men shared a brief smile. "If you do this, you'll be safe from them for the rest of your life. They wouldn't dare harm anyone with the kind of power I know you have within you."

"I don't know what to say." Rick looked a little stunned by the implications of what Davin had arranged, and he probably hadn't even caught on to all of it yet. Davin had deeper plans than even Rick suspected. This wouldn't be just to keep Rick safe, but also to allow him to live with them on equal footing. Truth be told, Rick would likely prove even more valuable to the Alvian race as a crystallographer than Davin—if he could begin by healing this crystal and proving himself in a spectacular way. Davin had no doubt Rick could do it. Now he just had to convince Rick.

Davin turned with Rick to face the damaged crystal.

"You can do this. Your power surpasses even mine." Davin spoke in a low, urgent voice, for Rick's ears alone. "I never told you this before, but what I said to them is true. You can do things I can't even contemplate. I believe it's because of your healing gift. Use it now. Show them what a human can do that even their best crystallographer can't."

"I hope you're right." Rick looked from the sick crystal to Davin and back again.

"I know I am." Davin gripped his shoulder, squeezing once in reassurance before letting go and stepping back. "Do us proud."

Rick stood before the Council Crystal, caught in its disharmony the moment he opened himself to it. If the Earth could cry, this was what it would sound like, he thought. He knew Davin and Callie believed in him. He knew without a doubt they thought he could do this, but Rick wasn't so sure. He'd never attempted something like this and didn't know if he had the strength or skill to complete such a monumental task.

But he knew he had to try.

For the sake of Callie. And Davin. And all the humans who might benefit from the aliens realizing they were worth more than just their value as guinea pigs. And for the Earth.

This crystal needed help. Like many of the people he'd healed, this small piece of the planet needed *his* help to heal and be strong once more. Rick couldn't turn away. Healing was what he'd been born to do.

With deliberate motions, he placed his hands on the pulsing, cracked core of the stone. His neck snapped back as the discordant energy flowed through him and he fought against the wave of pain, the cries of agony seemingly from the Earth itself.

Rick felt the power flowing through him. He felt his own power rise to meet it and morph it. He brought his will to bear on the swirling mass of energy, using touches of his healing gift, warned by previous tasks how a little of his healing gift multiplied exponentially as it reformed and bounced off the smooth planes of the crystal's inner matrix.

It took all his skill and concentration, but he was buoyed by the knowledge that out there, among the watchers, his resonance mate waited. He understood the concept so much better, now that he'd begun to decipher the song of the crystal. He felt the rightness of their personal energies meshing and intertwining and he could also feel the way Callie meshed with Davin. Neither bond was stronger nor more perfect than the other. Both were as they should be.

Rick lost himself in the song of the Earth, learning things as he taught the injured crystal how to grow and live again. Little by little, the harmony returned as he focused on each fracture, each dark spot on the otherwise white energy of the quartz. Like the living rock, his love for Callie and her love for Davin enriched them all—enriched the Earth itself.

He never thought it possible, but Rick learned things as he lost himself in the cracks and fissures of the quartz matrix. Ancient truths as old as the planet. He knew now that the Earth needed healing as much as its inhabitants. People like him were created to heal the Earth, but it gave back as well. Whatever benevolent power that oversaw both the Gaia spirit and the spirits of all beings, had a plan.

Rick saw only the tiniest hint of it as he nearly lost himself in the largest crystal he'd ever dared to touch, but he knew the truth of it. The small corner of the Master's Plan he was privileged to be part of—for just that tiny moment of communion—gave him knowledge he'd never sought nor would fully understand.

But he understood enough to know that whatever else was true, his love for Callie was part of the Master's Plan. As was her love for Davin and the deep and true respect each man held in their heart for the other.

Rick was lucky, in a way. He had a small amount of empathy that told him just how Davin felt about him, Callie and their new relationship. Rick saw that Davin had no such ability and that he'd need reassurance. As a healer, Rick could do no less than offer it—once he'd set this poor, ailing crystal to rights.

Pulling out of the matrix by slow degrees, Rick became aware once more of the silent chamber around him. Dancing light met his eyes as they refocused on the real world outside of the world of the matrix. Stunned expressions on Davin's and Callie's faces were his second vision of awareness. The Alvians wore varying degrees of interest on their calm facades. He could see now how empty they were, when compared to Davin. He was as they should be—full of life and emotion. They were nearly blank slates, going through the motions of life, but never really living.

Rick pulled his hands from the living crystal, glad to see it pulsing with renewed vigor and health. If he could believe his empathic senses, this little piece of the Earth felt almost...happy.

But such concepts were hard to apply to the vastness he had been privileged to glimpse while immersed so fully inside the matrix. He rested his hands at his side and felt the faintness of expended power rush over him.

Davin was there to prop him up, with Callie on his other side, emanating worry. She must've moved around the Council table while he'd been immersed. He took her hand in his, offering reassurance to counter her anxiety.

"Don't worry, baby. It's not that bad. Give me a minute, and I'll be okay."

"What just happened here?" Councilor Beyan asked.

Davin answered, still supporting Rick. "I believe it's what our ancestors would term a miracle. And this only proves my theory." Rick could feel Davin's smugness and joy, and Rick realized the Chief Engineer was playing a deeper game here than even he had guessed.

"What theory?" Councilor Gildereth wanted to know.

Rick felt his strength return and stood away from Davin's support. He spoke in a low tone, meant only for Davin's ears, though Callie undoubtedly heard too. "You're on, brother. Give them both barrels."

Davin spared him a grin before facing the Council with the air of a showman about to unveil his final and most impressive trick.

Bianca D'Arc

Davin grabbed at the opportunity that had been handed to them all. This is what he'd been waiting for—a chance to tell the Council and all Alvians just what they'd thrown away. He couldn't have planned it more perfectly and he would take every advantage of this twist of fate.

"Councilors," he began. "What you have just witnessed is something I have only read about in the histories of our race's greatest crystallographers of antiquity. It is what we would term a Master Working and it is something done only very rarely in our people's past. I freely admit, I could not have healed that crystal. I think Councilor Beyan will understand the complexities involved. And as she has intimate knowledge of my own strengths, weaknesses and abilities, she is perhaps best positioned to vouch for what I say."

The Council looked to their own. Councilor Beyan was the most qualified among them in matters of crystallography and did, in fact, have responsibility for much of the power grid through the engineering facilities she oversaw, including the biggest—Davin's Southern Engineering Facility.

"What the Chief Engineer says is true. I do not understand how a Breed could do what our most talented crystallographer could not. Please explain, Davin." Beyan turned the group's attention back to him and he bowed his head slightly in polite respect.

"Rick St. John is the most advanced pupil in the pilot program I set up, with the Council's permission, some time ago. There are several others who could equal my level of ability or somewhere just below, including my resonance mate, Callie. These are just the ones already in training. There are also many others of lesser strength that are still more apt than most of the Alvian candidates I've seen in the past decades. Simply put, crystal gift among the humans I have tested and trained is stronger and more prevalent than in Alvians of the past few generations."

"If what you say is true, do you have any hypothesis as to why?" Councilor Gildereth asked.

Davin nodded. "I have conducted a study, keeping careful records which reside on my facility's network. I would be pleased to make these observations available to you and any of the scientific community that has an interest in checking my data or taking the study further. I believe it is crucial to the continuance of our entire race to discover the root cause for the lack of crystal gift among our young. I have a theory, but as genetics is not my area of specialty, I would appreciate other scientists taking up the analysis."

"What is your theory?" Gildereth asked again.

"As you all know, I am a throwback, with all the emotions of our ancestors—perhaps tempered somewhat from the brutal aggression documented in our forefathers—but still emotions. Yet, despite that perceived flaw, I have the strongest crystal gift on this planet among our people. I did some research early in my career and gathered data on other known cases of throwbacks who had crystal talent. Eventually, I expanded my research to include all cases of documented throwbacks. All had crystal talent to some degree or other. Many were quite strong and lived out their lives—until insanity set in—as high-ranking crystallographers."

Mara 12 stepped forward from the crowd to face Davin, mild curiosity marring her features. "If I may address the Council?" She waited and received permission to speak. "I can confirm these facts. It is something I have also been researching. The incidence of genetic throwbacks does correlate to an elevated rate of crystal gift. Though what that implies for Breeds, I have yet to theorize."

"Then let me help you out," Davin said, facing Mara 12 in rude breach of Council etiquette, but he didn't care. "I believe emotion is key to crystal gift. By breeding out all emotion, we are killing ourselves. The humans have both emotion and some Alvian DNA. The two together creates optimal conditions for the development of the crystal gift." Gasps sounded from some of the onlookers. Few realized the word Breed stood for "half-breed" in the human tongue—a clever way for scientists like Mara 12 to disguise the fact that they had found Alvian DNA among the survivors of humanity. "This is something we need to consider carefully as we continue to colonize this planet."

"Is this true?" Councilor Gildereth pretended ignorance for the benefit of the vid pickups, no doubt. The Council was fully aware of the history of humanity.

Forced into a corner, Mara 12 had to come clean. "I have discovered the presence of Alvian DNA in some of the native population, it is true. To what extent our forefathers influenced humanity is still unclear."

"Unclear, my ass," Davin heard Harry's unmistakable voice in his mind, only just realizing the young man was seated among Mara 12's entourage. Davin caught the wink Harry sent him, trying not to laugh. This was going better than he'd expected.

Murmurs from the gallery met Mara 12's statement. Davin caught Callie's eye and she smiled at him. Her support meant the world to him. Rick came up behind her, shielding her and cupping her shoulders in his large palms. He looked stronger and seemed ready to protect her, should it become necessary. He nodded, the message of solidarity clear, as Davin turned back to the Council.

"Our people have been kept in ignorance too long. If we are to make a go of living on this planet—of continuing our way of life, indeed, our very race—we need to consider the ramifications of what we have done by draining all emotion from our genetic code. At the very least, we should cultivate and repair our relationship with the native inhabitants of this planet. Though most Alvians will never understand their emotional moods, we must comprehend that without them, within a few generations, our current way of life will be over. The crystal gift lost to us is strong in humanity and we will need every bit of it if we are to continue to grow as a society."

The Councilors seemed to take all that in, a few conferring privately among themselves before turning back. Councilor Hearn spoke for them all.

"You're right, Chief Engineer. Perhaps we have kept some of this information to ourselves for too long." Hearn looked over at his colleagues before facing the chamber once more. "We've been discussing a solution to this dilemma for some time and I think the moment to act is upon us. By order of the Council, all Breeds will be tested for crystal gift and those who prove to possess it in sufficient quantities will be invited to study crystallography. Chief Engineer, since your pilot program has proven successful, we ask that you expand your current program and oversee the creation of additional sites, as necessary, to accommodate however many of the Breeds are found fit for use as crystallographers."

"I can't believe it." Callie's whisper reached Davin's ears and he tried and failed to suppress a grin. It wasn't total victory, but it was a definite step forward. Humans would have at least a chance now, to live under better conditions and prove their worth. Alvian society moved in slow increments since emotion had been drained from the people. Slow deliberation marked almost every decision, unlike the hotheaded—and often disastrous—decisions made by their ancestors.

But they were moving forward, and in a direction that looked hopeful for humanity. That was something.

The Council meeting broke up after that, the level of conversation rising in the chamber as vid commentators repeated the startling revelations of the past hour. Davin, for one, was relieved it was over. He didn't want or need this kind of excitement in his everyday life. Political intrigue was not something he enjoyed, though he'd been sucked into it many times since he'd gained the position of Chief Engineer.

All he wanted now was to go home with Callie and Rick, and begin to build a new, happier, more secure life for the three of them. It would take some getting used to, but now that Rick had very publicly proven himself an even more powerful crystallographer than Davin, he hoped things would be better for them all.

There was a calmness to Rick now that hadn't been there before he wrestled with the crystal. Davin didn't know quite what to make of it. Perhaps it was only fatigue after using his psychic gifts. Davin wasn't sure, but he hoped it meant Rick was finally coming to terms with what must be. The three of them had to share their lives in order for them all to be happy. He knew full well that Callie's happiness dictated his own—and Rick's too.

Davin was ready to join his new family when Mara 12 caught up with him. Harry stood silently behind her, his expression suitably calm, but his eyes sparkled with triumph.

"You have my compliments, Chief Engineer. I didn't anticipate these events and the more subtle game you were playing beneath the surface. Congratulations."

"You may see it as a game, Mara 12," Davin said, trying to keep hold of his temper, "but I can assure you, to the humans in my program, their lives and living conditions are a very

227

serious matter, indeed."

Mara 12 waved away his words. To her, he knew, they meant less than nothing. She simply did not understand the emotion behind such serious circumstances.

"I cede your point, but my admiration of your political prowess stands. I will be more cautious next time we deal together. Your actions may have just cost me a large number of my test subjects. That is not something I welcome, nor was it a possible outcome I had anticipated. If I had known this would happen, I would rethink my willingness to help you."

"I understand, Mara 12, but I will let you in on a secret. None of this was planned. I had no idea the Council Crystal was so badly damaged. Please remember, I was on the run with no access to news for many days. When you said there were power fluctuations, I expected the normal grid interruptions that would happen should my facility go off-line. I had no idea this crystal had cracked. Everything that happened as a result of Rick's healing the crystal was serendipitous."

Mara 12 cocked her head to the side, thinking. "Intriguing," she finally answered. "No doubt, you consider this good fortune. I, on the other hand, could wish it had never happened. Now that the general populace has some idea of what the Breeds actually are, there will be many questions to answer and I have not yet had sufficient time to come up with definitive answers. I could wish for more time to study them and their effects on Alvian DNA, but will instead have to speed up my plans."

Davin wondered if she was talking about the top secret project in which Sinclair had participated. If so, he counted it as yet another blessing on this day of miracles. If more Alvians gained emotion, it could only be for the better as far as he was concerned. Mara 12 would bear close watching from here on out and Davin knew just the man for the job. Davin held Harry's gaze as Mara 12 turned to go.

"Don't worry," Harry said into his mind. *"I'll keep a close watch on her experiments. Now that I know what to look for, it should be easy enough. I'll be in touch soon."*

Davin wished he could speak freely, but there were too many watching. He nodded to Harry as he turned to go, but Harry surprised them all by stopping to hug his sister. Alvians all over the room perked up in question at his very un-Alvian demonstration.

"Love you, sis."

"Love you too, big brother."

Davin heard their whispered words before they parted, though only Rick was close enough to overhear. Murmurs followed Harry as he turned to go, but he only grinned at the questioning looks thrown his way.

The engineering facility was in chaos when Davin, Callie and Rick returned. A number of problems had arisen that needed Davin's personal attention.

"I'm sorry." He pulled Callie in for a quick kiss. "I need to get things back online."

"I can help," she was quick to volunteer, but he knew she was worried about Rick. He was still very shaky on his feet after healing the Council Crystal.

"No, my love. Take care of Rick. He needs you now. Though I do appreciate the offer." He kissed her again and she went back to Rick, supporting him under one arm as she led him off down the corridor toward the suite of rooms Davin and Callie had shared. Davin had plans to move them all to a larger, more secure suite, but the old set of rooms would do until the larger accommodations could be readied.

With a resigned sigh, he turned to the small platoon of lesser crystallographers, each of whom had a different problem to which only Davin could supply the answer. It would be a long night.

Rick woke to warmth. He was in a luxurious bed and this time, a soft female form was snuggled close. She was naked, as was he, and Rick knew immediately she was his dream come true. Callie. In his arms.

"Where's Davin?" he asked around a yawn as he felt Callie stir in his arms.

"Probably still heading off disaster on the grid."

"Poor guy." Rick's tone was obviously unsympathetic in a teasing way. "I guess that means I have you all to myself."

"Are you feeling better? You were kind of wiped after that

magic you did on the Council Crystal." Her drawn brows communicated her worry for him and he was touched.

"I feel fine, Callie. Good as new. But there is one thing that would make me feel even better." He stroked her back, ending by cupping her curvy ass.

She smiled up at him. "Oh? Whatever do you mean, Mr. St. John? Tell me and I'll do my best to see that you get...some."

"You'll give me some?" He rolled her onto her back, leaning over her prone form.

"If that's what you really want," she teased.

"You know I do, baby. I want some of this." He made her gasp by sliding one hand between her legs. Exploring fingers found her slit and pushed deep inside. She was wet and ready for him, as she always seemed to be. "Damn, girl. You must want it bad."

"I want you bad." She blinked up at him. "Does that count?"

"Oh, yeah," he agreed. "In the best possible way. Now spread those legs and show me your pussy. I want to taste it before I come inside you."

She gasped as he lowered his head, kissing his way down her body. He stopped off at her breasts, taking his time there while she writhed beneath him. He loved how responsive she was to his every touch. Leaving her nipples hard and wanting, he moved lower, helping her spread her already wide legs, pushing up and out so she was totally exposed to his gaze. The glistening pink of her made him want to lap at her like a cat, but his eager cock pushed him faster. Rick bent to take her swollen clit between his lips, worrying it with his tongue while she squirmed, almost out of control on the cushy bed.

"Rick!" she moaned as she reached a hard completion, but it wasn't as high as he would push her. No, he'd have her screaming the house down before he let her come the final time and followed her over the edge. This was only the beginning.

Touching her, he could sense when she was nearing another edge and he played with her, letting her come close, only to pull back. He knew the pleasure would be greater for it and he wanted to drive her as high as possible before joining with her. This would be the first time they made love alone in a bed. He wanted to do it right and give her an experience she would never forget.

For once, he wasn't holding back his emotions from her. Exposed by the energy drain of healing the crystal, his empathic sense—weaker than hers, but still present whenever he touched someone—seemed to call out to and connect with hers. There was a communion of sorts as their power meshed and melded, amplified and strengthened each other's feelings. The passion increased along with the desire and it wasn't long before Rick was on fire for her, unable to wait any longer.

"Callie, baby, tell me you're ready for me." His voice sounded like a plea to his own ears. He cleared his throat, lifting up to look into her eyes as he tried again. "Do you want me now, sweetheart? Do you want me as much as I want you?"

Callie smiled a slow, sexy smile that drove him up another notch. "Can't you feel it, Rick? You're burning me alive with your feelings."

"I'm sorry, baby. I can't hold them back. Healing the crystal did a number on me."

Callie raised herself to a sitting position and touched his cheek. She held his gaze with a serious expression. "I love feeling what you feel. I've been waiting for this moment, Rick, since the day I met you. Don't hold your emotions in check from me. Let them wash over me." Her eyes closed as her head lolled back. He let a wave of passion flow from him experimentally and she shivered. "Can't you feel what your emotions do to me? It's like an aphrodisiac and I want more." Callie raised her head and pulled him in for a long, wet kiss. He began to understand what she meant as her emotions bathed his weaker empathy with desire, passion and a fire unlike anything he'd ever experienced.

"I can't wait, Callie."

"I don't want you to wait, Rick." She gasped as he positioned her on the bed, spread before him as he knelt between her legs. "Come into me now. Let me feel you filling me."

Rick guided his cock to the place it most wanted to go, watching every last flutter of her nether lips as he approached. He loved the way she stretched around him, accepting his girth. He pulled back and pushed in once more, going a little deeper.

"Yes!" she cried, spurring him on as a wave of ecstasy broke over him. It was a mixture of his own and Callie's emotions, driving them both higher. Her warm wetness surrounded him, accepting him, taking his length in a welcoming slide that left him gasping as he seated himself fully within her tight depths. "Oh, Rick, it feels so good. *You* feel so good."

"I love the way you take me, baby. I love the tight stretch of your body around me. You were made for me."

"I was." Her whisper, combined with the waves of empathic passion crashing over them both, drove him to move. Rick lowered his torso to rub over hers as he began a driving rhythm that left her gasping. He watched her beautiful eyes glaze with pleasure as he stroked deep and high, reaching for that secret spot that would make her come like nothing else. "Rick!" she cried when he found it. He knew then just how to fuck to bring her the most sensation on every stroke.

Callie came three times in succession as Rick congratulated himself on holding off his own orgasm. He wanted this to be special, but his strength was fast running out and when she went over for the fourth time, he went with her, shouting her name as he pulsed deep within her. Dimly, he heard her chanting his name along with her love as they crested and came down slowly on the other side of the most amazing experience he'd ever shared with another being.

"I love you, Rick," he heard her whisper before unconsciousness claimed her. He didn't answer aloud, but his heart repeated the words over and over as he followed her into sleep.

Callie woke a few hours later. Rick was still with her, already awake.

"That was beautiful, darlin'," Rick said, kissing her hair as he snuggled her close at his side.

"Perfect in every way," she agreed, "except..."

"Yeah, I know. That damned Alvian wasn't here to watch. The pervert." Rick's chuckle reassured her, as did the emotion he now let her feel freely.

"I think you're getting used to him."

"That I am. Frightening as that thought is." Rick scratched his chin, the rasp of his beard stubble making scraping sounds. "He kind of grows on you."

Callie chuckled and reached to pull him down for a quick kiss that turned into a languorous exploration of his mouth. When she finally came up for air, she noted the worry that had crept into Rick's expression.

"The thing is," he spoke without her even having to ask him what was wrong. "I'm not sure if he's as okay with this proposed arrangement as you seem to think he is. I don't know. If the shoe was on the other foot...if I—"

"While I appreciate the sentiment, I have to remind you who the stronger empath is here." Callie cut him off. "Don't you think I'd know if he wasn't comfortable with our relationship? Sure, he was hesitant at first, but he's the one who made a study of resonance mating, and he's known my parents for a long time. He knew more about what to expect than you did. Let me ask you this—you seem almost resigned to sharing me with him now. What I want to know is, are you? Will you stay with us? Will you be my mate, just like he is?"

Rick looked skeptical, then folded under the pressure of her gaze. "I can't say no to you, sweetheart. You should know that by now. I still believe this kind of thing isn't right for most women, but with you, even the impossible suddenly becomes possible." He pulled her close, holding her gaze with his own. "I never dreamed I'd be a free man living among Alvians. I never thought I could love anyone as much as I love you. And I never believed I could be completely happy ever again."

Tears gathered in the depths of his eyes, but did not fall and she felt all the deep emotion welling too, in his soul. It made her breath catch. "But I saw something, when I was deep in the matrix of that Council Crystal, Callie. I touched the spirit of the Earth itself." Wonder shone in his eyes. "I know now what I was born to do. I'm a healer of people and of the Earth. Davin can help me do that and I can teach others. It's what I was put here to do. That, and love you."

"Oh, Rick." Callie let the tears fall that he would not—the joyous tears of discovery and of a love so deep, it defied all odds.

Davin found them kissing, in a deep embrace that made every crystal in the room shine as bright as the stars themselves. Watching them together made him not only hot and eager to join, but also touched something in his heart he hadn't expected to feel. They looked right together. As right as he felt when he held Callie in his arms.

"I didn't think it was possible to be this happy," Callie said as Rick pulled back, separating them.

"I feel the same, sweetheart."

"Well then," Davin said, alerting them to his presence in the room, "maybe my news will only add to the general euphoria." He moved into the room and sat on the edge of the bed at Callie's side. They were under the covers, but she turned to him and bestowed a smile that nearly stopped his heart with love.

"Is everything back to normal with the grid?" she asked.

Davin nodded. "Not completely normal. I don't think it'll settle down for a day or two yet, but it's good for now. You and Rick can help me tie up the last loose ends tomorrow, but right now, I need some sleep, and some loving. Perhaps not in that order."

"That's easily arranged." Callie's voice purred over his senses, enflaming him.

"I'll take you up on that, my love, but first my news." His gaze sought Rick, leaning up on one elbow behind Callie. "Rick, I made a few inquiries and am pleased to tell you that I've found your father."

"What?" Davin was pleased by the stunned look in Rick's eyes. So much had been taken from these humans, it made Davin feel good to be able to give back a little bit of what they'd lost.

"Zach St. John is on his way, as we speak. He'll be here tomorrow. Grady Prime is escorting him at my express request."

"Davin, I—" Rick's voice filled with emotion he had to visibly swallow back. "I don't know what to say."

Callie grasped one of each of their hands, squeezing tight as happy tears flooded her eyes. Davin felt about ten feet tall with the way she looked at him and Rick's gratitude was humbling.

"It was relatively easy to find him," Davin spoke. "He's been housed among soldiers all these years. Seems he impressed the Alvian commander who finally caught him, and was kept as a worker for the garrison."

"Damn," Rick said, shaking his head, "I knew it had to be something like that. Surrounded by soldiers was the only way they'd be able to keep my old man locked up."

"He'd earned the respect of the men, they said. I spoke to the Commander, a man called Rilan 19. The garrison where he was kept is on the other side of the eastern sea. Zach kept trying to escape in ever more creative ways until they convinced him he'd have a hard time working his way back to this hemisphere. After that, he seemed to settle in, more resigned to his fate."

"Does he, uh..." Rick had to clear his throat. "Does he know why he's coming here? Does he know about me?"

"I asked Grady Prime to tell him only what was necessary to gain his cooperation. I thought maybe it would be a nice surprise if you greeted his transport when it landed."

"God." Rick sat up, scrubbing a hand over his face. "I don't know what to say, Davin. I don't know how I can even begin to thank you."

Callie sat up and hugged Rick close with one arm. "This is going to be great, Rick. When we start having kids, they'll have lots of grandparents."

"Kids?" Rick turned white as the sheet pooling around his hips.

"Well, they're usually what results after the kind of night we just spent. Or hadn't you thought of that?"

"I—" Rick's jaw worked, but no words came out.

Davin decided to take pity on the man, since it looked like Callie was enjoying teasing him a bit too much. "That's for later consideration, Rick. Callie is taking preventative measures. We decided to have children only when we were both ready. Now we'll have to rethink our timetable, with you living here. Your wishes have to be considered too."

"I never once thought about having kids of my own." Rick shook his head.

"Well I hope you like the idea." Callie turned to face him, letting go of Davin's hand. "Because I come from a large family and I definitely want the same. That is, if Rick's decided to stay with us. What do you say, Rick? Are we a trio?"

There it was. The question he'd been both anticipating and dreading. He'd answered Callie when they were alone, but saying it in front of Davin was another matter entirely.

Before him, he saw a future unfolding that was brighter than anything he'd ever dreamed. Reuniting with his dad, having the ability to use his talents for the good of humanity, not to mention the love...

Callie's love was worth more to him than anything. The idea of having children with her was both stunning and tantalizing. He didn't know what his father would think of the arrangement, but Rick found it impossible to even contemplate a future without Callie in it. And where Callie went, so went Davin. Rick had to accept it all in order for them to be happy.

So be it.

"If you'll put up with me," Rick hugged her close, "I'll stay with you as long as you let me." He turned her to face him fully, noting the tears once again in her eyes. "I love you, Callie O'Hara."

"Oh, Rick. I love you too." Her voice was a breathless whisper against his cheek as she clutched his shoulders and hugged him tight.

Rick met Davin's gaze over Callie's head. "Are you okay with this, Davin? I mean, really okay?"

Davin's alien face broke into a wide grin. "I'm really okay with it, Rick. I never expected to find a resonance mate. Callie is my miracle, and if making her happy means sharing the joy we've found with you, then who am I to complain? Besides—" Davin stroked one hand over her hair, gazing at her with fire in his eyes, "—in case you've forgotten, I like to watch."

Rick chuckled at the way Callie's pulse leapt under his fingers. "You know, I think our Callie likes that idea. What do you say we do a little something to celebrate this momentous occasion?"

Davin stripped off his tunic and moved closer to Callie. "I think that's the best idea I've heard all day."

She delivered a smacking kiss to Rick's lips, then turned in his hold to give Davin the same. "You two have made me the happiest woman on the planet."

"Not yet," Davin said with a wicked grin.

"But we will." Rick completed the thought.

Epilogue

The transport landed light as a feather on one of the outer pads while Rick watched, his stomach churning with anxiety at what his father would have to say to him after all these years. Rick's heart was in his throat as the ramp lowered. Callie clutched his hand, squeezing once in reassurance before letting go and pushing him forward with a gentle hand on his back.

Rick walked out to meet the man, just now starting down the ramp with Grady Prime right behind him. Zach St. John looked about the same as Rick remembered, maybe a little older, but still fit and...wary.

Rick stepped out of the shadows cast by the big building behind him. He walked hesitantly, reluctant to face his father for the first time in years. They both stopped walking with about ten feet between them.

"Hi, Dad."

Blue eyes crinkled, then narrowed in suspicion. "Is that you, boy? Dear God. Is it really you?"

Rick wasn't sure who moved first, but a moment later, his father grabbed him in a bear hug. They pounded each other on the back, expressing without words how great it was to be together again.

How long they stayed that way, Rick wasn't sure. Eventually they broke apart and Callie was there, at his side, a beacon of warmth to soothe his confused emotions.

"Hello, Mr. St. John. I'm Callie O'Hara." Rick's father looked her over with a measuring eye.

"Are you the one responsible for the happy look on my son's face?"

Callie grinned and took Rick's arm. "I can't claim to be fully responsible for that, but I do my best to keep him looking that way."

"Son, what have you landed in here?" Zach looked around, his eyes lighting on the Alvians, most giving them a respectful amount of privacy.

"That's a long story, Dad. Damn," Rick hugged his father's shoulders, so glad to have him back he couldn't contain himself. "It's so good to see you."

"You've grown into a fine man, son." Zach cupped Rick's shoulder. "You always did have your mother's eyes."

Rick didn't know how to answer that. "You look the same as ever, Dad. I've missed you a lot."

"Me too, son. Me too." Zach nodded to the silent warrior a few yards behind them. "That Grady Prime told me I was reassigned here permanently. Is that your doing?" Zach was the same height as his son. They stayed arm in arm as they walked with Callie back toward the building. Davin waited there for them. One more hurdle to get over on this momentous day.

"Dad," Rick began hesitantly. "This is Davin's place. Davin's like no Alvian you've ever met, and he's gone to bat for humans more than once. He's responsible for all of this. We're safe here. We have the guarantee of the Alvian High Council on it."

"I can't imagine how you managed that." Zach St. John pulled away as they entered the door that was only large enough for one to pass through at a time.

Davin met them on the other side.

"Dad, this is Davin." Rick watched with apprehension as his father shook hands with Davin for the first time.

"Hot damn," Zach said, looking at his son with wide eyes. "You weren't kidding. Forgive me, Davin, but I have a little empathy. I hope you don't mind my saying you're nothing like any Alvian I've ever met."

Callie and Davin both laughed and the mood in the wide hallway lightened considerably. "I'm a very strong empath, Mr. St. John, as is my mother," Callie said. "Davin's been friendly with my family for a long time. He's what the Alvians call a 'throwback'. He has emotions, just like their people did before their geneticists started monkeying around with their DNA."

239

"It is said the warrior lines have more of the ancient aggression left in them than any of the others." Grady Prime had entered behind them and now joined the conversation.

Zach St. John looked thoughtfully around at all of them. "I was with soldiers mostly, and from time to time I would get echoes of emotion from them, but it wasn't much. I can honestly say your friend here is the closest thing to human I've ever encountered in an Alvian."

Davin inclined his head. "I'll take that as a compliment."

"Grady Prime." Zach turned to address the soldier. "I thank you for bringing me here. You have no idea how grateful I am to be reunited with my son. I wish it was something you could understand."

"Sometimes..." Grady Prime's face held an odd expression that seemed...almost...hopeful, "...I wish I could too." Silence greeted his statement until Grady Prime backed away. "I will go now. It is an honor to assist you, Chief Engineer. If you have need of me again, please do not hesitate to call on me." Grady Prime shocked them all by touching Callie's hair with something like fondness. "Keep this little one safe. She is special to many people."

Rick and Davin nodded in unison, but it was Davin who spoke. "We'll take care of her, Grady Prime. Thanks again for all of your help."

The soldier reversed and left through the door, back toward his waiting ship.

"So what exactly is going on here?" Zach asked in a suspicious tone. "I'm getting strange impressions from all three of you and my boy's about to bust a gut with worry. Whatever it is, it can't be that bad, Rick."

Rick shifted on his feet uncomfortably. "Wait 'til you hear it before you say that, Dad. See, it's like this—"

But Callie spoke over him, cutting him off. "I love your son, Mr. St. John, but I also love Davin. We're what the Alvians call resonance mates. All three of us. Well," she amended, "both of them resonate with me. Rick has this crazy idea you're going to object to the fact that we're a trio. I know it's not like it was in the old days, but my parents have a multi-partner marriage that works really well for them. I think Davin, Rick and I can make it work for us too. In fact, I know we can."

All eyes turned to Zach St. John. "Give me your hand, Callie."

She reached out to the older man, letting him take her hand between both of his. Rick's father closed his eyes and tilted his head, as if considering.

"I'm more of a touch empath, like my son," he said as he released her hand. "I feel your love for them both and the strength of your convictions."

Callie smiled. "You're better at this than Rick is."

"Hey now," Rick objected, but in a teasing way.

"I sensed both Rick's and Davin's feelings the moment we shook hands. I'll admit, I was a little concerned until I touched you, Callie. You're the glue that binds this relationship together." Zach put his hand on Rick's shoulder. "I know why you think I'd object and I would, under other circumstances, but this seems like the one exception that just might work, son. Personally, as long as you're all happy, I have nothing to say on the matter. I'm just glad to have you back, Rick. I never thought I'd see you again."

"Hell, Dad. I always hoped, but I never dared dream. It was Davin who found you and brought you here."

"Then I owe you an even greater debt of gratitude," Zach said to Davin.

Davin bowed his head in acknowledgment, but said nothing.

"I knew you'd be as nice as your son, Mr. St. John." Callie looped her arm through his and started down the hall, leaving it to her men to follow behind.

Rick spared a quick look for Davin. "I can never thank you enough, Davin, for all of this."

"We're in this together now, Rick. For better or worse." Rick thought it prophetic that Davin echoed part of the old marriage promises as he watched Callie saunter down the hall in front of them. "We'll share the job of keeping her happy for the rest of our days."

Rick had to smile at that thought. "There are worse things I can think of." Davin chuckled at the small joke. For an alien, he really wasn't half bad.

With both of them to protect and love Callie, and now his father back safe and sound, the future looked brighter than it ever had. Callie turned her head to smile at him and his heart knew, whatever came, they'd face it—all of them—together.

About the Author

A life-long martial arts enthusiast, Bianca enjoys a number of hobbies and interests that keep her busy and entertained, such as playing the guitar, shopping, painting, shopping, skiing, shopping, road trips, and did we say...um...shopping? A bargain hunter through and through, Bianca loves the thrill of the hunt for that excellent price on quality items, though she's hardly a fashionista. She likes nothing better than curling up by the fire with a good book, or better yet, by the computer, writing a good book.

To learn more about Bianca D'Arc, please visit www.biancadarc.com. Send an email to Bianca at bianca@biancadarc.com or join her Yahoo! group to join in the fun with Bianca and other readers! http://groups.yahoo.com/group/BiancaDArc/

An abused woman has the power to unite werefolk, fey and vampire against an evil that would see them all dead—if she can learn to love again.

Sweeter Than Wine
© *2007 Bianca D'Arc*

Christy lies near death after a brutal beating by her estranged husband. Her preternatural friends reach a desperate conclusion: The only way to save her is to turn her. Sebastian steps forward to take on the burden of being her Maker.

For him it's no burden at all. She draws him as no other woman has for centuries. With the help of a werecougar friend, Sebastian teaches Christy about her new life and abilities, making certain she is as strong as he can make her. Only then can she face her abusive ex-husband and put her old life behind her. But Christy's ex-husband is involved in something more dangerous than any of them had guessed.

Vampire, *were*, and even a fey knight must work together to put an end to the threatening evil. To overcome her past, help keep the darkness at bay, and fight for a new life with Sebastian, Christy must draw on all of her new-found strength.

Will it be enough?

Warning, this title contains explicit sex, graphic language, ménage a trois, hot neck biting and werecougar stroking.

Available now in ebook and print from Samhain Publishing.

Enjoy the following excerpt from Sweeter Than Wine...

Christina woke in slow increments, like a kitten just learning about the world around it. Sebastian watched her from the side of the large bed, waiting for the moment when she'd realize she wasn't alone.

"I bet you're hungry." He was enchanted by the sleepy look in her eyes as she met his gaze. Rubbing her tummy, she looked like she was considering his words.

"I feel strange."

He nodded and moved closer, sitting on the edge of the bed. "That's to be expected when you're newly turned."

"Then it wasn't a dream?"

"No, my dear. It was most certainly real." He dipped his head closer, smiling so she could see his fangs. He was hungry too, it seemed. "You've been deep in healing sleep for more than two days. That's longer than most of the newly turned, but you were gravely injured, so I encouraged your sleep." He tugged at the sheet that covered her, inching it away. "I've decided on a course of action some might consider reckless." He paused. "Do you trust me?"

She seemed to think that one over before answering. "I think so."

"What I'm going to ask of you will seem strange, but I need you to believe it is for your own welfare that I've even considered this." He pulled the sheet a little lower.

"Now you're frightening me, Sebastian."

"That's not my intent. But I need you to know that what comes next is necessary for your future. I want you to be strong enough to deal with Jeff Kinsey on your own. I believe standing up to him—and winning—is the only way to face the rest of your years, now that you are immortal. If you let him win, even the smallest confrontation, it will set a tone for your new life that could prove disastrous."

"Did I mention you'd already scared me enough?"

Sebastian was glad to see a spark of humor in her wary eyes. It made him feel a little better about what he was about to do, though other aspects of his plan still made him uneasy. There was jealousy for one thing. It was likely to eat him alive before long. Good thing the task could be accomplished quickly. He knew he couldn't take too much of this.

"I'm sorry, Christina. What I propose will not hurt. On the contrary, it will bring you great pleasure, but it is somewhat...risqué. I know from your friends that you've never been very adventurous sexually. That will have to change."

She looked wary, but receptive. "What exactly are you talking about?"

"Your body is fully healed now, and its chemistry forever altered. Now it's time for your lessons to begin."

"Lessons?"

"I promised to teach you everything you need to know to survive in your changed state. Those lessons begin now, with our most basic needs—blood and lust. You need to feed." He dipped his head, kissing her savagely. He didn't mean to do it, but her soft lips were so close, so inviting, he couldn't resist.

Sebastian reveled in the sweet taste of her, delving deep with his tongue as her petite fangs began to emerge. He ran his tongue over them, encouraging their arrival. He'd forgotten how it felt to kiss one of his own kind. It was beyond erotic. It was nearly orgasmic in itself.

When she jumped, he pulled back, looking past her beautiful, bare body to see what had scared her. Sebastian understood her alarm when he saw Matt. He'd come in and prowled right up to the bed, taking a seat near the foot as if he belonged there, while Sebastian had been distracted. It was a shock to realize he'd been so lost in her kiss, he hadn't even sensed Matt's arrival. Matt's knowing wink didn't go a long way to soothe Sebastian's self-recrimination, but it did make him smile. The lad was audacious, but Christina needed a little nudge to guide her on this path. Before the night was through, Sebastian knew she'd need to put all her inhibitions behind her and Matt Redstone was just the creature to help her do it.

"I invited a mortal friend to help you learn how to feed both bodily and psychically." He waved one hand toward Matt, releasing her slowly. "He is *were*. You might note the difference in his scent from ordinary mortals. He'll make an excellent first feeding for you to grow strong and he's agreed to let us use him as our guinea pig for this evening. It's a rare honor. You should be thankful."

Christy looked at the gorgeous, muscular man who sat on the edge of her bed and began stroking her legs. "Um, thank you?"

She didn't know what to think. On the one hand, she'd never slept around. On the other, she'd never been this horny in her life. It had to do with whatever Sebastian had done to save her life. She felt different in startling ways. Liquid fire raced through her veins and straight to her womb, making her yearn in a way she never had before.

Cunning topaz eyes smiled up at her. "You're very welcome, sweet thing. It's been a long time since I had vampire pussy." He licked his lips, daring to smack them at her. She liked the sparkle in his gaze and could tell right away this handsome stranger was a bit of a tease. He drew her, but at the same time she was afraid of her own response. She didn't know this man. Was Sebastian going to sit by and let him touch her—perhaps even take her—just like that?

"Sebastian?" Her voice rose along with her distress.

Reassuring hands stroked her back, helping her sit up. "Don't fear anything that will happen here this night. A vampire's first feeding is one of the most important of her existence. That Matt has agreed to let you feed from him tonight is no small thing. A portion of his inherent cunning, agility, and strength will forever be passed on to you. Like I said, it's a great honor."

"But is he going to um..." she felt heat stain her cheeks, "...will he want to have sex with me?"

Matt shifted to sit between her legs. "I'm going to fuck your brains out, sweetheart, and eat this pretty pussy 'til you come in my mouth."

"Sebastian!" The objection came out on a shocked gasp.

To be honest, though, she had to admit the new hunger wasn't only for the blood she could actually hear coursing through this strange, savage man's veins. He was handsome and muscular in a way she'd never seen in person. His golden hair practically invited her fingers to run through it, and he had the most gorgeous, bright, inquisitive eyes.

"It's all right, Christina." Sebastian's hypnotic voice soothed her. "It's only fair that Matt gain something from giving you his blood. By lapping your fluids, he will temporarily attain some of our healing and regenerative abilities to augment his own. It's a fair exchange."

"Who is he?" She was upset both at Sebastian's cavalier attitude and his assumptions about her willingness to sleep with a complete stranger. But even more upsetting was her body's response. She wanted to know how that muscular body would feel over her—inside her—fucking her. The thought was deliciously forbidden and altogether shocking. She shook her head, but clarity refused to come. So she appealed to Sebastian—her lifeline in this world gone wild. "How do you expect me to be intimate with someone I don't even know? That may be normal for you, but it's not for me. Not by a long shot!"

"Sorry, ma'am." Matt grinned and held out one hand for her to shake, still sitting between her thighs. "I'm Matt Redstone. Like Sebastian said, I'm *were*, and the youngest brother of the leader of the cougar clan."

She shook his hand as if in a trance. This was probably the strangest situation she'd ever been in. Bar none.

"What is *were*? What does that mean?"

Matt Redstone shot an amused look up at Sebastian. "She doesn't know anything yet, does she?"

Her touch is heavenly. Her kiss, deadly. To mate with her means certain death.

Black Widow
© 2008 Mackenzie McKade

After a brutal attack by a huge, dog-like creature, Tammy is left clinging to life by a thread. Her last memory is of her rescuer asking her if she wants to live. She awakes to a nightmare, bound in chains, nearly paralyzed by terror—and with a strange sensual creature slinking beneath her skin, screaming with hunger for only two things. Blood. And sex.

Roark and Marcellus, leaders of the werewolves and vampires, come together to destroy the results of a night gone terribly wrong. As a result of the attack, Tammy has become a hybrid—part wolf and part vampire—and to complicate things, she's in heat. The transformation has thrown her into a sexual frenzy that makes her a virtual black widow. For the sake of their people, Tammy must die.

Yet they can't bring themselves to kill her. Instead, Roark and Marcellus find themselves trapped in the femme fatale's web of seduction. Her touch is heavenly...her kiss, deadly. To complicate things, they discover she is mate to each of them.

Soul-wrenching desire reigns over their struggle for dominance and possession, forging a unique bond between the immortals. Together Roark and Marcellus will fight to save the woman they love from the people they are pledged to protect.

Warning, this title contains the following: hot, explicit and a little kinky ménage sex, graphic violence and language, and explores the impact of combining werewolf and vampire blood. The results are dangerously delicious!

Available now in ebook and print from Samhain Publishing.

Enjoy the following excerpt Black Widow...

Tammy was trapped between sleep and that moment when her conscious mind begged for control. *Sleep.* That's all she wanted. Just ten more minutes before she had to face the day, rise and go to work. Was it Tuesday morning? She had no idea as she fought the threads of wakefulness threatening to pull her from slumber. Maybe she'd call in sick. Hard as she tried, sounds and smells began to seep through the mental wall she had erected.

The first to break through was the scent of male musk. *Dream,* she rationalized. Tammy slept alone. What she would give for it to be real. She'd turn over and slowly licked her way across the man's body, every succulent inch. A tightening fluttered in her belly. A moan parted her lips as the ache in her stomach grew. Need made a lousy bed partner and so did hunger. When was the last time she ate? With the thought, something clawed at her insides. A craving rose so quickly she groaned.

Chocolate? *No.*

Meat? Her mouth began to water.

Blood? The pain inside her sharpened.

Okay. Now that's odd, she thought even as visions of her body entwined with two strange men popped in her head. Now this was a dream made in heaven. Not one, but two men. *Yummy.* The warm smell of the heater kicking on dissolved the image. Her eyes open on a sigh. She blinked once, twice, and then again.

A cry of distress stung Tammy's throat. This wasn't her room. Panic rose swiftly engulfing her like a wave pulling her under. For the love of God, she was naked and bound.

She jerked her head up as she fought her bindings. The shuffling of feet drew her attention across the room. She wasn't alone. Fear washed over her a second time. At the same time her senses jumped like live wires striking different polar ends. A million questions assailed her. The most acute—how was she going to escape?

The men seemed unaware of her existence as they argued.

Testosterone rolled off them in sheets. For some unknown reason their fervent scent made every nerve ending inside her come alive, heating her body like a furnace. She had to taste them, feel them against her skin and between her thighs, now.

Tammy tensed. What was wrong with her? She should be concerned for her life, not fantasizing about fucking her kidnappers. But try as she did, she couldn't erase the need that screamed to be fed.

In her sexual frenzy, Tammy thought she heard the auburn-haired man say something about letting her die. Her breath caught. Panic took hold once more. Quietly but firmly she pulled against her bonds. When she heard the dark-haired man call her an abomination it was like cold water dousing a fire. She went rigid with anger that quenched her arousal but did nothing for the hunger gnawing in her belly.

"Release me now," she growled, low and menacing. The tempered voice was not her own. Just as fast as her anger had risen memories flashed, snatching her breath away.

A wolf. The attack. She remembered the pain, the fight— dying. A kaleidoscope of scenes continued, making love to two men, a wolf, then blood—the men's blood. God it had tasted so good.

Her stomach pitched. For a moment she thought she would vomit. Instead acid rolled like an angry sea causing a burn to develop in her chest and throat. A whimper squeezed from her parted lips.

When both men's stares scanned across her skin, her mind froze, but her body responded. Her nipples drew tight. An ache developed between her thighs, the result a flood of desire she couldn't control.

Mixed emotions assailed her. Her immediate reaction was to free herself, run and hide. At the same time she wanted them next to her, to feel their strong hands roam her body, to feel their cocks buried inside her, and to taste them upon her tongue. The hunger was so great her spasms ignited a chain reaction that overtook her. She groaned, a raspy sound, washing away the mental conflict. Here one moment and gone the next, she felt the muscles in her body relax. Some freaky-ass thing was going on inside her—she didn't feel right, and then a noise like a kitten's purr slid off her tongue.

Her fingers splayed wide, her wrists held firmly by the manacles. *"Venez à moi."* *Come to me?* She mentally translated the words as she spoke them. Her French lessons were paying off. Yet the sexy voice belonged to someone else. She should have been frightened, but for some reason wasn't.

Almost as if he were in a trance, the buff man in jeans took a step toward her. His face was absent of all expression. As he drew closer excitement filtered through her. She shuttered her eyelids. *"Venez à moi, mon prince."* My prince. She liked how it rolled off her tongue. French was a beautiful language.

Her breasts filled with need, heavy and ripe. She couldn't wait for the moment of contact. She craved him like she had craved no other's touch. Thick eyelashes swept her cheekbones. Her body undulated, her hips swaying, invitingly.

What is happening to me? But the thought didn't linger longer than a heartbeat. She wanted this man and his friend.

A shiver of need made her next purr staccato, distinct breaks, so it came out an alluring mating call. Heat flared across both men's faces. The man in black didn't move, but the other one stepped closer, as if he couldn't resist.

Tammy's back arched as teasing rays of her arousal shuddered through her body. Rattling chains stopped her from reaching out, seeking her pleasure.

"Lanier, I wouldn't get any closer," warned the tall, lean man. "She's hard to resist. I know." He reached down and cupped his erection.

Still the auburn-haired man called Lanier stepped nearer—

If her hands were free she could have touched and savored him. "Are you afraid of me?" Her mouth drew into a pout. She tilted her head from left to right needing to be free of the collar around her neck. "All I want to do is play. Won't you please release me? I promise you won't regret it."

Where this teasing, sexual woman came from Tammy had no idea. All she knew was that she needed to satisfy the lustful ache in her body. Not to mention, she was hungry. She cocked her head, listening to each stranger's heartbeat. Healthy and strong.

Her fingers splayed, curling as if to emphasize her long fingernails. "But I can't touch you," she whimpered. "And I want to touch you both so badly." Her hips swayed side to side enticingly.

Again, Tammy's breath caught. Sanity briefly surfaced once more as she wondered what was happening to her. This wasn't like her—not that she hadn't secretly wanted to be seductive and charming. Looks? Yeah, she had them, but experience—zip.

Tammy wasn't promiscuous, just the opposite. Yet her body felt more in control than her mind. She desired these men more than anything she'd ever wanted.

"Kiss me." Her voice was a plea.

Lanier appeared caught in her web. His pupils were dilated as he stepped close enough she could feel his masculine heat. It warmed her blood like a fire was set beneath her. She couldn't wait to feel his embrace, the caress of his hands against her flesh. Couldn't wait for the moment his cock parted her folds and filled her.

Suddenly a spasm clenched her belly and threw her body into convulsions. Pain splintered in all directions as a drawing sensation like a knot being pulled tighter and tighter twisted inside her.

A sharp, breathy cry pushed from her mouth. "It hurts. Oh God, it hurts." She jerked against her bindings, the metal biting into her wrists and ankles, as a fiery burn raced through her body.

She couldn't quiet the involuntary muscular contractions pulling and pushing on her insides, threatening to rip her in two. She squeezed and released her vaginal muscles, attempting to lessen the throb between her thighs. But it did no good.

"Shit," Lanier cried as he ran to her.

The minute his hands touched her waist the pain inside Tammy eased, but not entirely. She brushed against his body as he folded his frame around her.

The rapid pulse in his neck called to her. Her mouth salivated. But it was the bulge pressing into her belly that made her cry out. "Please help me."

Donne glanced at Lanier.

"Her needs are sexual. It happens to all the young wolves as they come of age. Her transformation must have thrown her into a heat," Lanier said.

Heat? The thought disappeared as her stomach growled and the sound of Lanier's blood flowing through his veins became a symphony in her ears. She could hear the swish of his life essence as the chambers of his heart opened and closed. His breathing seemed to melt into hers, almost as if they were becoming one.

Donne's eyes widened. "Are you telling me she needs to be bred—fucked?"

Lanier held her firmly against his body.

Blood. Tammy sucked in a breath, fighting to think of something other than sinking her teeth into the vein pulsing in his neck.

"Fucked." He watched her guardedly. "And thanks to you, fed."

GET IT NOW

MyBookStoreAndMore.com

GREAT EBOOKS, GREAT DEALS . . . AND MORE!

Don't wait to run to the bookstore down the street, or
waste time shopping online at one of the "big boys." Now,
all your favorite Samhain authors are all in one place—at
MyBookStoreAndMore.com. Stop by today and discover
great deals on Samhain—and a whole lot more!

WWW.SAMHAINPUBLISHING.COM

GREAT
CHEAP
FUN

Discover eBooks!

THE FASTEST WAY TO GET THE HOTTEST NAMES

Get your favorite authors on your favorite reader, long before they're
out in print! Ebooks from Samhain go wherever you go, and work with
whatever you carry—Palm, PDF, Mobi, and more.